D1349060

OTHERS

Also by James Herbert

The Rats
The Fog
The Survivor
Fluke
The Spear
The Dark
Lair
The Jonah
Shrine
Domain
Moon
The Magic Cottage
Sepulchre
Haunted
Creed
Portent
The Ghosts of Sleath
'48
Others

Graphic Novels

The City
(Illustrated by Ian Miller)

Non-fiction

By Horror Haunted
(Edited by Stephen Jones)

James Herbert's Dark Places
(Photographs by Paul Barkshire)

JAMES HERBERT

OTHERS

MACMILLAN

First published 1999 by Macmillan

an imprint of Macmillan Publishers Ltd
25 Eccleston Place, London SW1W 9NF
Basingstoke and Oxford

Associated companies throughout the world

ISBN 0 333 76117 0 (Hardback)
ISBN 0 333 76136 7 (Trade paperback)

Copyright © James Herbert 1999

3 5 7 9 8 6 4 2

A CIP catalogue record for this book is available from
the British Library.

Typeset by SetSystems Ltd, Saffron Walden, Essex
Printed and bound in Great Britain by
Mackays of Chatham plc, Chatham, Kent

Only in this world can there be no perfection.

His is the House of Pain.
His is the Hand that makes.
His is the Hand that wounds.
His is the Hand that heals.

H. G. Wells,
The Island of Doctor Moreau

1

My redemption began in Hell.

It was a day like any other – except there are no days in that singular (in both senses of the words) place. No minutes, no hours, weeks, or years. No seconds either. There is no time in Hell, you see. There just *is*. That's the hell of it.

There I ruminated under the faintest light from above, nameless, Godless, with no sense of humour at all – I existed as a wretched and self-sorry soul, all reflection and no projection – contemplating the base, wasted life I'd once lived. Regrets? Too many to mention, but occasion enough to remember them all. Credits? Not enough to dwell upon. No, the balance was tilted in the worst direction and at the most extreme angle. Legions in this (literally) God-forsaken place still couldn't figure out what they'd done wrong – or, more accurately, why it was deemed so damned offensive – while others understood only too well. The former would come to know eventually, but in the meantime, theirs was a different kind of torment. As I pondered my own iniquities, a light suddenly brightened a corner of my dark 'cell'.

Two of them appeared, tall and seraphic, their radiance pushing back the shadows around me, guarding themselves against contamination from this murky realm I inhabited (interesting how the ancient artists intuitively had got it right when they depicted bright auras enveloping the holy spirits on their sojourns into the infectious world of mankind) and I was blinded until they wished their dimmers to a more comfortable level. Both wore annoyingly benevolent smiles.

'Good day to you,' one of them said as though time had relevance.

I nodded back, wary and too surprised by their visit to appreciate the break in the routine.

'We hope we didn't disturb you,' greeted the other one, neither sarcasm nor irony in his manner.

'Glad of the company,' I returned, all nervous humility and dread.

The first entity, essence – *angel* if you like – sensed my fear. 'Don't be alarmed. We're here to comfort, not chastise.'

Chastise? Nobody had chastised me since I'd arrived. The torment was too subtle and yes, too *drastic*, for that.

'Not more punishment, then?' I asked half-pleadingly.

'Oh, we wouldn't say that,' replied the second, and they both glanced at each other.

'Something punishing perhaps, but not really punishment,' said the first.

I groaned. 'Something worse than this?'

'Not worse. I told you we're here to comfort you. No, this is something infinitely better.'

He smiled down at me and I took in a countenance so serene, so pure, that tears blurred my vision.

'A chance,' he announced before straightening again.

My thoughts, as well as my emotions, raced. A chance? A chance for what? To leave this place? To attain a new level? A chance to escape the perpetual misery of an existence without hope? What did he – *it* – mean?

He knew my thoughts. 'All of those things,' he said, beckoning me to rise so that I wouldn't have to gaze up at him any more. 'But more importantly, an opportunity to make amends.'

Instead of rising I knelt before them both. 'Anything,' I said. 'I'll do anything.'

'I wonder,' was his response.

'It would be a harsh test.' The second one gently loosened my grip on his robe. 'And it's more probable that you'll fail. If that is the outcome, then there really is no hope for you.'

'I don't understand.' I looked from one to the other.

No 1 took me by the elbow and drew me up. 'We have a tradition on the, er, uppermost level.'

'The Good Place?'

He gave a slight bow.

'Heaven?'

His smile twitched. 'If you like.'

'Anything,' I pleaded. 'Just tell me what you want me to do.' I admit, I was weeping floods by now. You had to know what Hell is like.

'Calm yourself,' he soothed. 'Stay your tears and listen.'

Angel 2 started to explain. 'Every half-millennium we are allowed to choose a few souls for . . .'

'We call it the Five Hundred Year Plenary Indulgence . . .' No 1 interrupted helpfully.

'. . . whereby all grievous and venal sins of the chosen souls are forgiven, their spirits become untainted once more. As they were before Earthly birth. They are able . . .'

'. . . eventually . . .'

'. . . to enter the Kingdom and at last find their peace.'

It was too much for me. I sank to my knees again, disturbing the vapours that swirled low to the floor of my cubette. 'You've chosen me . . .' I burbled as my hands again caught the hems of their gowns.

I heard a throat clearing, a sound of disapproval, and immediately let go, afraid of irritating these wise and wonderful creatures. I remained doubled over though, my nose disappearing into the mists.

'You and one or two others,' Angel 2 corrected.

'Thank you, oh thank – '

No 1 cut me short. 'In your lifetime you were thoroughly wicked and your punishment here is richly deserved.'

'I know, I kn– ' It was my own sobs, like sharp hiccups, that interrupted the self-mortification.

No 1 had paused. 'Yes, yes, it's never too late for tears, but please save them for after we've gone,' he admonished, a little impatiently I thought, given the stress I was under.

Well, wailing, gnashing of teeth and the beating of breasts was the norm in this place, but I guess it could be upsetting – or just plain tedious – for visitors. I snuffled into my hand and choked back further lamentation. If they didn't want woe, then woe there wouldn't be. A few snivelling whimpers maybe, just to show I was truly contrite, but nothing distracting. Besides, I was desperate to hear what was on offer.

'You were blessed with so many gifts for your test-time on Earth, yet you squandered them all, used them for your own self-gratification.'

'Yes, I know, I know,' I agreed with a barely-repressed sniffle.

'You were guilty of hedonism . . .'

'Yes.'

'. . . sensualism . . .'

'Yes.'

'. . . eudaemonism . . .'

'Er . . .'

'. . . and you used your charm, your wit and your exceptional presence to cheat and humble those around you. Duplicity and betrayal was your canon, to lie and abuse was your doctrine. You debased the worthy and downtrod the already downtrodden.'

'Well, I . . .'

Angel 2 added his own condemnation. 'A libertine and a roué.'

'Both a philanderer and a gigolo.'

'Indeed, a rake of the lowest order.' No 2 didn't want to be outdone.

'You were a great star in a celluloid firmament. A moving star . . .'

'Uh, mov*ie* star, actually,' I corrected.

'. . . in the place they call Holy Wood.'

I felt it unwise to correct him again; no point in ruffling his feathers (just an expression – they don't really have wings. They don't really have bodies or voices either, but let's not get pedantic).

'Women adored you, men admired you.'

'Until they got to know you,' No 2 added darkly. 'The people worshipped your debonair image; to them you were a devil-may-care sophisticate, whose bluff exterior secreted a caring and sensitive core. Or so they thought. The public only knew you for the black and white image you portrayed.'

And they *hadn't* come to chastise me?

'But most wickedly of all, you caused premature death and suicide. You caused despair and yes, even insanity to the ones who loved you most and who forgave your amorality and hardness of heart.'

I offered no excuses. I had once before, at my Judgement, and they'd got me nowhere. This time I kept my mouth shut.

From their thunderous countenances I thought they'd changed their minds about giving me a second chance, but it was Angel 2 who threw some light into the shade: 'However, you did have some – *not many mind* – redeeming qualities.'

I kept my lips clamped tight, even though a small, tingling excitement was beginning to lift my spirit once more.

'And it was those few – very few – redeeming qualities,' he went on, ' that gave us cause to review your case. It seems you were not altogether a *bad* person, although there are those among us who disagree about that. In fact it was the Final Arbiter – you know *Who* I mean by that – who made the decision to allow you another chance. You might just save your own soul if . . .' and he made it sound like a big *IF* '. . . you are willing to take up the challenge.' His raised hand halted further gibberings from me. 'True repentance is not so easy, you know. Hell isn't necessarily just here, it can be found in other places, and if you go back . . .'

'Go back?' My body snapped up so suddenly that you

might have heard my spine crack – *if* I'd had a spine and *if* I'd had a body. 'You mean . . .'

They nodded as one and there was an odd sadness to their demeanour. 'It's a most serious thing,' No 1 said mournfully and No 2 repeated just as mournfully, 'A most serious thing.'

'For if you fail, you will be lost to us forever, you will never be allowed another opportunity to save your soul. Your damnation will truly be eternal . . .'

'And even worse than this,' his partner added.

I gulped. 'Worse?'

'Oh, much worse. Infinitely worse. Perdurably worse.' Angel 2 was shaking his head in pity. 'So think carefully before you agree to a new life and the harsh reveille it will bring.'

'I . . . I won't go back as myself?'

'There has only been one Resurrection – two if you count Lazarus, and eventually he had to give up his body again. Besides, you left your Earthly vessel almost fifty – in human-kind terms – years ago. You'd create quite a stir if you turned up in it once more.'

Fifty years? It could have been fifty thousand for all I knew.

'You'll find that your old world has changed considerably since you left it, and part of your atonement will be the loss of the privileges and gifts you once had, so we urge you again to think carefully before you decide.'

It took me all of two timeless seconds to make up my mind. But I chose my words with more care than I'd made the decision. 'Let me make amends,' I begged. 'Please give me the chance of a new Judgement.'

The Angels continued to regard me pityingly. 'There will be conditions,' No 1 said.

'Just tell me what I have to do.'

'One of those conditions is that you won't know.'

'But how can I – '

'You will choose what is right. Or perhaps you will choose what is wrong. It will be entirely up to you.'

And so saying they left me. Just wafted away so that I stared into darkness and shadows once more. Then I lowered my head and wailed.

All this, of course, metaphorically speaking.

2

She began hesitantly, her gaze never leaving mine, even as
she drew a long dark cigarette from a pearl and silver case.
She tapped the filtered end unnecessarily against the metal,
an old-fashioned gesture that made me smile – inwardly.
Shelly – she had already impressed on me there was no 'e'
before the 'y' – Ripstone looked anywhere between thirty-
five and forty, one of those not pretty but handsome women
who had time and money to keep their figures trim and their
skin soft. Only a faint regiment of fine lines marching across
her upper lip and spreading from the outer corners of sad,
mascaraed eyes spoilt the illusion, but that was only on close
inspection – and I'd been inspecting her closely from the
moment she'd walked into my office to sit in the chair facing
my desk. Bottle-blonde hair – ash-blonde, I suppose you'd
call it – the tips, curling beneath her chin, struggling to meet
below the jawline as if to hide those other wrinkles, those
mean, tell-tale give-the-game-away neck furrows that were
the bane of maturing women. Her neat grey suit was Escada,
or a fair copy of, and her high-heels Italian (I was good at
that kind of thing), but her voice, whose vowels became
more flattened and her mid-word *t*s more absent as our
meeting progressed, was ill-disguised estuary (I figured
southside Thames, maybe Gravesend or Dartford, no further
east than that – accents were another thing I was good at).
Shelly Ripstone exuded new money, both in apparel and
voice – even her scent was Poison – and I had no hang-up
with that. In fact, I kind of liked it: it made her more human,

8

more vulnerable, someone with whom I could empathize. Let's face it, we all try to be more than we are and there's no harm in that.

She took a thin Dunhill lighter from her purse and lit the cigarette. 'D'you mind?' she said as an afterthought.

I shook my head. 'Go ahead.'

'Would you . . . ?' She lifted the pearl and silver case from the purse again and offered it towards me, another hint at her origins (the wealthy middle classes rarely shared their straights with strangers).

I shook my head again and she seemed fascinated by the awkwardness of the movement. Mint-flavoured smoke drifted across the desk at me.

'Can I ask who recommended my agency?' I enquired to interrupt the apparent attraction.

She was suddenly aware she shouldn't be staring like that. 'Oh. Etta Kaesbach. She said you were the best.'

I uttered a short 'ah' of understanding. Good old Etta. Etta Kaesbach was a first-rate solicitor who'd passed a lot of work my way over the years. In fact, she was the one who'd helped me most when I first set up business as an enquiry agent. She had great heart and a contrary streak that dared anyone to challenge her recommendation. It was embarrassing for me sometimes, embarrassing for the undecided prospective client too, but usually their surprise worked in my favour – nobody liked to appear discriminatory in these PC days – and once they'd realized how pro I was, there was no problem.

'Is Ms – ' I hated the *Ms*, but it was expected ' – Kaesbach your lawyer?' I asked.

'No. But her senior partner was once my late husband's.' She blew a stream of blue smoke which dispersed half-way across my desktop. 'Gerald died five months ago. Heart attack. His heart had never been strong. It was over very quickly.' She offered the last bit of information as if it were a blessing, and perhaps it was. Still the memory was fresh enough to upset her: her eyes lost focus for a moment, moisture softening their hue. And for some reason her face reddened, as if embarrassment played a part too.

'Would you like some coffee, Mrs Ripstone?' I wanted to give her time to regain her composure. 'Tea?'

'No. No, thank you. I'm fine.'

'Okay . . .' That was fine by me also. It would have been nice to impress clients by using the intercom on my desk and asking my secretary to bring us refreshments, only I didn't have an intercom and I didn't have a secretary. Sometimes Henry would shift himself to bring me a hot drink or a fruitjuice, depending on whether it was one of his health-drive weeks, or, when young Philo was around, I could yell through the open doorway for him to get busy with a brew, but neither option was very ritzy, and to do it myself was even less so. I opened a notepad on my desk and reached for a felt-tip.

'If you could just outline what this is about and I can ask questions as we go,' I said, Pentel poised.

She straightened her shoulders, which by now had become hunched. 'Well, I told you my husband, Gerald Ripstone, died five months ago,' she began, and I jotted down the name and the month he'd passed away.

'You'd been married how long . . . ?'

'Oh, sixteen years, I think. Yes, it would've been sixteen years this August.' She exhaled more smoke and watched the cloud for a few seconds. 'He was a good man, my Gerald. He could be pretty ruthless in business – he exported refrigeration units, you know, cold storage containers – but generally he was good to me. I was his secretary before we were married.'

'Were either of you married before?' The question was just out of curiosity, not relevant to anything as far as I knew at this stage; I like to get a full picture, that's all.

She eyed me sharply. 'I wasn't. But yes, Gerald was, and yes, he did leave his first wife for me.' She dared a judgement, but I had no problem with it. Why should I?' 'He was a good man, Mr Dismas, a little – ' little was the kind of word where her *t*s went AWOL '– bit hard on me sometimes, but only when I'd done or said something stupid, especially when we were in company. Gerald never liked to feel foolish or embarrassed, especially if I was the one showing him up. He was a very proud man. A very . . . a very rigid man and, I suppose, old-fashioned in some ways.'

'Children? D'you have any?' Again I asked for no particular reason, just a way of getting her to open up, but the question stopped her dead. She glanced away and it was a relief to escape her carelessly veiled gaze at last.

'No,' she replied after a pause. 'No kids. Gerald always thought it was me; y'know, that I was to blame. But it wasn't me. I was sure of that, although I never let him know.'

'You had tests?'

'Didn't need to.'

I sensed we were finally getting to the point of her visit. (Yep, I'm good at that kind of thing too.)

'It's the reason I'm here, Mr Dismas,' she confirmed.

Ah, I thought. 'I see,' I said.

Now she looked directly into my one good eye. Oddly she didn't proceed; she had to be prompted yet again.

'You do have a child, then,' I ventured.

She looked at the tip of her cigarette held in her lap and I pushed the ashtray across the desk towards her. She tapped ash into it, a hurried, jerky gesture.

'I think so,' she said quietly.

She thought so . . . 'I don't understand, Mrs Ripstone.'

'Could we . . . could we have the office door closed?' she asked.

'Of course.' I lumbered round the desk, my limp not too bad at that time of day; it'd grow worse as the day wore on, depending on how tired I got. As I was closing the door Henry looked up from his desk and raised his eyebrows; I gave a small shrug. Clients were entitled to all the confidentiality they demanded, and then some; that was the first rule in the private investigation business. Henry's balding head was already bowed over his accounts again before the door clicked shut.

'Okay, Mrs Ripstone, we can't be overheard,' I assured her as I returned to my seat. 'This is strictly between you and me, although other members of my team will have to be brought in if I decide to take your case and if the subsequent investigation requires extra hands. Even then, any personal information will always be kept in a locked briefcase carried only by myself, or it will never leave the precincts of these offices.' I indicated a row of four grey filing cabinets to my left. 'While on the premises, your file will be kept under lock and key as a matter of routine. If particularly sensitive, that file can be locked away in our multi-cylinder, combination-lock Stratford Clarendon safe which, incidentally, is bolted to the floor.' I pointed to the big metal box against the wall behind her. 'And only myself and my first assistant know the combination.'

If she was impressed, she didn't show it; I think her thoughts were too inward to pay attention to my blatherings. She needed another deep drag on the cigarette before she could proceed. A blue haze was beginning to fill the room, but that was okay – I enjoyed smoky atmospheres.

'I had a baby two years before I met Gerald and I was single. A son. My name was Teasdale then. Shelly Teasdale.' She blurted it out, as if it had to be said in a rush because she still felt some guilt, some shame even. 'He never knew ... I never told Gerald about the birth,' she added. 'I didn't think it was necessary.'

I nodded sagely; it seemed the right thing for me to do.

'But now I want to find my baby,' she said, leaning forward on the desk.

'Well, hardly a baby any more. You said eighteen years ago ...?'

'He's a young man now, I know that. But I only knew him as a baby.'

'And you've had no contact with him since? Look, I have to be frank with you here. The only people who can help you find your son are the authorities who arranged the adoption or for the boy to be taken into care, whichever the case. Barnardo's would be your best bet, although there are special agencies that deal with this sort of thing. Even then, it would be up to the boy if he wanted to see you. Eighteen years is a long time to be disowned by your own . . .' I didn't have the heart to finish; the poor woman was distressed enough.

She was clutching the cigarette in both hands and shaking her head, slowly, deliberately, as if she didn't want to hear. Her eyes were liquid as she said: 'You don't understand. They told me he was dead. There was something wrong with the baby at birth. He didn't survive.'

'I'm afraid you're right – I don't understand. If the baby died, why would you – ?'

'Because they lied. My baby didn't die. They said he was born with too many abnormalities to live long. They told me he was dead within minutes of the birth.'

'You must have seen it . . . him . . . for yourself.'

'No. It was a difficult birth, I'd been in labour for more than twenty-four hours. I was exhausted, only half-conscious when he finally arrived. They took him from me immediately, but I heard him, I heard his cries. They were . . . different, somehow, but I definitely heard them. They were very strong.'

I tried to be gentle. 'That may be so,' I said softly, 'but that doesn't mean the child didn't die soon afterwards. Did you see him again?'

'I told you, I didn't see him at all.' The tears were beginning to spill over and ruin her mascara line.

I hoped she took my small groan for a sigh as I sat back

in my chair – not a very comfortable position for me, incidentally. 'I'm sorry, I still don't get it. Why would they tell you the baby was dead if that wasn't so? It doesn't make sense. What kind of hospital was it anyway?'

'An ordinary National Health hospital in Dartford. The Dartford General.'

'Well, there you are, there wouldn't be anything sinister going on in an NHS place, nor any other type of hospital for that matter. I wonder . . . uh, there's no easy way of saying this. I wonder if the death of your husband hasn't left you overwrought? You've lost a loved one unexpectedly and tragically and I assume you're alone, so maybe now you're reaching for another possibility, one that tells you that the son you had all those years ago and thought was dead might still be alive. You're full of grief, remorse, and dare I say, guilt? Guilt that you never told Mr Ripstone, you kept it a secret for eighteen years, and guilt that you might have abandoned your only child.'

She stabbed the cigarette into the ashtray, her fingers trembling. 'I'm not a neurotic widow, Mr Dismas, despite what you might think. You don't know the full story yet.'

She took a small handkerchief with lace edges from her purse and dabbed at her eyes, now smudging the running mascara. The tears ceased though, and her voice became steady again as she looked me directly in the eye (I think she was getting used to me now that the initial shock had passed). 'Do you believe in clairvoyancy, Mr Dismas?' she said.

I groaned again, inwardly this time, already guessing where this was headed. I had enough problems dealing with reality without bringing hokum into my life. I didn't want to upset her any more, though, so I replied: 'I've heard a few interesting stories about such things over the years. Let's face it, Brighton has more than its fair share of fortune tellers and psychics, not to mention New Age and alternative medicine practitioners.' (And not to mention private enquiry agencies, which was why I wasn't keen to lose a prospective client, no matter how off-the-wall they might be; competition was too fierce for that.)

'Then you do believe certain people have psychic powers?' she pressed on.

'Telepathy, a sixth sense, that kind of thing?' I shrugged noncommittally. 'It's a possibility, but I wouldn't know for sure.'

'But if I told you that when Gerald died I consulted a clairvoyant, you wouldn't laugh at me and think me stupid.'

'Of course not. Nothing unusual about that kind of thing these days. In fact, I've heard some of these people – clairvoyants, mediums, psychics, whatever you'd care to call them – can bring a lot of comfort to the bereaved. The one or two I know around town seem harmless enough.'

'They can do more than just comfort. Some of them can heal the sick just by thought or touch.'

She was a believer all right.

'You mean faith-healing? Well, I'm not too sure about – '

'Don't dismiss it so easily.'

Tetchy about it too. 'Many of them can look into a person's future as well as their past. Some can know your thoughts just by looking at you and without your saying a word.'

Yeah, and some can con you into parting with cash by providing all manner of useless information. 'Can I take it, then, that you've consulted such a person, Mrs Ripstone?'

'Gerald's death left me in a bad way,' she replied by way of answer or an excuse, I wasn't sure which. 'I missed him so much and his death came so quickly and so horribly. He was an awkward man sometimes and he had his black moods. But he cared for me. I *know* he really cared for me, despite some of the things he said, the things he did . . .' Her tiny handkerchief had become a scrunched-up ball in her fist. A large, diamond-cluster ring on one of her fingers caught the light from the window behind me. 'I'm still not over it, Mr Dismas. His death, I mean.'

'It can take a while,' I commiserated, 'maybe a couple of years to get over the loss of a loved one, and even then you're not really over it. You just learn to cope.'

'You've been through it too?' She seemed almost hopeful.

'Uh, no. No, it's only what I hear.'

'Oh.' She wiped the dampness from her cheeks, then squared her shoulders as if determined to get a grip on herself. 'It was so hard to accept that Gerald was gone at first. I think I went a little bit crazy with grief. I locked myself away, saw no one, talked to no one, wouldn't even answer the telephone for a while. And then a feeling came over me – I don't know how to describe it. I just woke one day and felt there was something I could do about my loss, that if there really was something called the "soul", as the Church tells us, then perhaps I could contact Gerald again. I didn't have to be entirely on my own.'

Uh-oh, I thought.

'I hadn't really believed in spiritualism before, you know, contacting the dead? But at the same time, I'd never *dis*believed in it. I just hadn't given it much thought. D'you understand?'

'Sure,' I answered. 'Most people don't like to think about death until it comes close in some way or other. So that was when you decided to approach a medium?'

'Not at first. It wasn't a sudden urge, anything like that. It just come on gradually, a sort of feeling I should contact Gerald. And I wanted to find a good clairvoyant, a genuine one, not one of them phonies.' Estuary kept breaking out despite her efforts to contain it. 'Lucky for – *luckily* for me, one of my friends knew of someone who didn't live too far away.'

'You wouldn't have to look far in Brighton.'

'Well, this one lived in Kemp Town.'

(Kemp Town is an adjunct of Brighton, although it likes to keep a separate identity.)

'Her name's Louise Broomfield,' Shelly Ripstone continued. 'You've heard of her?'

I shook my head.

'She's quite well-known. In those sort of circles, I mean.'

'You went to see her.' I tried not to let my impatience show.

'I got her phone number and I rang. Apparently she doesn't just see anybody, she has to talk to them first. She knew I was distressed right away.'

There's a surprise, I thought.

'And she could feel there was something to tell me. She knew just by our conversation on the telephone.'

A light tap on the door just then. It opened a little way and Philo, my youngest employee, and Sam Spade wannabe albeit a brown one, poked his head round.

'Sorry to interrupt,' he said cheerfully, his short black hair glistening with gel. 'You wanted to know about the writ this morning.'

I used Philo a lot for process serving, especially if there might be some running after the recipient to do (and as process serving took up half the agency's business, on some days there was a *lot* of running to do).

'Any problems?' I asked, looking past Shelly Ripstone. The particular debt dodger Philo had had to confront was more slippery than most – I'd had dealings with this character before – but the kid had to learn some time, and the hard way was often the best.

'Well, he pretended to be his own brother, but I recognized him from the Polaroid you gave me. He wouldn't touch the papers, so I dropped them at his feet in the hallway, then did a fade.'

'You're sure you got the right man?'

'Definite.'

I gave him a lop-sided grin. 'Okay, make out your notes

for the affidavit right now so you don't forget the details. Then Henry's got a trace for you to work on, only telephone stuff, but it might be complicated. I'll catch up with you later.'

He took a last look at the back of Shelly Ripstone, appraised her ash-blonde hair, raised his eyebrows a couple of times at me, then disappeared from the doorway. The door closed quietly behind him.

I apologized for the interruption before prompting my prospective client once more. 'You went to see this, er, Louise . . .'

'Broomfield,' she finished for me and I wrote the name down on the pad.

'Okay.' I waited for her to continue.

'She was wonderful. And she's a faith healer too. There was something about her, a sort of . . .' she searched for the appropriate word '. . . a *goodness*, a sort of . . .' she struggled for another description.

'Compassion?' I suggested.

'Yes, that's it. I sensed it as soon as she opened the front door. You know she hugged me right there on the doorstep, before either one of us had said a word. That broke me.' Tears were brimming again at the memory and she swiftly dabbed at her eyes with the soggy hanky. 'I'm sorry. I'm an emotional person.' She sniffed a couple of times as evidence.

'It's all right. Take your time.'

A snuffle to end the sniffs, then she regained control. 'Louise took me into a room at the back of the house, a bright little room, walls and ceiling painted pale blue. I felt at peace as soon as I entered it.'

With most prospective clients you learned to cut to the chase pretty fast, getting to the facts without too much embellishment. Some, though, I'd learned to let tell their story in their own way, guiding them with the odd soft prod here and there. Shelly Ripstone fell into the latter category; she'd get to it at her own speed.

'What was she like, this medium?' Medium or clairvoyant,

it made little difference to me. What I think I wanted to know at this point was whether or not Louise Broomfield was genuine, and any information about her might help me decide. I would naturally distrust anyone who adorned themselves with pendants or crucifixes and dressed in black as symbols of office. That was showbiz, artifacts of illusion, and not for the serious-minded. There were quite a few hucksters around town and, I had to admit, some of them I liked; in general, though, I had an aversion to robes and regalia of any kind, especially when they were to do with the Church.

'Louise is very ordinary. More like a kindly counsellor than a clairvoyant. She makes you feel . . . well, good inside. She understood what I was going through right away and she let me have a good cry before asking me anything.'

'You told her about the death of your husband?'

'She already knew.'

I didn't push her. It would have been easy enough to conclude Shelly Ripstone was grieving, inevitably for someone she'd recently lost. Guessing it was for her late husband would have been easy enough by minimum probing.

'So she contacted Gerald for you?'

The question from me was genuine enough, despite an in-built cynicism towards anyone who claimed they could communicate with 'the other side'. Even if I didn't believe it, it was evident that this woman across the desk did.

'No. She contacted my son.'

'But you said you thought your son was still alive.'

'It's how I now *know* he is. I'd always had that feeling my baby hadn't died. Intuition, a mother's instinct – I don't know what it was, but it was always there, always with me. And Louise said I'd been right to believe it all this time.'

'I thought clairvoyants could only communicate with spirits, not with the living.'

'Like lots of people, you're mistaken. Louise can pick up the thoughts of people who might even be thousands of miles away. Living people, I mean. She can heal just by thinking of a sick person who could be on the other side of the world. She can "see" the auras of people she talks to. She told me she had communicated with a little boy who'd been in a coma for two years and who still showed no signs of recovering. Sometimes she can tell if a person is going to die soon, even if that person doesn't know they're sick. Her mind reached my son, through me, just by my being there. She picked up his presence.'

Shelly Ripstone leaned close across the desk, her anguish overriding her nerves of me. Her eyes were pleading, regarding me purely as someone who could help her and not as some misshapen thing to be pitied, or repulsed by. 'Louise fainted away in front of me, Mr Dismas. Whatever it was she sensed, whatever it was she saw in her mind, it caused her to collapse. And when she came round she wouldn't – couldn't – speak of it. She just kept telling me over and over again that I had to find my son before it was too late. That if I didn't, something terrible – *something awful* – was going to happen. And it would happen very soon.'

3

It was at least another half-hour before I finally showed Shelly Ripstone out. Earlier, her loud weeping had brought Henry to the door, enquiring if he could be of any assistance, his real motive just plain nosiness, and I'd shooed him away. In private again, I rose from my desk and patted the distressed woman's shoulder (was that the slightest shudder I felt run through her, or just a sob-spasm?) and offered her my own dry handkerchief. She took it gratefully and eventually stifled the tears.

I think it was sympathy rather than the fee I'd charge that made me agree to take on her case. Truth is, I thought an investigation wouldn't amount to much anyway, that the search for her lost son would be a wild goose chase – hospitals just didn't lie about newly-born babies, even if there was no supporting father involved. I explained this to Shelly Ripstone, *née* Shelly Teasdale, but she insisted my personal view wasn't important as long as I did my job properly. Fair enough, I told her, and promised that all the agency's professional skills would be put into force to resolve the matter one way or the other; it was her money, so it was her shout. A little cynical, I know, but it cheered her up considerably.

We talked some more, with me taking notes and my new client still snuffling as she supplied the details: address at the time of her pregnancy all those years back, the address of the Dartford General Hospital where she'd given birth (together with some unfortunate news concerning that

21

particular place), Louise Broomfield's contact address and phone number. We also agreed on my fee and expenses. When she left she was in better shape, although not much better: those smudged eyes were still anxious and her fist clenched the borrowed handkerchief as if to wring it dry. Nevertheless, there was a glimmer of hope in those eyes when I promised to call her the moment I had anything to report.

On the way downstairs to the ground floor she had to edge past the large frame of Ida Lampton, my third and last employee, who was ascending the creaky staircase with heavy breaths and even heavier steps. Standing at the office door I watched Ida turn her head and stare after our attractive client as she descended the next flight of stairs; no chance, I thought, and Ida looked up to catch me grinning. She smiled back and shrugged her meaty shoulders, then came all the way up, bringing her plastic bags full of light shopping with her, for all the world looking like a favourite maiden aunt returning from her morning's shop. It was a great guise, especially for someone hired as store detective for the week.

I stepped aside to let her through, then closed the door marked Dismas Investigations behind us. When I turned, three sets of interested eyes were focused on me.

So. I'm Nick (Nicholas) Dismas and I run the Dismas Investigations agency, a two-room office with leaning walls and crooked door frames a couple of floors above a charity shop a few doors along from Brighton's Theatre Royal. In the heart of the seaside town, we're close to the train station, shops, seafront, and more importantly, a crush of solicitors' offices, from which we get most of our business. Note it's an investigations agency, not a detective agency: we don't 'detect' anything – that's for the big boys, who have more contacts, generally richer clients (in particular, companies and financial institutions) and who earn a whole lot more from a higher scale of fees than we humble investigators. Also – unlike us – they quite often get involved in criminal cases. The one thing we do have in common, though, is that neither party has any real power or authority: we're ordinary citizens with no official status whatsoever.

The private investigator's job generally involves process serving (handling writs and summonses and the like), tracing (tracking down certain people who had decided to go 'missing', usually because of financial or domestic difficulties), status and credit reports, accident and insurance enquiries, repossessions, debt collecting, surveillance (which includes anything from watching individuals or premises, to joining a company as an employee in order to catch out pilferers or industrial spies, to following errant husbands or wives). Mostly mundane, even boring, work that requires patience, care and an eye for detail. A sense of humour sometimes helps, too.

Henry Solomon was the agency bookkeeper and administrator, who occasionally took on fieldwork. He was tall, hooknosed, bespectacled (in fact, he was one of those types whose glasses seemed to be built into their heads – you couldn't imagine the face without the attachment), balding, with a midriff bulge that mocked his overall leanness. He dressed neatly and conservatively, although when the mood took him he sported colourful braces and socks, or a flashy bow-tie, sometimes – when the mood *really* took him – all three. Henry was mad on old movies (in fact he looked a bit like the dead actor Henry Fonda) and ballroom dancing (watching, not partaking of) and lived with his elderly mother in the Kemp Town. He enjoyed a gin and tonic, although never to excess, and loved to try and catch me out on movie trivia. His downside was that he hated blacks, Asians, the French and Chinese, and socialists; to be honest, he was the only Jewish Nazi I'd ever met. His sense of humour was waspish-acerbic, but his basic nature – *despite* those imperfections mentioned – was benign (folks are complicated, right?).

Ida Lampton, the big woman who'd just climbed the stairs and who looked like that maiden aunt with her short greying hair and plump face, was my main asset. Equally good at serving summonses and injunctions or repossessing unpaid-for goods, she also made a great store detective, especially when dressed as she was that day in light summer frock and cardigan, with sensible brogues for walking. Six-foot one, big-boned and broad of girth (more than fifteen but less than seventeen stone was her last admission regarding weight), Ida could play the heavy – in trousers, neck scarf and reefer jacket you could be forgiven for taking her for a man – or the sweetheart (useful for debt counselling and collecting). In the latter guise she could be pleasantly persuasive, in the former she was goddamn intimidating.

I'd first clapped eye on Ida in a Brighton gay club called the Greased Zipper (no subtlety there, then), where she was serving behind the well-packed bar and I was searching for a runaway youth who was known to frequent such haunts, despite his tender age. His parents, my clients, were frantic and only too willing to accept his burgeoning lifestyle if only he would return to the nest, and I was showing his photograph around to either uninterested or excitable, mock-eager male clubbers, some of whom snatched the picture to show their giggling clique. As in any other city or big town club, straight or gay, there are many variations in type among members – the quiet, the flamboyant, the drunks, the troublemakers, the hard men and women – and in this particular one (I'd done the rounds that night) a combination of the last two types, all leathers and glory moustaches and naked arms (and that was just the women – joke), had decided I was an affront to their delicate (despite their muscles and blue jaws) sensitivities. If they'd stuck to verbals everything would have been okay – I could always handle that – but they'd become physical, shoving me around, giving

me no chance to back off either with wit or reason before
things turned any nastier.

Now I'm no pushover, despite my problems, but before I
could retaliate, aware I'd come off worse and not giving a
damn anyway, lovely big Ida stepped in. Five minutes before
she'd given the photo I carried time and attention, even
though she was mobbed at the bar, genuinely sorry she
wasn't able to provide me with a lead on the missing kid
(she was only too aware of the predators that stalked the
streets here for fresh, inexperienced meat), and now she'd
noticed the trouble I was in. A swift knee into one bully-boy's
leathered crotch and a sharp big-boned elbow into another's
powdered nose settled the matter quickly enough (I learned
later that Ida was also engaged as club bouncer as well as
barmaid). One of the boy-bitches had screamed blue hell
and Ida grabbed my arm to steer me towards the door.
Outside I'd jabbered my gratitude and given her my card in
case she happened to see the youth I was searching for. Two
days later she'd called in with a sighting of the runaway
selling copies of the *Big Issue* outside a Virgin record store,
which led to my taking his parents directly to him (the
record store had become his regular pitch). After contact he
was their problem, but I had become interested in Ida
herself. That she could take care of herself there was no
doubt; that she had many contacts all over town soon became
evident. I offered her a job with the firm and, after she'd
consulted her live-in partner of twenty years, a sweet, gentle
woman who taught pre-school infants in a small village eight
miles outside Brighton and to whom I was soon introduced
over a Little Harvester Sunday lunch, Ida agreed to give it a
try. That was six years ago and she'd been with me ever
since.

Young Philo Churchill was the newcomer to the agency,
the sometimes hopeless but ever-enthusiastic novice. It's
usually a mistake to take on young apprentices in this game
– in fact, most agencies won't touch them – because once

they've learned everything from you, every trick in the book, every procedure to be followed, often making themselves a pain-in-the-butt in the process by asking too many questions and fouling up too many times, they strike out on their own, setting up their own agency and taking some of your clients with them, promising a cheaper deal and more (ha!) care. But what the hell, Philo had left school at seventeen with seven GCSEs and two A levels and had vainly been searching for work for two-and-a-half years before turning up on my doorstep. Yep, I felt sorry for him. A little ashamed too, because I knew the fact that he was black – a light brown tone actually – hadn't helped him in the job market. Besides, I needed an extra hand – the workload was good at that time – and he was willing to accept low wages. Almost twenty, he was a good-looking kid whose grandparents had arrived in Southampton shortly after the Second World War, when the country was in desperate need of young, manual labourers. They'd done their bit, and so had their offspring son, who eventually had married a Greek girl; now Philo, English bred and born – as English as his surname might suggest, in fact – wanted to do his bit, if only that residual prejudice, rump of a sorry past but still rampant in certain low quarters, would so allow. Philo hadn't sought work to prove himself worthy as an Englishman; no, he'd never suffered from that foolish kind of race-paranoia. He simply wanted to work because that was the normal thing to do. Besides, he was ambitious.

Philo dressed smartly, despite his meagre earnings, and he looked good. Even Henry was impressed by his keenness, and working together, Henry, Ida and Philo, well, they made a good team.

So that just leaves me, Nicholas Dismas.

I was found, thirty-two years ago, among the dustbins behind a nuns' convent in a poorer part of London. Found by the convent's caretaker/handyman when he took out the trash early one cold winter's morning. God knows what he thought of the misshapen little gnome lying there among the bins, barely a few hours old and not even wrapped in a blanket but swaddled in yesterday's newspaper, although without doubt it must have given him one hell of a shock. Perhaps he even crossed himself, while muttering a prayer and wondering what demon had had the temerity to leave its hideous spawn on holy ground.

I was born a monster, you see.

I'm not shamed by the term, nor embarrassed. Saddened, of course. Made desperately bloody miserable by it. But that's the way it goes. It's what I am in most people's terms.

Doctors told me in later life that my physical condition was probably due to *birth trauma*. I'm not diseased at all, there was never any sign of spina bifida or any form of deficiency: I was just born malformed. And as I grew older, the deformities augmented, became more defined and ever more distorted. The infant monster ripened into a grotesque.

My forehead overlapped my eyes, a Neanderthal protuberance that frightened children and dogs; my jaw grew more pointed, my mouth more leering, lips more twisted. The curve of my spine increased and veered to the right so that my shoulder was huge, the blade amalgamating with the hump of my back. I crouched further and further forward until crooked was my normal walking, sitting, resting stance, and my right leg was slightly – oh thank *You* God, only *slightly* – withered, so that I walked with a hobbling lurch. Even my chest was disfigured, breastbone and upper ribs on one side overlapping their neighbours, and hair spread down my back to form a tail between my buttocks, one that I kept shorn regularly, a DIY job because I'd have hated for anyone else to see my naked body.

Would the hair on my head were that thick, but no, His torment – did I *thank* God a moment ago, albeit ironically? – was far too comprehensive to allow such favour; it hung in loose drab strands over my scalp and forehead, the bushiness of my eyebrows mocking its very sparsity. My ears, too large even for this large cranium, looked as though they'd been chewed by a couple of unfriendly Rottweilers.

But there was nothing wrong with my brain, no lumps or dents in the bone had damaged its fibres; no, only bitterness bent my thoughts. My nose was flattened, but its shape was no worse than the nose of an incompetent pugilist's, and my hearing, despite the gnarled receivers, was keen, as was the vision in my one grey/brown-speckled eye (its twin, the left one, was useless, mutilated in an incident which occurred in my younger years). I wasn't tall, but was by no means a dwarf; somewhat below average height, I suppose, which was hardly surprising considering how crooked I was. So on the plus side, I was smart, could see and hear comparatively well, had an acute sense of smell, and my arms and left leg were exceptionally strong (nature compensates, right? Hah!). Despite these small compensations, it was difficult for me to believe that life was God's precious gift. In fact, was my wretched body an indictment of His will? Did He issue some of us with faulty meat-machines on purpose? Or was it a mistake, an oversight? Or truly deliberate, all part of His Master Plan? Who knows? I only knew my *mistake* – if *mistake* it was – was worse than most, not as bad as some. I hardly felt grateful for that.

In the early years I used to wonder about my mother, mostly as I lay in my narrow cot at night in the dormitory of the boys' home they – the authorities – had sent me to. Was she like me, a hunchbacked monstrosity, or was it my unknown father who bore the mark? Perhaps they were both like me. You know, it takes one to love another? Maybe they'd been freaks in some age-old circus show, the kind that would be banned for being politically incorrect these days (and how I agreed with that!). I didn't often think of *him*, though. I don't know why; he just wasn't part of the reverie. My thoughts were nearly always of her alone.

In my fantasies, my mother was a princess, or the beautiful daughter of some wealthy lord, and it was they, the King and

Queen, or the lord, who had forced her to give up the child who had been born with such hideous deformity. The shame for such grand people would have been too much to contemplate. So I'd been stolen away while she was sleeping, or perhaps dragged from her outstretched arms, her pleas, her tearful protests, ignored; and then I'd been lost somewhere, given to the captain of the guard or, more probably, the lowly groundsman to take me away to some faraway place to be left there with nothing to identify my august status. But someday she would defy all those around her and she would search and eventually find me. Then she would claim me for her own and we'd never be separated again. The tears of pleasure and misery those romanticisms would bring me.

As I grew older, such fancies dimmed to be replaced by the thought that my mother had had no one to help her in her desperate straits, that the unwanted pregnancy was the last straw in circumstances of abject poverty, and she had been forced to leave me on the nuns' back doorstep, knowing they would not reject me, that I would be cared for if not by the nuns, then by the State, until I became a man.

And as I grew older still and unhappiness had moulded (and even mouldered) my psyche, that fantasy too, had faded. My mother had been shamed and repelled by the variant she had given birth to – perhaps she had even sensed my awfulness while I was still in her belly – and had dumped me as soon as the umbilical cord had been cut. She neither cared for me, nor was she curious about me: the search had never been undertaken and I was never to be claimed.

I believed all this until other visions started coming to me, uncertain revelations mixed with night-time dreams that made me wonder if the bitter discontent I had felt all these years, the resentment, the loneliness that only my kind could ever know, was finally leading to madness. Then again, they might only have been due to the drugs.

*

Philo was the first to speak: 'So what was *her* trip?'

'You'd think she would've invested in bawl-proof mascara,' Henry added in his waspish manner. 'All Coco and no class.'

'Poison, actually,' I corrected.

'Hmn, with a nose like yours it's a wonder you can tell.'

I could take that kind of remark from Henry – unless it was on a bad day, that is.

Ida flopped her bulky frame into our one and only guest's chair and exhaled a rasping breath. She crossed her ankle over her knee and eased off a shoe. She rubbed her toes. 'Who did her wrong? Is the lady after revenge or recompense, Dis?'

'Nothing like that. Shelly Ripstone is a grieving widow.'

Henry peered winsomely through his spectacles as if interested in the woman's status, that she just *might* be the one for him. We all knew that was pretence though, but we were never quite sure if Henry knew we knew. 'Of course, she is reasonably attractive, despite her kitschy style.'

Ida shot me a secretive glance, then let her eyeballs swivel towards heaven.

'What is it then?' said Philo, sitting on the corner of Henry's desk. Henry frowned and moved his accounts books further away from the black youngster's butt. 'Problems with the will? Dodgy relatives turning up for a share?'

'A trace,' I informed them all. 'A baby son she hasn't seen for eighteen years.' The answer was met by a collective groan.

'I thought we never took on a trace for anyone missing more than ten years,' Ida grumbled.

She was right: that kind of contact rarely earned out – too many phone calls, too many document searches, too many blind alleys; and often the client's reluctance to pay the bill when we came up with zilch. To make matters worse as far as this particular assignment was concerned, we didn't even have a photograph – let alone a description – of what the mark once looked like (and even if we had, what use would a picture of a baby be?).

Now I broke the *really* good news. 'Our biggest stumbling block is that her son may not be alive anyway.'

'Yes, I'd say that was a definite snag to finding him for his poor dear mum.' Henry, as caustic as ever. 'Dead people rarely turn up again, do they?'

Ida removed her other shoe and wriggled the toes on that foot. 'In fact, that should make it easier. There would be a record of his death somewhere.'

'There is,' I said. 'Or, there was. The hospital where the baby was born. Problem is when Mrs Ripstone – her name was Shelly Teasdale when she had the baby, by the way – tried to track down those records herself, she discovered the hospital no longer exists. It burnt down ten years ago and all the records, along with several patients and medical staff, went up with it.'

Henry slid his fingers beneath the glasses and massaged his closed eyes. 'Er, you're losing me here. Did – does – the mother know her son is dead or what?'

'She was informed of the baby's death minutes, maybe only seconds, after it was born.'

Now he was shaking his head wearily. 'Then why on earth has she come to us?'

The reason sounded even more crazy when I heard myself telling them.

4

Before heading home that evening to my basement flat on the other side of Brighton, I made a little detour. I'd taken an instruction the previous week from a building society for a house repossession and had gone along with a court bailiff, who was the only one with the legal authority to repo the particular property, and I'd stood by while he went about his business. Fortunately, the occupants who'd reneged on their £90,000 loan from the Halifax had already skipped, so there was no problem with eviction. Less fortunate though, for the creditor that is, those same people had trashed the house before leaving.

Now I know it's easy to feel sorry for anyone turned out of their home, but the truth of it is it generally *isn't* their home. They've borrowed the money, a large amount at that, and refused – yes, *refused*, in this case – to pay it back. So the home wasn't rightfully theirs in the first place. The building society had done its best with the debtor, a guy in his early forties who, it was later discovered, had a habit of running one business after another into liquidation, every time setting up again a few months later under a different company name. When he'd approached the Halifax, his current business had looked pretty healthy – on paper, at least – so the building society had no problem with advancing him the loan. It wasn't long before his business went belly-up, though. Almost a year of letters, phone calls and personal visits by the building society people failed to produce a satisfactory resolution – our debtor always promised to pay the next month's mortgage and somehow make up the rest over a period of time; but he never did. And as I'd been sent round to see him a couple of times, more as a counsellor than a debt collector, I knew he never would. He was a fly-by-night builder who had a record (I eventually discovered) of letting down clients with shoddy workmanship, overcharging and, more often than not, beginning a job and not completing it. There were genuine villains around town that I respected more than this joker, and my advice to the creditor had been to claim the property before the debt rose any higher. As it turned out, the errant builder was smarter than all of us – he disappeared within a week of my last visit.

So this one I wasn't sorry for at all. And when I'd arrived with the bailiff, whose duty it was to force entry if necessary, I even hated the bastard. Not only had he and presumably his wife and two strapping teenage sons wrecked the inside of the house – skirting boards and door frames were ripped off, light fixtures, sockets, even the fuse box, torn from the walls and ceilings, toilet bowls and sinks smashed – but they'd also smeared the walls with special graffiti. Special? Oh yes, because this moron and his retard family had had a fine old time leaving messages especially for me.

On this particular evening I could have sent one of the others – Henry or Ida – to check out the house, but frankly I hadn't wanted them to see the ugly and obscene drawings with which the clan from hell had daubed the battered walls. More shame than embarrassment, I think. Embarrassment about my physical irregularities was something I'd managed to get over a long time ago; shame, though, was something different, and a little harder to shake off. Those spray-can daubings had been bad enough, because they were grotesque cartoons, warped but so badly executed they were almost abstruse; but one of the family, one of the boys, I think (I'd hate to think it could be the woman) had an undoubted talent for art, and I don't mean of the primitive kind. The draughtsman of the brood had used a brush and gloss paint (so much harder to remove or coat over) and his depiction of my misshapen body was exaggerated only enough to emphasize but not to distort. It's lurid accuracy was what made it so humiliating.

Just why the artist had decided to paint me naked and why he should depict my genitals so enormous and mangled (the one *big* overstatement he'd allowed himself), I had no idea, except to surmise that the obliquity of the imagination can far exceed any aberration of the physical. And exactly why he'd depicted me copulating with something that might just have been a pig (talented though he was, farmyard animals were not his forte) God alone knew.

No, I'd been shamed before the bailiff and his crew and I had no desire to be shamed further before my own colleagues and friends. I wanted to spare them that.

After the bailiff and his men had left I'd turned off the house's water supply by the stopcock – water had been flowing down the stairs from the bathroom for at least two days, I figured – before emptying the hot tank by running water from the tap into the kitchen's metal sink (the only sink that hadn't been smashed). After that, I'd switched off the electricity from the broken main fuse box, then turned off the gas by the tap on the meter's main feed out (I suppose I should have been grateful that these lunatics hadn't tampered with that or left the gas stove turned on). Any telephones that had been there were gone, so I used my mobile to ring a local handyman I hired regularly to change doorlocks, board up windows, and carry out any other jobs that would make the property more secure; personally, I had no argument with squatters, but building societies, banks and landlords in general detested them, so it was part of my brief to keep them out. Lastly, I'd taken an inventory of anything inside the house that might be worth selling on, so that the creditor could at least recoup something towards the damage caused. Unfortunately, nothing of much value had been left behind.

That evening – it was a Monday – I'd returned to the empty, vandalized house to check everything was still in order and that my handyman had done his job properly. It's location was in the rougher part of Kemp Town, the building itself set in a terrace of similar type properties down a narrow turning, and I let myself in with the shiny new key. Because of the boarded windows it was dark inside, like winter dusk, and there was the mouldy stench of damp everywhere.

Any of the undamaged furniture that had been left behind had been removed by the bailiff's men, and my steps along the gloomy hallway had that echoey resonance peculiar to empty buildings. There was enough natural light seeping through the small, dusty, arched window over the front door, as well as from the unboarded landing window above, for me to see my way, but still I took out the pencil-thin torch I always carried in my jacket pocket and switched on its beam. First I ventured into the front parlour, checking the window boards, making sure they were secure enough. My workmen had done an excellent job as usual, only a narrow shaft of light shining through the middle join. Next I examined the kitchen, trying the dry taps even though the stopcock was off. My report to the building society would state that I'd visited the reclaimed property a second time to make sure everything was in order, all services shut down, the house itself impregnable to the casual intruder. The cost of alarms and stronger defences was prohibitive to the creditor, who had already lost enough on their unwise loan, and my report would say that the precautions now taken were satisfactory. It was when I was checking the bolts on the back door that I heard the noise from upstairs.

It had sounded like something breaking.

I swore under my breath. Surely nobody had forced entry so soon. The squatters' grapevine in Brighton was finely tuned – they even had their own advice bureau – but I'd considered this place a reasonably hard nut to crack.

The sound again, sharp, tight, over-loud in the empty building. Outside a seagull gave out a startled shriek as though it, too, had been alarmed by the sudden noise.

I left the kitchen and shone the slim torch beam up the hallway stairs, treading cautiously as I went, for some reason wary of my own footsteps. Stupid, I told myself silently. I wasn't the intruder.

'Okay,' I hollered up the stairs. 'Who's there and what the hell are you doing on private property?'

That should be enough to send them scurrying for the nearest window, I figured. Obviously the trespasser or tres-passers had found their way in from a garden window at the back of the premises, a window I'd thought not worth boarding. I paused at the foot of the stairs, waiting for more sounds, hopefully of running feet. Nothing stirred, though.

I'd have to investigate. I'd have to go up there. Probably it was only neighbourhood kids up to mischief, aware that the property was vacant. Even more likely, it was an animal of some kind, maybe a cat on the prowl, or mice searching for food. Could even be rats. I shuddered.

'All right, I'm coming up,' I called out reluctantly, wanting to give whoever or whatever the chance to make a getaway. I didn't want trouble – my fee didn't warrant it.

I began to climb, the damp stair-carpet spongy beneath my feet. Mildew had already begun to set in and the smell was unpleasant. Come on, make a break for it, I said to myself, a voiceless plea to the intruder above, and the dusty stair-rail was shaky under my grip (in their rage, the vengeful builder and his tribe had obviously tried to loosen it).

Half-way up and the noise came again, only this time even louder, almost like the sharp report of a pistol being dis-charged. It brought me to a halt.

Dust motes swirled in the beam of light from the torch as I aimed it at the landing ahead. Did I really want this? Did I *need* it? Much better to retrace my steps and leave the house entirely. Inform the police of the break-in and let them get on with it. Like I said, I wasn't paid enough to put myself in danger. Unfortunately, if nothing else, I'm a pro. Part of my contract with the Halifax was to make the building secure, so it was my responsibility to keep the place free of intruders. Although right then I tried to resist the idea, I knew I had a duty towards my client. God damn it, why hadn't I gone straight home from the office?

The thought suddenly occurred to me that perhaps the debtor himself had returned to reclaim something he'd forgotten during his moonlight flit. I prayed that was not the case. He'd already unleashed his wrath on the building itself and I didn't want what was left over taken out on me. The graffiti had been enough to deal with.

Then I thought, what the fuck, and headed on upwards again, working up a steam of anger as I went. Yes, I hoped it was the bastard builder and I hoped his sicko son was with him, because I had something to tell him about his particular artistic gift, a whole lot to say about his mean-minded, bigoted, self-fucking-expression in gloss paint. I stamped the stairs, squelching liquid from the carpet with my heavy footfalls, and pulled at the fragile banister rail, causing it to rock to and fro.

Where are you? I called out in my mind only. *Don't mess with me*, I warned, still in my mind. *Don't be fooled by my appearance, I can handle myself all right.* Ah, the power – the self-deception! – of anger.

I rounded the bend in the stairs, reached the landing, looked this way and that, craning the whole of my upper body in that awkward movement of mine.

'Come on you bastards!' I shouted aloud this time, invigorated (or fooled) by my own temper. *'You want trouble, you've got it!'* All bravado, of course, but it had carried me through before under similar circumstances; a bit of bluster could sometimes save you a whole lot of hassle.

But the landing was empty. The evening sun shone through the grimy window at the far end, reflecting off the wall over the stairs with its word-graffiti, the Neanderthals' imagination obviously having run out of ideas for illustrations by the time they'd reached the upper level. Even so, the scrawled letters were equally obscene.

There were three open doorways along the landing, one behind me, the other two on my left. The cracking sound exploded again and I almost hopped into the air.

It had been even louder than before and seemed to come from the middle room. I stayed a moment or two, trying to analyse the sound. It was brittle, acute, a sound that cleaved the still, damp air, now more like the crack of a whip than a pistol shot. I made for the open doorway.

And stopped at its entrance, shocked rigid by what I saw across the darkened room.

Then, as the large cracked mirror on the wall opposite fragmented into a thousand more pieces, I stumbled backwards, terrified and aghast by what I'd seen in its fractured reflection, the hideous images, the grotesques mouthing silent screams, curious oddities whose malformed limbs seemed to claw at the glass from the other side. And I screamed myself and heard the sound, the *only* sound in that terrible tenebrous twilight. And I backed away from the room as I screamed, moving fast, my bent spine breaking the frail banister behind me, so that I plunged into the stairwell below, thudding against the sodden carpet, rolling down, over and over, head over hump, until I reached the bottom.

I wasn't knocked unconscious, but I was dazed, my one good eye deliberately closed again after observing the hallway revolving around me. The pain of landing had hit me instantly and as I lay there it gathered force rather than subsided.

I whimpered first, and then I moaned. Oh dear Lord, that fucking hurt.

I sucked in a large draught of musky air, then resumed moaning, for a short time the shock of the fall outweighing the fright I'd received inside the upstairs room. But quickly the fright claimed the upper hand and I began pushing myself along the hallway towards the front door. I didn't get far though: the dizziness and gathering pain soon brought me short. Hunched there, on knees and elbows, I drew in more breaths and closed my eye once more.

The worst of the pain eventually passed, along with the giddiness, and I managed to lift my oversized head a little.

What the hell was that up there?

I blinked, blinked again.

What the hell had I seen in that mirror?

My panic began to ease as I considered the question. Unfortunately, my heart still thumped too hard and too quickly, my hands and arms continued to tremble against the carpet. Shapes, horrible, disgusting shapes – that's what I'd seen. It was almost as if the room itself had been alive with monsters that could only be seen as reflections in the broken mirror. A long shudder ran through me, seeming to start with my head and shoulders and coursing right down to the soles of my feet. It couldn't be. The room had been empty. I would have heard those things before I'd even entered the room if they had truly been there. No, something had triggered my imagination. Maybe my *own* distorted reflections, multiplied by the fractured glass, were the images that gaped at me across the darkened room. Or maybe it was just another acid flashback, a lingering chemical imbalance among the complex neurons of my brain. Lord knows, it wouldn't be the first time.

Not entirely convinced by either solution, I mentally began to explore my limbs and body, wondering if anything had become broken or detached in the fall. I breathed more easily when everything appeared to be intact; well, as intact as it ever could be. I pushed myself back against the wall and rested there awhile.

I let a minute pass by, then another, knowing what I had to do if only for peace of mind. I had to go back up there and take a second look. No rush though. I had all the time in the world.

I hesitated at the top of the stairs. I really didn't want to go inside that room again. There was no percentage, no incentive. No gain. Not really part of the job description. Except I had to; for my own satisfaction.

I'd suffered flashbacks before, a result of too much Eighties acid, but they'd never been as nightmarish as this. And the last one had been well over a year ago and had involved hundreds of thousands of dancing legs, a black and white Busby Berkeley extravaganza of torso-less limbs and sparkling sequins, a Grand Guignol musical of severed parts danced to a full Latin-rhythm orchestra. Where that peculiarly horrid fantasy was dredged from, I'd no idea – probably from watching too many Thirties musicals on TV while tripped out on A – but it had been patently unreal, easy to cope with, unlike this latest vision – *hallucination*? No, there had been something all too real about those mutants in the mirror.

I inspected the broken landing rail before moving on, a delaying tactic, I guess. I must have hit it with some force to smash right through, even though the mounting had been weakened by the last tenant. That was going to be added to my damage report, just another item the absent builder would have to pay for when the building society finally caught up with him. Time-wasting over, my gaze drifted towards the open doorway.

It was so dark in there because, as the middle room, it was windowless, only light from the landing window seeping into the open doorway. I edged closer, unwillingly, treading carefully while not exactly creeping. This time I peered round the door very slowly.

The mirror on the dingy wall opposite had broken into myriad pieces, yet still held together like a great big jigsaw of silvered glass. And it was my own image I saw reflected there, my own fearsome self mirrored a thousand times or more, my imperfections multiplied; and even though I could not understand why the glass had shattered at my approach, I now realized that it had been my own hideousness, viewed in a new and awesome way, which had shocked me so.

I stood transfixed, watching myself in this jagged confederation of plagiarized horrors, this horrendous coalition of likenesses, and after a while I began to weep.

5

I got back to my flat late, having lingered in a bar on the way. Not one of my regular haunts – too many friends and acquaintances would have wanted to gab, even buy me a drink or two, and I had a need to be alone with my own thoughts, my own personal misery. After five Bushmills Malt and three Buds, I'd left, stepping out into the warm night and turning towards the seafront, the salt-breeze almost clearing the fug from my head, which was something I hadn't wanted. I needed that alcohol haze between myself and my demons, needed it to restrain them, lest their grip clung too tight, held me in terror till dawn. They had come knocking before, more than once, possessing me through the night, mesmerizing, haunting me; and with daylight, I had never understood why.

Hobbling along the coast road, I listened to the voices of people, youngsters in the main, rising from the open areas outside clubs and cafés along the lower promenade. For years the arches between the town's two piers had lain neglected and derelict until a bright local councillor had worked his butt off attracting investors to a scheme by which the area would be revamped. Now it had metamorphosed into a lively boulevard of clubs, bars, cafés and craft shops, where locals and tourists mingled on mild evenings and the younger ones, too many of them high on Special K or GHB, raved to their particular caste of Jungle or Techno, Nu Energy or Drum 'n' Bass, Trance or Speed, Hip Hop or Big Beat, Waltz or Foxtrot (just kidding). Ironically, it was both what I needed and didn't need at that moment: the noise, the shrieks, and the babble of life was good, and, together with the bright lights, told me that life was incessant and encompassing; and that, in itself, let me know how alone I was. An outsider. Always had been, always would be.

In that lachrymose mood, I moved on, eventually reaching the steps to my basement flat. My home was situated in one of the seaside town's broad, sweeping crescents, a hilly green park at its centre, the main thoroughfare and the sea itself bounding the open end. It was a terrific location, most of the tall, white Regency properties – some in better condition than others – nowadays split up into flats or grand apartments, the residents a mixture of rent-paying youngsters and high-earning owners. Vehicles lined both sides of the horseshoe road, many of them double-parked, but still the vista from the apex of the curve was breathtaking, day or night. Descending the stone stairway to my front door, I drunkenly scratched the wood around the keyhole with the key's tip before inserting it. I pushed my way in, flicking the lightswitch quickly as I hurried down the short hallway to the bathroom where I kept part of my stash. My hands shook like a regular druggy's – which, take my word for it, I wasn't, not really – as I reached inside the bathroom cabinet and scrabbled with the lid of the Elastoplast tin. Somehow I managed not to spill the contents as the lid came off.

Inside, instead of plasters, were my ready-mades (Sunday afternoons was generally reserved for rolling enough joints to get me through the week), comprising of two varieties, some rolled in brown cigarette skins (papers), the others in white. The Skunk – in this case Kali Mist, named after the Hindu goddess of destruction – was for when I was really strung out, and the other, white-skinned, was more gentle, a good Jamaican sinsemilla. Tonight I chose the brown.

Lighting up, I went through to the small furniture-crowded sitting-room and poured myself another Highland Malt, this one a Dalmore, before drawing the curtains of the barred windows a little and flopping on to a cushion-strewn sofa. Anticipation as the smoke burned its way down my throat was almost as pleasant as the mellowness that I knew would quickly follow. No rush involved, just an easy sinking into a better place, and while waiting for the mood change the drug and alcohol hopefully would bring about, I surveyed my surrounds, something I often did when my emotions were low, my perspective hopeless. Two small versions of magnificent sculptures stood at each end of the sideboard, Rodin's *Eternal Spring*, a dark bronze whose male and female figures were wonderfully natural on one side, and Epstein's *Genesis*, an anti-naturalistic carving of a pregnant woman, an elongated hand stretched across her swollen belly, a piece that was the very antithesis of its opposite neighbour but no less beautiful. Adorning the wall over the room's mean little fireplace was a wood-framed print of Agnolo Bronzino's *Eleonora da Toledo and Her Son*, the mother serene in her beauty, the young boy placid in his innocence, and on the mantelshelf below was a miniature copy of Hepworth's *Mother and Child*, an abstract carving in marble, all fluid lines and pierced stone (make what you will of my choice, its romanticism, the obvious underlying yearning – I only knew that they took my mind on journeys). I sipped whisky between the drags.

Sleep, helped along by a couple of Motivals before I turned in, was uneventful that night. Rather than fall into another dimension where everything was troubled and plausible only in the dream state (which was my usual sleep pattern), I drifted off into oblivion instead, cares and worries excluded, fantasies barred. Even my hangover next day was tolerable, and although I suffered a few hurts and bruises from the tumble I'd taken, there seemed to be no real harm done (thank you squidgy stair-carpet).

I wet-shaved in front of the bathroom mirror, used to the

ugliness that stared back at me; used to it, yes, but never willingly accepting that countenance, still disturbed and saddened by it, even after all these years. An everyday ritual like shaving was still a routine torture. Once, when I was on heavy stuff like Ice – crystal meth – another face would sometimes regard me from beyond the glass, one that watched me with two good eyes and whose features were regular, though too blurred for recognition. That ill-defined but handsome countenance had hinted at something too evasive to remember properly, too vague to focus upon, yet still filled me with a strange, elusive regret. Regret *and* guilt. At one time those emotions had become so overwhelming I'd turned away from hallucinatory substances completely – what good was a high whose sidekick was profound but unaccountable remorse? Maybe a shrink would have some answers, albeit predictable ones: cut out the bad stuff, think positive, drugs altered and eventually deteriorated your mind state. You take the drugs to escape your own reality, but in the comedowns the reality only becomes more depressing, and the stronger the substance, the harsher the aftermath. Well, I'd already cut out the heavy stuff, because it scared me too much, and I didn't need a shrink to tell me so. In fact, Acid, Charlie and Amphets had been easy to dump, and I'd never used H anyway – heroin was too addictive for someone like me who constantly sought escape. My main gig nowadays was Skunk and booze. Hell, I'd spit in your eye if you even offered me E. Sure, I knew it was considered smart to be part of that scene, but I also knew that those poor suckers were the losers in the long run (and that was their problem – it took time to find out). No diatribe here, no preaching; just the hard facts.

Naturally, more than one psychologist – not psychiatrist; nobody's ever thought me crazy – had tried to get me on their metaphorical couch, assuming I had to have some kind – *any* kind – of inner turmoil because of my 'impaired' physique; and maybe I had – *of course I bloody had* – but I'd never felt the need, or even the urge, to discuss it with the medical profession – or anyone else, for that matter. My mind was my own territory. Let doctors prescribe medicines and pain-killers for the afflictions my physique brought me, but my thoughts were private, they belonged to me alone. Tormented I might be, but it was my own personal torment, invisible to outsiders, unlike my deformities, which were on show for all the world to see. Besides, I had the constant and irrevocable feeling that no shrink would ever understand, let alone resolve, the reason for my lifelong disquiet, this unease that was always with me and which grew more ponderous as the years went by. They'd assumed my troubled mind was due to my dysfunctional form, and I knew – don't ask me how I knew, I just *did* – the issue was far more complex than that.

Self-discovery had never been an indulgence of mine. That earlier time of fierce drug-taking had always had two clear purposes: pleasure and escape. With both there came a 'lifting', a supposed ascent on to a higher plane where creative thought is enhanced and where you feel at one with all around you, at one with the essence of life itself. Huh! Try it enough and you'll discover it's a false concept; that, rather than being a great mind-expanding experience, it's ultimately a closing down of avenues of reason, an occlusion of actuality, and so a limiting of the thought process. At the time you may think you're on the road to perception, to Nirvana even, but in truth you're travelling blind alleys (although instead of heading towards a dead end, you're on the way to cerebral dissipation). Am I sure? Sure I'm sure. Just look around at all the deadheads left over from the sixties, the mental cadavers of the drugs revolution, those once creative musicians and artists and writers, and even businessmen and financiers, their powers of creativity long since withered, their drive stultified, not through passing years but through damaged brain cells and enfeebled resolve. You know who I mean, those dried-up facsimiles of their former selves, their talent mere echoes. Many – of those who survived, that is – are rarely heard from, they seem to exist in some intellective timewarp, while the bleatings from those still in the public eye tend to be an embarrassment.

Anyway, for me the comedowns that followed the highs were too disenchanting to bear and the pursuit itself too ineffectual, meaningless and self-deceiving, to desire. Besides all this, the cost was too great, both to pocket and body (let alone the mind).

These days, I stuck mainly to cannabis and booze for no other reason than to dull my own wretchedness.

I retraced last night's route to the office, on the way passing by the bar I'd swilled in last night, not even giving its locked door a second glance, and stopping to breakfast at one of those archway café's along the boulevard. The sun was already working up to a steady blast, the slight sea breeze cooling the few holiday-makers who were about so early. The sea itself was a fresh blue, dark on the horizon, white caps breaking easily along the shoreline; one or two sunbathers were already stretched out on towels on the pebbled beach, but these were probably office workers or hotel staff, catching the early morning heat before commencing duties for the day. Watching sky-weaving seagulls as I sipped lip-burning coffee at an outside table, I felt a calmness come upon me. I wasn't at peace with myself – I'd never known what that was like – but at least the trauma of the previous night had settled, and the illusion in the broken mirror had become precisely that to my rational mind: an *illusion* caused by fragmented glass and embellished by the darkness of that windowless room. Why had it shattered completely at my approach? Easy. The former occupier had already smashed it and my footfalls had caused the final meltdown. I refused to consider the fact that I'd witnessed an *explosion* of glass – that just wasn't part of my rationale on that warm civilized morning.

A craft-shop owner gave me a wave as she opened her

shutters, the young waiter who'd served me breakfast loitered for a friendly chat. As I climbed the steep ramp to the upper road, another acquaintance hailed me from the doorway of the Old Ship hotel. I returned a brisk salute and went on my way.

Looking as I did, I was more noticeable than most around town, and hence had become part of its scenery, a familiar figure to the locals; and that was no bad thing in my line of work, because it made me well enough known to gain people's confidence and so much easier for me to pursue enquiries. A lot of these people were eager to talk to me, either out of some guilt-ridden pity (there for the grace of God, and all that . . .), or because they were ashamed of the repugnance I aroused in them and felt noble when they were able to hide it. Maybe I'm being a little over-cynical here, but I can only explain the vibes I got from them. Some – a certain few – were unabashed at how I looked, and I received genuine warmth from them, while others – there's always the opposite extreme to anything – never even tried to conceal their loathing of me. All in all, though, I was generally accepted and only the tourists and out-of-towners tended to give me the hard, or at best, discreet, stare. Kids were always a problem, but then I'd learned to accept that.

Cutting through the Lanes, a pedestrian area of narrow turnings and alleyways filled with antique, jewellery and gift shops, I crossed a broad thoroughfare and turned off into the road that led past the old Regency theatre and the Royal Pavilion's park opposite. The theatre's display boards advertised an 'all-new *Rocky Horror Show!*', not quite my taste in live performance, but the kind of thing that brought in the holiday-makers and locals (especially the kids and weirdos) in droves; next week might be a Gilbert and Sullivan, or a murder mystery, or even a ballet. Variety, in the broad sense, is what kept the place going. My mood considerably brightened by the sunshine and 'hail goodfellows' along the way, I climbed the creaky stairs to the agency.

'Okay,' greeted Henry, who always seemed to beat me into the office, no matter how early I arrived, from his desk. 'In which movie did Cary Grant say his male co-star resembled Ralph Bellamy and who was that co-star?'

I groaned at the regular ritual, not quite ready for it so soon in the day. Nevertheless the answer came to me before I'd even reached my office door.

'Easy,' I told him with a smug grin. '*His Girl Friday*, and the co-star *was* Ralph Bellamy.'

Henry wasn't pleased. He went back to his paperwork, grumbling darkly under his breath.

I went around my own desk and studied the day's agenda, which I usually scheduled in a large diary before leaving the office the previous night. Ida would have gone straight to store duty and Philo, when he arrived in about half-an-hour's time, breathless and over-heated from his dash from the bus stop and ascent of the stairs, would be busy for most of the day with an assignment that meant catching the train to London. I wanted him to pay a call on the General Registrar Office, where there should be a record of baby Ripstone/ Teasdale's birth, as temporary as that condition might have been.

As I hit the first cigarette of the day I thought of the baby's mother, Shelly Ripstone, and wondered why she was so positive her son was still alive. Just on the word of a possibly fake clairvoyant? Didn't make sense. And something else that didn't make sense was why I shared the same intuition.

6

I was on my second repo of the day when I got the call from Philo on my mobile.

The first of the two vehicle repossessions had been for a BMW, which unfortunately was parked in the driveway of an upmarket residence situated in a plusher part of Brighton's suburbia. The car's owner – or non-owner, because he hadn't kept up his payments – was one of those flash businessmen who knew all the answers, someone who did well by living on his wits and running up debts. He was aware of his rights and was only too pleased to inform me of them when I rang his doorbell and showed him the letter of authorization from the credit company that empowered me to take the BMW away. With a self-satisfied grin he'd snatched the letter from me and torn it to pieces (that was okay, I had three photo-copies, two of them in my briefcase). Standing on his door-step, he towered over me, yet still he stretched himself to full height (I could see him pivoting on the balls of his feet) in an effort to intimidate me even more. I got that kind of thing all the time: people either patronized me, letting me know my deformities meant nothing at all to them, that I was just one of the chaps, or they got nasty and made the most of what they considered my shortcomings. Either way, it made no difference to me: I was there to do a job, that's all there was to it.

This debtor had been expecting my call, no doubt fore-warned by a prior visit from the finance company's own man, and his only surprise was my appearance itself. He hadn't bothered to lie by telling me the cheque was in the post, or that the lender and he had come to some agreement about the unpaid sums only an hour or so before I'd arrived; no, he didn't bother because he knew that legally I couldn't touch the BMW while it was on private property, i.e. his own driveway. If I tried to repossess, I'd be guilty of taking and driving away without consent, and the police held a dim view of auto theft, whatever the circumstances. However, in such cases there is an answer as far as the poor old repossessor who, after all, is only trying to do his job, is concerned: you turned the tables, reversed the situation. I stuck a copy of the authorization letter under the windscreen wiper and informed the defaulter, who remained on the doorstep, hands in pockets, grin mouldering into a scowl, that the vehicle had been officially repossessed by the finance company and that if he took it out on the public highway (my address was as formal as this) it would constitute an arrestable offence because he was no longer the legal owner. The police would be informed and if he were to be stopped by them, he, himself, would be charged with taking away and driving without the owner's consent.

That ruse hadn't pleased him one bit, but I knew as he slammed his front door on me that by the time I returned next day he would have seen sense and given in to the inevitable. He might throw the keys at me, but at least I'd be able to drive the BMW away.

My second 'bust' that day was a lot easier. The car was a Golf GTi and I had expected some trouble: you can usually tell by the vehicle the kind of person the driver is likely to be and a sports model invariably meant 'aggressive'. So I was delighted that the GTi was parked in the roadway and even more delighted that when I knocked on the debtor's front door, there was nobody in. Pushing the authorization letter through the letterbox, I went back to the car and opened the driver's door with the Slim Jim (a thin metal strip that slides down easily between the window glass and rubber sealing strip, its hook contacting the doorhandle locking pin and opening it by a sharp pull) I always carried on such occasions. Once inside, it was almost as easy, although it took a little longer, to hot wire the ignition and drive off. It was as I was pulling away from the kerb that Philo's call came through on my mobile.

'Dismas,' I said.

'Dis?'

'Philo?'

'Yeah. Just left the Family Record Centre. At the GRO?'

'Yes, I know, Philo.' I pictured him outside the registrar office, mobile phone, compliments of the agency, clamped against his ear to cut out the sound of busy London traffic. 'I'm in a repo at the moment, so give me a couple of seconds to get round the corner.'

I didn't want the debtor returning to find me driving away the vehicle he still considered his own. Like I say, GTi drivers often mean trouble and I could do without that today. Parking around the corner and tucking nicely between a Metro and a Volvo estate, I retrieved my mobile from the passenger seat.

'Still there, Philo? Good.' I took a look around the street before switching off the car's engine. 'So what's the story?'

'That's just it, Dis. There isn't one. No birth or death certificate for the Ripstone – sorry, the Teasdale – baby was ever issued as far as they can tell at the registrar office.'

'That's impossible. Our client had the child and it was delivered at the Dartford General.'

'Well, you know the place burned down.'

'Sure but that was some years later.'

'Yeah, but the point is that the records can't be checked at the point of source if there was an error or oversight at this end. That's what they've just told me.'

'There's another GRO in Southport; we can check with them.'

'Uh-uh. Already did. They did it here for me. No record of the baby there either.'

I sat in silence for a moment, trying to make sense of it all. Was Shelly Ripstone *née* Teasdale lying? But why should she, what was there to gain? Could she be deluding herself, imagining she'd given birth all those years ago? No, she was overwrought at the loss of her husband, but she didn't seem crazy or hysterical. I wondered if the clairvoyant, this Louise Broomfield, had planted the thought in Shelly's troubled mind. Some kind of auto-suggestion. What would be the point of that, though? I shook my head in mild frustration: I had no answers.

'Dis?'

'Sorry, Philo, just thinking.'

'What d'you want me to do?'

'Get yourself off to the Search Room at Companies House. It isn't far from where you are now.'

In the investigation business you always tried to kill two or three birds with one stone to justify the expense of long excursions; it was important to cover the expense in time and travel for the agency. In this case, one of the national banks' local branches in Hove had asked me to look into the commercial background of a prospective client who was seeking a substantial loan for a new business venture and the bank had a feeling that other branches and different brand banks had been approached by the same man before for similar type loans, but under different company names. They were aware that money had been lost on those deals and didn't want the same to happen to them. Reluctant to turn away a future and apparently well-heeled client, they were, nonetheless, proceeding with extreme caution. Hence my agency's assignment.

'Sure thing,' Philo came back at me. 'I've got the details. Anything else while I'm up here?'

'Can't think of anything. Just get the train back as soon as you've finished – no loitering around the fleshpots. Keep away from Soho. I need to work on a report for the bank tonight, if poss.' I didn't, but neither did I want my apprentice roaming the big city on my time.

'Right, Boss. Catch you later.'

The line went dead and I switched off the mobile. Because of my hump, my face was only inches away from the steering wheel and I leaned even further forward, resting my forehead against the warm, hard plastic for a moment or two. What the hell was Shelly Ripstone playing at? Why waste my time and her money? I straightened again – that is, I straightened as much as possible – and lit a cigarette. I could end the assignment there and then, call her with my apologies and close the case. But something – I didn't know what: instinct, intuition, I had no idea – prevented me from doing so. It was an odd reaction at the time, but it makes sense to me now.

The first thing I had to do before making any final decision, I told myself, was to find out more about Shelly Ripstone herself. And there was one particular person who could help me with that.

I tapped numbers into the mobile.

Early that evening we met at Brown's, one of the seaside town's trendy eateries, where the waiters and waitresses were hip and friendly. Etta was a few minutes late and stood briefly by the door, searching the tables for me. I gave her a wave and she returned a smile.

Etta Kaesbach was slim, almost skinny, with long brown hair and intelligent eyes. I'd always be grateful to her for helping me set up business in the first place, giving me the chance to do work for her firm of solicitors after I'd bombarded her with letters, mailshots and phone calls. She'd been the first solicitor – and it was from this profession that most private investigations agencies got their work – to provide me with the opportunity of proving my worth, not, she once told me when we'd got to know each other better, because of my obvious disabilities, but because of my overwhelming enthusiasm (yes, I had been over-anxiously keen in those early days, eager for the work, desperate to show I could do a difficult job as well, if not better, than the best of my particular trade).

She sat opposite me at the round table, her face a little flushed from her obvious dash from her office to meet me. Etta's hair was held back from her forehead by a child's hairgrip, not a slide, and her hazel eyes were encircled by round, wireframed spectacles, somewhat like ancient National Health specs, but which were Armani and probably cost well over two hundred quid. Perched on her fine, straight nose, they actually softened the intelligence of her face rather than enhanced it, and the absence of lipstick on lips that were already a pretty shade of pink, as well as nicely defined, combined with the neat-but-dated hairstyle, gave her a fresh attractiveness that was easy on the eye (literally in my case). She wore a deep-brown soft velvet jacket over a flowing maroon skirt, the collar of her beige shirt/blouse overlapping the jacket lapels. Etta was in her mid-thirties, although she looked ten years younger, had one disastrous marriage behind her – it had only lasted eighteen months, due mainly, she admitted, to dedication to her own career (although I knew there was more to it than that; she'd chosen a real bastard for a partner) – and had suffered poor on-and-off relationships since. As far as I knew, there was no man in her life at the moment and, I have to own up, I'd often dreamt of playing a larger part in her life myself, but had never had the nerve, nor the encouragement from her, to make a move in that direction. I was too scared of spoiling things between us. And too afraid of rejection.

A young girl in white shirt and black leggings was at the table before Etta had placed her briefcase by her chair.

'Hi,' greeted the waitress, all sleeked-back hair and stunning smile. 'What can I get you?'

'Just coffee, regular.' Etta smiled back, then glanced at my brandy glass. 'One of those might be useful too.'

'You'll need to order some food if you want alcohol,' I said, indicating the remaining half of my chicken salad sandwich, brown bread, no mayonnaise.

'That's okay,' said the waitress obligingly. 'We'll count yours as the meal. Unless you'd like something to eat?' She raised her eyebrows at Etta.

'No thanks. Coffee and a brandy will be fine.' Etta smiled back, then returned her attention to me as the waitress left us.

'Busy day?' I enquired.

Etta rolled her eyes. 'Like all others. You switching from whisky these days?'

'Needed something a little more substantial.' I sipped the brandy to show how necessary it really was.

'Having problems, Dis?' It wasn't an idle question; those hazel eyes were full of concern.

'Uh, no, nothing drastic.' The episode last night with the broken mirror wasn't one I cared to relate.

'Nothing to do with the new client I sent you, I hope.' She pulled a wisp of hair away from her mouth.

'Shelly Ripstone? Uh-uh, she's fine. But I did want to talk to you about her.'

'So I gathered from your phone call. Oh Lord, I hope I haven't sent you trouble. I thought it might be an easy one for you, a straightforward trace.'

'And so it should have been,' I reassured her. 'Thanks again, by the way.' I meant for the continuing work and she acknowledged with a shrug.

'You're the one who's helping me out, Dis. I'd hate to refer a good client to the wrong agency.'

I gave Etta my lop-sided grin. 'So long as you know it's always appreciated.'

'Are you getting sentimental in your old age, Dis?' She

was smiling too, but she watched me keenly, a little puzzled I suppose.

'God forbid,' I joked. 'You'd only take advantage.' I was suddenly embarrassed by the sexual connotation of that remark – like as *if* – and I quickly moved on. 'I only wondered if you could tell me more about Shelly Ripstone.'

Etta gave me a surprised look as the waitress arrived back at our table with her coffee and brandy. I quickly drained my own glass and tipped it towards the girl. 'Sorry, I should've asked a minute ago.'

'No problem.' No strain at all in the waitress's smile. 'Back in a moment.'

I put the empty glass down and returned Etta's gaze. 'S'okay, Mrs Ripstone isn't being difficult. I'd just like to know some more about her background. We drew a blank on tracing her baby at the first hurdle and I wondered how badly she'd take it.'

'I see.' I could tell Etta didn't quite believe what I'd said, but she seemed prepared to indulge me. 'What did Mrs Ripstone tell you when she came to your office?'

'She was distraught, missing her late husband. I gathered she was afraid of being left alone in the world and the thought of finding her long lost son seemed to provide her with some comfort. I told her a trace on the child wouldn't be easy after all these years, but she didn't want to hear it. I guess getting her son back might have compensated for the loss of her husband in some way, so I was sympathetic.'

Etta gave a small shake of her head before sipping the coffee and it was my turn to be surprised, this time by her cynical smile. A fresh brandy was placed before me and I nodded a thanks to the waitress as she retrieved my dead glass. Picking up the new brandy, I held it towards my companion and Etta lifted her own glass. We clinked them together, a minor ritual I always believed in when I was with a friend.

'She didn't tell me it all, did she?' I said, and Etta was hesitant.

'Oh, what the hell, she is a mutual client, so I think it's okay to share a confidence with you. But it *is* in confidence, right?'

'Hey, it's me you're talking to. When have I ever broken a confidence?'

'Yes, I know, you're a pro. And in this case, I think it might be useful for you to hear the whole story. It won't help you find the missing child – if there *is* one – but you'll at least understand why it's so important to Shelly Ripstone.'

'So it isn't just because she's a lonely widow.'

'Well, that might be part of it, but there's also a much more material side to the whole thing.'

Becoming more interested, I leaned forward on the table.

'Did she tell you how her husband died?' Etta asked.

I raised my eyebrows, not an easy thing for me to do. 'She said he'd had a heart attack.'

'She didn't explain the circumstances?'

I shook my head slowly, wondering.

'No, I suppose there's no reason why she should have.' Etta put down the brandy and sipped coffee again. Whirling ceiling fans sent down cool, welcoming breezes. 'It was downright embarrassing for her, in fact.'

'Come on, Etta, get to it.'

'Gerald Ripstone had a heart attack while he and his wife were, uh, well you know, Dis . . .'

'While they were making love?' I grinned again. 'Not good for her, maybe, but not a bad way for him to go.'

'He shouldn't have been at it at all, his doctor had warned him to take things easy.'

'I thought the heart attack was a one-off, the first and fatal one.'

'She told you that? No, Gerald had been suffering from a heart condition for some time. He really should have been more careful. At least, he shouldn't have used Viagra, especially combined with the drugs he was on.'

'Well, I guess it's natural enough for a man to want his own wife, no matter how debilitated he is. And his wife is an attractive woman.'

'That's as maybe. I'm more inclined to think that Shelly persuaded him to use the pill. As for Gerald, he was desperate for a son and heir. Needed someone to leave his business to, someone who'd carry on his name. Incidentally, you won't know the worst part about that night. The embarrassing part, that is.'

Now I was intrigued and moved even further across the table towards Etta, my back so bent I must have resembled a turtle.

'I'm not sure I should tell you about this, mutual client or not.' She looked down into her coffee cup, just a little flustered.

'You can't stop there, Etta. What'll it take to bribe you?'

She sighed. 'You won't let it go anyway, will you?'

I shook my head. 'You know you want to tell me.'

She smiled, revealing small, even teeth. 'Yes, I do, you bastard.' She took a nip of brandy, grimaced, and chased the taste away with coffee. 'Okay. You've heard of couples becoming locked together during intercourse?'

My turn to grin again. 'I've witnessed dogs in that awkward state, but I always thought it was a myth as far as we humans were concerned.'

'No, it isn't, actually. It's not common, but it happens – ask any experienced doctor. Sometimes a woman might panic for some reason or other while copulating and then becomes incapable of relaxing her legs, which become locked tight.'

A young mother on the next table feeding a toddler chocolate ice-cream from a glass dish glanced over. The little boy, sporting a brown moustache and beard, smacked his lips impatiently until he caught his mother's attention once more.

Etta lowered her voice. 'The abdominal muscles become locked too, as well as the muscles around the vagina.'

'Nice,' I commented.

'Not really. The man's working part is gripped so tightly he just can't break free, no matter how he tries. And I think the blood concentration in the penis because of the Viagra Gerald was using might have made things even more difficult. Personally, I think he took more than one pill and was locked in tight as a result.'

'Pretty humiliating when you have to call in the fire brigade.'

'No, it requires hospital treatment.' Etta's face was quite serious. 'The woman, and maybe the man too by that time, has to be given a muscle relaxant so they can be separated.'

I made an 'ouch' sound.

'It can quite often happen if the male partner has a heart attack while . . . well, while on the job. The sexual act itself raises the blood pressure, which is dangerous for anyone with a heart condition, and the woman's fright when she realizes her lover is dying on top of her is enough to send the relevant muscles into spasms.'

I needed a cigarette, but Etta wasn't a smoker and I'd chosen the non-smoking area of the restaurant in deference to her. Instead, I drained my second brandy.

'Surely the Ripstones would have been aware that the strain might be too much for Gerald,' I said.

'You'd have thought so, wouldn't you? Perhaps Shelly wanted her husband even more than he wanted her that night.'

'And he couldn't resist.'

'Or she made it impossible for him to resist.'

'She wouldn't have – ' I began to protest.

'Shelly wanted his child too. She had a special reason to.'

'If she thought she might lose her husband at any time, I suppose it's understandable. A child might compensate – '

Again, Etta interrupted. 'Without an heir, she stood to lose half Gerald's fortune.'

I pulled back a little, one good eye staring at my companion. 'You want to explain that for me?'

'When the Ripstones were first married, Gerald made a will through our firm leaving everything – his wealth, the business – to his wife and any children they subsequently might have.'

'Only they didn't get to have any kids.'

'Correct. And they were never likely to. Not together, at any rate.'

I looked askance.

'Gerald Ripstone was sterile. He consulted a specialist after a few years of marriage and no offspring, and discovered he was incapable of siring an heir. He kept it to himself, never told his wife.'

'Wait. How d'you know all this?'

'Eventually, Gerald confided in his lawyer, the senior partner of my firm, who'd become a good personal friend over the years. Howard Benson, my boss, gave me the information when I queried a specific clause in Gerald Ripstone's will, the part dealing with inheritance.'

'But why wouldn't he tell his own wife? From the way she blubbered in my office she must have thought the world of him. Surely the fact that he was firing blanks wouldn't have mattered to her?'

Etta shrugged. 'Who knows why? Pride? Embarrassment? The way you've just expressed it shows how the male of the species views that kind of thing. You know what men are like, Dis.'

Well no, I didn't, not in that respect, anyway. Sexual prowess or high fertility having never been an area of contemplation for me.

'The point is,' Etta went on, 'Shelly was never aware that she couldn't have a child by her husband. But here's the weird thing: Gerald loved her so much and cared about the continuance of his business enough for him not to worry by whom she had a child so long as there was someone around to take care of both after he was gone. Unfortunately, he didn't have enough confidence in his wife's business acumen or her ability to survive without him.'

'I can't decide if the guy was eccentric or admirable.'

'Probably a bit of both. If you ask me it was his way of dealing with his own guilt and self-imposed shame.'

People are complex, right? Lord knows, I've dealt with enough oddballs, both professionally and personally, to be aware of how complicated we mortals are.

'Okay,' I admitted. 'Curious, but it makes some kind of psychological sense. It was his way of compensating for something he deemed his fault. What I don't understand though, is why they didn't adopt?'

'I think it was because he wanted the child to be part of one of them. If it couldn't come from his loins, then at least it would be from Shelly's womb. However, I do know they were finally looking into the matter of adoption – Gerald dearly wanted a boy – just before he died. They left it too late.'

Her coffee was almost gone and I asked if she'd like another. She declined and twirled the brandy glass around by its stem. She took a sip before placing it back on the table.

'In his will,' Etta said, 'Gerald gave his blessing to any new partner that Shelly might find. All part of his guilt trip, I suppose, and his obsession for the continuation of his business, which he seemed to regard as his own epitaph.'

'But even if she had a child soon, a baby couldn't run a business. It doesn't make sense.'

'That's why everything has been put into a trust for now.'

'What? The money *and* the business?'

'Yep.'

'The trustee . . . ?'

'The bank that helped Gerald set up business in the first place. The one that likes to say yes unless you're asking for overdraft facilities. He'd always maintained a good working relationship with that particular bank.'

'I can see how Shelly would be just a little upset with that arrangement. It's treating her like a child herself.'

'She was more than a little upset. She yelled blue murder when the terms of the will were read out to her.'

'So the trustee looks after the business until the child is old enough to take over.'

'And if it's a boy, all the better.'

I let it all sink in, drawing back from the table and staring into space. The waiters and waitresses had gathered in a clique by the bar, occasionally breaking into laughter at a shared joke. The toddler at the next table grizzled for more ice-cream, while his mother wiped the mess from his face with a napkin. The restaurant's glass door opened and a couple of wide-eyed tourists wandered through, looking around as if not knowing what to do next; one of the waiters quickly joined them and showed the way to an empty table. A gabble of Dutch or German drifted our way.

'So that's why she's so keen to find her missing son,' I murmured at last.

'Shelly? I would think so, although I've tried to convince her she'll be well taken care of without the worry of dealing with a business she doesn't understand. She seems to have got it into her head that she'd be better off by being independent of the bank, and in a way, I can see her point. Why should she have to be accountable for every penny she spends and every business decision she makes to some faceless wonders at head office?'

'Wait a minute.' A new thought had struck me. 'This clairvoyant thing. You knew about it, didn't you?'

Etta nodded. 'Yes, Shelly was very excited. That's why

she wanted the name of a reputable private investigation agency.'

'But did she visit Louise Broomfield seeking some kind of consolation for the loss of her husband, or has she always suspected her baby had lived and wanted help in finding him?'

'What does it matter?'

'I'm just wondering if the clairvoyant picked up Shelly's desperation, somehow tuned into the *thought* of a missing child. Isn't that how this kind of thing works, by extrasensory perception? Maybe Shelly just passed the idea on to this other woman.'

'Dis, as I said: what does it matter? Your work is done as far as this case is concerned. When you rang me earlier today you said there was no record of the baby's birth, let alone its death. Submit your fee and forget about it.'

I wished it could be that simple. Unfortunately, something was nagging at me, something I couldn't get a handle on. Some creepy little voice way back in the deeper recesses of my mind was telling me I was more involved that I dared to imagine.

7

'James Stewart.'

'You got it wrong this time. It was Gary Cooper.'

Henry shook his head vehemently. 'No. I'm telling you it was James Stewart.'

'You're thinking of *Mr Smith Goes to Washington*, not *Mr Deeds Goes to Town. Deeds* was made in '36 and *Smith* in '39, same year as *Destry Rides Again.*'

That gave Henry cause for pause, but not for long. 'Henry Fonda was *Smith Goes to Washington.*'

'No, you dope. Fonda was *Young Mr Lincoln.*'

'Okay, okay. So who played *The Thin Man*?' My accountant's eyes narrowed behind his thin glasses and he grinned with expected triumph.

'William Powell, of course.'

'No! *That* was James Stewart!' He banged the desk with the flat of his hand, triumph complete as far as he was concerned.

'Sorry, Henry, but James Stewart was in *After the Thin Man*, made two years later, and he was the villain; William Powell was still playing the thin guy, Nick Charles, and Myrna Loy was his partner, Nora. His dog was called Asta, by the way, played by Asta the dog.' I tried not to gloat.

Henry's mouth was open, his jaw loose. He quickly regathered his wits though. 'Answer me this one, then. What Roger Corman B movie did Jack Nicholson star in?'

'Ah, you know I don't have a clue about modern movies,' I returned disgustedly.

'Modern? *Modern?* This was Sixties stuff, my friend.'

'Yeah well, anything made after the Forties escapes me. I prefer the really old ones.'

'God, anyone would think you were ancient.'

'I just like the black and white style. Films had class in those days. Men and women dressed right and sex was suggested and all the sexier for it, and there was no profanity then. Didn't need it: the story was everything.'

'It was the Edgar Allan Poe one, wasn't it?'

We both turned to look at Ida, who was sitting in the visitors' chair, stirring her mug of tea with a plastic spoon.

'What?' I said.

'Directed by Roger Corman, starring Jack Nicholson. He was a soldier or something. Bit part. You know – the horror film, *The Pit and the Pendulum.*'

'Oh don't you start!' Henry was gritting his teeth, his fists clenched. 'It was *The Raven. The* bloody *Raven*, okay?'

'Yes, but Nicholson was in the other one, too,' Ida offered helpfully.

'No he bloody wasn't!' Henry always got wound up over movies; he considered himself the oracle as far as the silver screen was concerned.

I'm not sure if Philo was deliberately winding Henry up, but he chipped in with a grin: 'No, Jack Nicholson was in *Fall of the House of Usher.* That was the one he had a small part in.'

'He didn't! *He didn't!* He didn't come anywhere near it!'

That was it as far as the rest of us were concerned. Ida broke into a fit of giggling first, closely followed by Philo. I was just chuckling. Henry gripped the edge of his desk, glaring at all of us, not quite sure yet if the tease was deliberate. Watching Henry, usually so calm and rational, even during his racial diatribes, lose his rag over something so trivial was always fun.

He gave up in disgust, his only way out. 'All right, we've all got plenty to do today, so why don't we just get on?'

I put my empty coffee mug down beside the plastic kettle, which resided on top of a filing cabinet (it was Philo's job to do the washing up in the small loo just off the main office), then lumbered towards Henry's desk. It would have been awkward for me to sit on its corner, so I leaned back against it instead, arms folded over my misshapen chest.

'Ida, you've got a status report for our old client, the Ownback Catalogue company. They need to know if there's any chance of getting their money from a customer who's suddenly gone sour on them. Henry has the details.'

Our accountant and administrator, still miffed, handed a typewritten brief from the catalogue company to Ida, who took it and began noting the details.

'Check with the receiver's office if the debtor is bankrupt and the County Court Office to find out if there's any out-standing judgements against him,' Henry instructed her.

'I *have* done this sort of thing before, Henry,' Ida reminded him, still scanning the two-page letter.

'You'll need to pay the debtor a visit on this one,' I advised, only because I wanted the option followed up. 'If he's uncoop-erative, talk to his neighbours – and let him know you're prepared to do that; he might just want to save himself the embarrassment.'

'Want me to pad out the report?'

'Shouldn't have to. By the time you've checked on what car or cars he runs, his personal possessions, whether he's paying rent or mortgage on his home, if he works full-time or is he on the dole, you'll have enough to fill a couple of pages.' It's a common practice in this business to make sure the client feels they're getting value for money, even on – no, *especially* on – a negative result like a non-trace.

I shifted attention to Philo, who had one foot on the desk he shared with Ida and was polishing his already glossy black shoe with a duster. 'Henry has an accident report for you, Beau Brummell.'

'Stewart Granger and Elizabeth Taylor,' Henry chipped in,

anxious to regain his authority as movie-buff of the century. 'Peter Ustinov played the Prince of Wales. Or was it Robert Morley . . . ?' He appeared deeply worried at this fresh uncertainty.

'Yeah, yeah,' I growled. 'Playtime's over, Henry. As you said, we've got a busy day.'

Philo's brown eyes, meanwhile, had lit up. Accident reports were tedious to do, but for a novice, it was a step up. This was the first one I'd allowed him to carry out on his own.

'It's an NOF, of course.' Henry's mind was back on the job, but there was a certain coolness in his voice that let our apprentice know he wasn't yet forgiven for his part in the tease. 'No Obvious Fault,' he added, just in case the acronym wasn't clear to Philo (Henry loved acronyms – they lent him authority). 'It's cheaper for the insurance company to use us to investigate the RTA – "Road Traffic Accident" – than loss adjusters, and it's cheaper for us to use *you*.' The last emphasis was unnecessary, but Henry was never one to forgive easily. 'You're to meet our client's driver at the scene of the accident, so take the standard interview sheet with you – that way you won't forget to ask the right questions, will you?'

'What else will you need, Philo?' I quickly asked, more to smooth over Henry's sarcasm than to test the kid.

'Camera, surveyor's tape measure, and pen and pad for sketches,' Philo answered immediately.

'SLR camera *and* the Polaroid, dummy,' Henry corrected. 'You never know, the SLR shots might not come out.'

It was a valid reminder, despite the sneer that went with it. I'd taken scene-of-accident photographs myself with no film in the main camera, and high street developing was always a risk. 'Three sketches at least, and let me see the report before you send it off to the client. In fact, let me sign it.'

Still pleased about the assignment, Philo nodded, a smile brightening his good-looking face.

'Report the facts only,' Henry warned, 'not your opinion, or the driver's version of what happened.'

'Gotcha.' Philo was already reaching into a low cupboard for the cameras and film.

'What're your plans for the day, Dis?' Ida enquired as she pulled on a light summer jacket and took an umbrella – it was raining outside – from the coat stand.

'Couple of debt negotiations this morning.' I held a Credit Consumer's Licence, categories D and E, which allowed me officially to come up with ways a debtor might solve their financial problems. Usually it was simply to suggest they pay off a little at a time on a regular basis, or at least by laying down a lump sum towards the whole amount. Sometimes there was a more complicated process to go through, the main object being to keep the whole thing away from the courts, which was always expensive and time-consuming for all parties, including myself as far as time was concerned. I preferred counselling these people, many of them in debt through no real fault of their own – a sudden loss of earnings, a death in the family – to demanding they pay up, and category D allowed for debt adjusting as well as advising, while E was what actually empowered me to collect payment if at all possible. These jobs frequently took time and patience, but if the agency handled enough of them through the year, they were quite lucrative. Sometimes it bothered me, this chasing people for money, even though I knew that many debtors were either crooks or irresponsible, and if they fell into neither of these categories, then better to deal with me than the bailiff. Ultimately, I was there to help, not to threaten or take things away.

'And what about our Mrs Ripstone?' Was there just a hint of malicious glee behind Henry's smile? 'Are you going to keep the poor woman hanging on?'

'No, Henry.' I turned to face him. 'I'm going to ring her right now and tell her there's nothing more we can do. Unless you'd like to tell her for me?'

He shook his head slowly and deliberately. 'That's what being the boss is all about,' he said.

'Thanks for reminding me.'

I went into my office and, still oddly uneasy with my decision, I picked up the phone.

8

It was around 10.30 that night that I stepped outside the pub in a side street near the seafront, the steady drizzle that had marred the day over with for the moment, but the streets still shiny damp. The noise from the saloon bar behind me died with the closing of the door and I took in great lungfuls of almost pure sea air, exhaling long and hard to rid my lungs of the residue cigarette fumes they'd been collecting over the past couple of hours. I felt only a little better now, the irritating sense of dissatisfaction that had been dogging me for most of the day dulled by booze and company. A burst of laughter behind me was raucous enough to pass through the thick wood and glass of the pub door and I was pretty sure it wasn't at my expense: I knew nearly all the regulars, who were mainly of the – how shall I put it? – of the 'exotic' variety; young and not so young gay men, pensioned-off chorus boys of untold age but with fabulous stories to tell, cultured antique dealers who'd had other careers in their prime, but who now saw this last profession as a means of genteel employment for themselves and their (invariably younger) partners. There were shammers and schemers, duckers and divers, women who love women, the lonely and the disparate. A good bunch. And whenever I entered that bar I was greeted with friendly calls rather than odd stares.

The air may have been moist, but it was warm; warm and scented with the aroma of sea and salt. As I began to walk towards the front, depression settled over me like a well-worn cloak, and even the bright promenade lights at the end of the long, narrow street failed to offer any cheer. Moving along the glistening pavement I wondered why this mood of – what? I couldn't focus on it. Inadequacy, perhaps? – had pursued me all day. Since I'd first opened my eye that morning, in fact. Since my conclusion that there really was nothing more I could do for Shelly Ripstone.

When I'd rung her earlier, she'd pleaded with me to stay on the case, even phoned me back seconds after I'd broken off the call. She'd offered to double my fee if only I would agree to continue the search for her lost son, and nothing I said would convince her that it would be pointless, that the child – and now I was beginning to doubt there ever was a child – had died only minutes or seconds after being born. Doctors didn't lie. The authorities might, but then why should they in such a case?

Shelly had become more distressed. Didn't I understand that a mother intuitively, *instinctively*, knew these things? And besides, the clairvoyant, Louise Broomfield, also had no doubts that her son was still alive. The evidence – or lack of it – said otherwise, I told her, but that had made her more aggressive. Pleadings became insults. But fine, I'd had plenty of those in my time. Firmly, and quite politely, I said my goodbyes and replaced the receiver.

This time she didn't ring back.

I could, of course, have mentioned the fact that she had not been entirely open with me, that maybe – well, quite likely – her motivation had more to do with her late husband's money than maternal love. But that would have been rude of me. And unnecessary.

Even so, this night I reviewed the case in my mind as I shuffled on towards the sea, yet still I could make no sense of her claim. Even if Shelly Ripstone *née* Teasdale had given birth eighteen years ago and the hospital had been razed to the ground some time afterwards, the baby's short existence would still have been noted by the General Registrar Office. But it seemed nothing at all had been documented, neither at the London office nor the one at Southport, where all such records were kept after the closedown of Somerset House in the capital. Also, in adult tracing the method is relatively simple, even if the disappearance is intentional (I rule out murder and dismemberment here); credit card purchases, the electoral roll, National Insurance number, bank statements, car registration, friends and associates – all conspire to track down an absconder; but when there is no life history, when there isn't even any evidence that the subject of the trace was ever born in the first place except for the word of a bereaved widow of dubious (although understandable) motivation and possibly of distracted mind, then finding that person is next to impossible.

There was *nothing* I could do. I'd only waste time and the client's money, and I'd never been into that kind of scam. No, I'd made the right decision. The assignment was a dodo, a dead duck. The agency had done all it could. So what was nagging at me? Why couldn't I let it go?

'Spare some change, chief?'

I'd almost passed by the figure huddled in a doorway before his voice, both plaintive and cheerful at the same time, brought me to a halt. I peered closer, searching for a face among the darkness and rags, but only when the headlights of a car crawling down the narrow street lit us both up did I find one. Wide, friendly eyes looked up at me and I realized the beggar was a kid, somewhere between seventeen and twenty, with spiky hair and a ring through his nose and grime on his skin that looked more than a week old. The sleeves of his ragged jumper were pulled over his hands, even though there was no coolness to the night, and his well-worn boots were metal-tipped and too hardy for the season.

'Just for a bit of food, like,' he said, working for whatever I was prepared to give him. He seemed uncomfortable under my scrutiny, perhaps with my features. What he couldn't appreciate, though, was that I was only doing my job. Even half-drunk, I did what I always did when I came upon vagrants or beggars (not necessarily the same thing): I gave them the once-over – all of us at the agency did – trying to catch any resemblance to photographs on our files, old images of persons gone astray, missing youths, absent husbands, absconded wives, even mothers or fathers who'd decided normal society wasn't all it was cracked up to be. You never knew when you might strike it lucky.

He became uncertain, having had a good look at me as the glare from the headlights had peaked before moving on. He appeared very uncomfortable now that we were in the shadows again. He drew up his boots and curled up in the doorway, his body seeming to shrink.

'It's okay,' I said quietly – soothingly, I hoped. 'When did you last eat?' It was important for me to know.

He didn't answer straight away. His neck craned from the untidy bundle of clothes, and he looked around the doorway's corners, up and down the street, as if searching out other company. This was a lonely little side road though.

'This morning,' he answered at last, his face featureless in the gloom. He cleared his throat, a nervous rasp.

I sighed and rummaged through my pockets, finding only a pound coin and a few odd pence. 'Fuckit,' I grumbled to myself and reached inside my jacket for my wallet. Pulling out a ten-pound note, I sensed a fresh, a more trusting, alertness about the boy.

'Promise me you'll get yourself something to eat, okay?' I thrust the note towards him and he accepted it with both hands.

'Bloodyell,' he said in a low breath. 'Thanks, man. I mean, really – thanks.'

'Sure.' I stepped away from him. 'Remember: food. Right?'

I could just make out the nodding of his head before I turned away, already wondering if he'd stick to the handout's condition, or if he'd head straight for his regular supplier.

A tenner wouldn't buy him much, so maybe he'd just drink it away. I let it go: I could only make the offer – the rest was up to him. I'd learned a long time ago it was all you could do.

As I neared the seafront there was more activity. Tourists strolled arm in arm along the broad pavements that edged the wide King's Road, many of them still in shorts and T-shirts, despite the earlier drizzle and the lateness of the hour, all of this – the people, the coast road, the edge of the beach below the promenade railings – lit up by street lamps and festive lights, lights from hotels, restaurants, the big cinema and theatre complex, lights from traffic rushing by as if late for curfew. And noise came from all directions, the jabber of crowds and their laughter, and muted music from bars and clubs, the conversations of diners drifting from open doorways.

I stepped over a puddled gutter that rainbowed oil or spilt petrol in its waters, and waited anxiously for a break in the traffic, a chance to cross the broad expanse of road at my own lively but slow speed. The gay lights of the Palace Pier stretched out into the blackness, their mirror image on the sea below dancing with every wave that rushed to shore. The pier resembled an ocean liner in celebratory mood.

Taking my chance, I made it to the centre of the road, then waited for a gap in the opposite lane's flow. Faces stared out at me from passing cars, one or two vehicles even slowing down so that their occupants could take a more leisurely look, and I saw myself with their eyes, a ridiculous stunted shape, bent as if cowering in the roadway, a clown of a figure whose mask was not funny in transient headlights, its shadows too severe, mien too crooked, the body too unseemly. Laughter passed me by as I waited; someone even took the trouble to wind down a passenger window and call out to me, call out something I didn't quite hear and did not want to hear. I seized the moment to hobble the rest of the way, my bad leg dragging across tarmac as it does when I'm tired or inebriated, my left arm waving in the air ahead for balance. I arrived safely but a little dead in heart.

A group, a horde, of language students – Brighton is always full of language students – paused to allow me through, the hush in their voices as I avoided touching any of them making their alien whispers easy to comprehend. I lowered my head even more, ashamed, vulnerable – naked under their gaze – not even my alcohol haze dimming the ocular assault, and I kept moving until I reached the ornate rail overlooking the lower promenade and beach. There I leaned, my chest pressed against hard metal, my only eye watching the blackness of the sea's horizon, a barely visible dark against dark, and I concentrated on that alone so that self-pity would not overwhelm me. My breath came in short heaves and my hands clenched the rail tightly until my thoughts, my feelings, began to settle; not calm – I didn't feel calm at all – but to quieten down, become absorbed into me so that my hands on that rail no longer trembled, so that my gasps steadied, my breathing became deeper, more even. With the quietening, there soon came the question: why had I panicked so quickly, so easily? Ridicule was something I'd borne for as long as I could remember and pity for the same length of time, but I'd learned to cope; hadn't accepted, could never accept either insult, but I'd learned to endure. So why this abrupt overpowering fright? Why had my mental equilibrium, that hard-earned stability gained only after a lifetime of abuse and sniggers and curious glances if not downright ogling and well-meaning but so often *de*meaning patronization, why had it so swiftly deserted me? Had I only kidded myself that I'd adapted to all those jibes and kindnesses? Well no, because I knew I'd only ever placed a barrier between myself and the prejudices and good intentions of others. I suppose my surprise tonight was that the shield was gossamer-thin instead of cast-iron thick. Even the whisky and beer I'd consumed that night had failed to dull the senses, to thicken that self-preserving defence even more.

An urge to be nearer the sea overcame me (because the sea was clean and as far away from people as I could get?) and I lurched from the railings, heading towards the ramp that led to the boulevard below. I was aware that my shambling walk was exaggerated by weariness – and yes, no excuses, by alcohol too – the limp now a parody of my normal gait, my hump even more rounded. Crouched and shuffling, I hastened down towards the beach, momentum increased by the slope's angle.

The ramp was wide enough for wheelchairs and delivery vans alike, but not user-friendly for hunchbacks of awkward stride, and I steered myself to one side so that I could slide my hand along its rail, steadying myself, occasionally gripping to control the descent. Near the bottom, customers were overflowing from the Zap club, milling around its door, spilling out on to the level boulevard. Getting in my way.

Now I deliberately kept my head bowed, my one eye watching other people's feet as the noise from the club's open door became horrendous, the chatter of voices around me intimidating. I could tell by the shifting of legs that some of the crowd were anxious not to become an obstacle in my way; others failed to notice me though, only becoming aware when I tried desperately, solicitously, to nudge by without giving offence. A girl's shriek was followed by laughter, a male's derision followed by embarrassed shushes.

At last I was through, but as I raised my head to see the way ahead I was confronted by the customers of the Cuba Bar, a large section of its patronage seated at tables arranged in an open area outside the bar itself. I slunk around them, regretting my impulse to reach the seashore, aware that not only did people *en masse* stare harder but that they felt anonymous enough to voice their humour or shock. Several of them pointed me out, and one or two shouted comments, and only when my feet crunched pebbles did I stop running.

I sneaked away from the bright lights towards sweet covering darkness, away from mocking sounds and cries of pity, making my way diagonally across the beach so that I'd also be moving closer to home in my sea quest. Noise behind me became a general hum of voices and music, the stony shore grew dimmer with every shuffling pace, and I'd almost reached my tidal sanctuary when I heard the insult that was the worst of all, the one I dreaded because it was never the end of it, it was always the precursor to further torment.

'Oi, fuckin Quasimodo!'

They were sitting around in a circle on the stones, unnoticed in my rush, difficult to see in their mainly dark attire. They drank from cans of beer but the smell that drifted across our neutral ground was pure weed; their spliffs glowed in the gloom, bright one moment, a dull amber the next, each burning dot thick with Jamaican promise. I ignored the call, hurrying on, my feet sliding on the little pebble hills that spoiled any rhythm I could build, but something large and hard struck the hump of my back. The stone clunked on to the beach and I went on.

'The bells, the bells!' someone behind me wailed to much snickering.

I stopped, hung my head, closed my eye for a moment, then turned to face them.

I was between the group and the boulevard, between it and the broad stretch of light from the roadway above, so that as they collectively stood, some moving sluggishly as though heavy with dope and booze, one, the nearest to me, rising almost sprightly, fired by youth's arrogance, I could see their shapes in the muted illumination, could take in their leathers and amulets, their spiked collars, their freaked hair and high, laced boots. They were an unlovely bunch.

I could just make out the peppy one's leering grin, no mercy in that expression.

'Going swimming, Quozzie? Only swim at night, do yer?'

The others enjoyed the taunt, adding their own drolleries.

'Didn't know the freak show was in town.' 'What yer do for sex, date a spazzie?' 'Didn't know abortions could walk about.' You know, remarks of that ilk, and others that were plain degenerate. Every one seemed to inspire the next, and the gang had great fun.

'Oh shit,' I said quietly to myself, then turned away and began moving again, not rushing, just taking it steady, not wanting them to see how much I was shaking. Shaking with rage, with fear, with impotence.

A beer can hit me this time, half full so that liquid spilt into my hair, ran down the back of my neck.

'Hey, we're talkin to you, 'umpback!'

I didn't reply. I kept going.

Footsteps crunching after me.

Knowing I couldn't outrun them, I whirled around and it must have been my expression that stopped them dead, shadows formed by the dim light probably deepening my scowl, maybe even making me look fearsome.

'Listen to me,' I said, allowing anger to override my nervousness. 'I'm not bothering you, so just leave me alone. Okay?'

But the sprightly one, the arrogant one, the one I assumed was the leader, swaggered towards me, features screwed up into a grimace that was as ugly as mine.

'You got it wrong, Quozzie. You are botherin us.'

Another step closer allowed me to see a face so full of loathing and bigotry that it surely must have poisoned this one's soul; it came in waves, a silent rant against everything this zealot thought of as abnormal and not up to the perceived order of things. Although my gaze never left those venomous eyes, I was aware that the others were outflanking me so that soon I was surrounded. I took a step back; my main tormentor took a step forward.

I sensed no euphoria among them, no laid-back pleasantry that the fat Jamaicans and drink should have induced, and I began to suspect they had all been on something harder earlier that evening, maybe Ice, which was the drug of the moment in Brighton around that time, a street methamphetamine, pure crystal shit that gave a big rush that ultimately and invariably fucked up the brain with its worsening withdrawals. Sometimes the tweakers freaked out with meth psychosis and hallucinations, and that was never a time to be around them.

I consoled myself with the thought that this merry little band of junkheads could just as easily be on GHB, or Liquid Ecstasy, both popular drugs around the clubs, whose comedowns sometimes could be scary as well; then again, they could be on the nutter stuff, Special K. Whichever, I figured their smoking mixed with booze was their way of making the descent easy on themselves. Only it didn't seem to be working: aggression was bristling from this mob.

'Look,' I said placatingly, hoping the tremble in my voice wasn't too noticeable, 'what d'you want from me? D'you want money? I've got money. I can give you some.' I reached for my wallet, an action replay of a short time earlier when I'd willingly offered charity to the beggar. I wasn't proud of myself at that moment, but if that was what it took to get me off the hook, then so be it.

'Yeah, we want money.'

Eyes looked greedily at the notes in my hand. 'But we don't want some, we want all of it.'

My wallet, as well as the notes, was snatched away and when I reacted, reflexively reaching out to grab it back (cash was one thing, credit cards and driving licence was another) something whacked against my head. I think it must have been another, even larger, stone from the beach, because I heard it crack as it struck my temple, and it hit me so hard I fell to my knees.

My brain went numb for a second or two and I brought both hands up to the wound, rocking there on the beach on my knees. I remember crying out, pleading with them to stop it there and then, not to let it go further, that I was hurt enough, but then they were on me, kicking, punching, pounding me until everything became a blur – everything except the pain – and I was tumbling, tumbling forward and curling into a foetus position, a frightened, confused, malformed thing scrunched up as small as I could make myself, there to be pummelled and humbled because I was an oddity, because I was an oddity with money, because I was an oddity with money who wouldn't fight back.

I don't know how long it went on for – a thousand years, two minutes? In its way, it was a lifetime – but I heard them calling me names, snarling their hatred, screeching their bile, and I absorbed it, let the pain and the name-calling sink into my system, so that soon my body and my mind had swallowed it whole, and then I allowed it – blows and words – to deaden me. That was the only way I could make it tolerable.

And when it was finally over and the five leather and amulet clad girls had walked off, I cursed them under my breath and prayed that one day the sickness inside each and every one of them would cause them to suffer the way I had suffered that night.

It began to spit with rain again.

9

The wet stone steps to my basement flat were treacherous in my condition, mainly because my vision was still bleary with tears of self-pity and humiliation and my limbs were stiff, the joints almost locked; each movement, each lumbering step, took willpower, each draw of breath took an effort. Both body and mind were in a wretched state.

Practically falling against the front door, I dug inside my trouser pocket for the key and then, for the second time in two days, scraped its point over the paintwork to locate the hole. Once inside, I fell back against the closed door and blubbered there in the darkness. I was hurt, but by now I knew it wasn't badly, and although I'd lost the cash, the girl-gang had contemptuously tossed the wallet back at me; it had struck my head, then lay open on the pebbles beside me. They hadn't been interested in the credit cards, just the money for their next fix. No, I wasn't crying because of the physical pain they caused me, nor the loss of hard-earned cash; I wept because of the dagger thrusts of their derision, their unconscionable and conscienceless verbal assault. And I cried because of their gender and their youth – two at least could have been no more than fourteen or fifteen years old. I had been broken by a team of young girls and it wasn't their blows that had weakened me, left me foetal on the beach, absorbing every punch from their fists, every slap from their hands, every kick from their high-laced boots; no, it was the viciousness of their barbs that had struck so deep, words so vile and uncompromising that it seemed as if my muscles and my mind had atrophied, had become useless and limp. It was their disgust that had defeated me.

'Oh God, why, why?' I heard myself mumble between sobs. And when I asked again, it came as a shout, a *demand* for an answer, and the question was full of loathing for myself and the Supreme Being who had created me, for I was not questioning the attack on me that night, not challenging the violence dealt to my miserable twisted body, but asking why I had been born this way, why had He created me as a monster to be reviled or pitied but never to be accepted as a normal human. How did He justify such cruelly protracted torment, a lifetime's punishment which would only end when my lungs gasped no more breaths and my heart lost its beat? I *needed* to know. I *had* to know. Yet even as I raged, implored, I was aware there would be, could be, no response, because no matter how often I'd asked – how often I'd *begged* – the question in the past, never, never, never even in my deepest despair – and this was one such moment – had an answer been given.

And eventually, as I crouched there and the last tears flushed from the undamaged ducts of my one good eye, I berated myself for believing there *was* a God to give any such rhyme or reason. Nothing – No Thing – no Heavenly Creature, no Ruler of Heaven and Earth, no Divine Deity, no Almighty, no Omnipresence, no Allah, Elohim, Yahweh, or Jehovah, would ever devise such a hellish torture. Maybe a Devil could, but surely no God?

Finally, miserably, I dragged myself up from the floor and lumbered along the short hallway to the kitchen, where I flicked on the light-switch and knelt before a low cupboard. Opening it, my hand scrabbled around behind the tins of baked beans and pineapple chunks and all the other easy-cook packages sad, single people keep stored for instant sustenance, until I felt what I was searching for: a medium-sized square-shaped, coffee jar. I pulled it out and held it to my chest while I wiped the dampness from my face with the sleeve of my jacket.

This was my special stash, used only on specific occasions; not for celebrations, nor social gatherings, but for when I needed it most – like tonight. I used it infrequently, because it was highly addictive and I couldn't afford to become highly addicted. Snow. Coke. C. Charlie. Cocaine. A cheap commodity nowadays compared to some other drugs, but still prohibitive for the likes of me. Beneficial though, at certain times. The quick rush would take me through to the other side of this trauma, the sense of wellbeing would overwhelm all else. I'd become a man again.

I took the jar through to the bathroom, unscrewed the lid and placed both on the glass shelf in front of the mirror, all routine and carried out in semi-darkness. Only then did I pull the string that operated the bare light-bulb over my head.

Dipping my fingers into the coarse coffee grains I drew out a tightly sealed plastic bag, inside which was another tightly sealed plastic bag. I unsealed the first, extracted the second, opened it and carefully poured a portion of the white powder on to a clear area of the glass shelf, my right hand trembling so badly I had to steady it with my left. I took a razor blade from the medicine cabinet beside the wall mirror and left it next to the little white hill of euphoria, of instant Nirvana, of deceptive redress, while I returned to the kitchen to get a straw. A dozen of them stood in a long plastic tumbler on a high shelf and I had to stand on tip-toe to reach them. I pulled out one and snipped it in half with scissors from a cupboard drawer before hobbling back to the bathroom.

My hand still shaking, I used the razor blade to make thin uneven lines of the coke, then bent forward with the brightly striped straw stuck half-way up my nose. I sucked up white bliss like an anteater snorting lines of ants, working my way along the short rows, thumb against the clear nostril, until only a scattering of fine dust remained. The high hit me almost immediately, a rush that was like nothing else on this earth for quick, appeasing pleasure and I jerked upright (as upright as my body would allow), still inhaling as I did so, my good eye closing as the exultation flooded my brain and a lightness swept through me.

I let out a long sigh and removed the straw, my other hand gripping the edge of the sink, the trembling already beginning to calm itself as my whole being relaxed into a wonderfully silky warmth. Pain still throbbed, but it was accommodated, harboured within a better sensation. I moaned aloud and went with the flow, my chest swelling as my misery detached itself from my psyche and floated to another place, still in reach but sequestered for the moment. The rapture swept through me and I accepted it gratefully, my poor misshapen head rocking back, my lips split into a grin of joy, my eyelids closed so that a few more tears were squeezed between them.

But when I lowered my head and opened my eye again another's face was staring out at me from the bathroom mirror.

I staggered, just a step backwards, my gaze never shifting from the figure that stood watching me from the realm beyond the glass.

I knew that face. I knew those strong, handsome features, the deep, brown eyes framed by heavy, almost feminine, lashes, the classic and very masculine shape of the nose, the lips so defined and sensual in their half-smile, the jutting, cleft chin, so rugged in its appeal, softened only slightly by that carnal mouth. Somehow I recognized the smoothed-back black hair, sleek and glossy in the mirrored light, and the heavy eyebrows, beautifully shaped over those watchful, amused eyes.

I knew this person.

Those broad shoulders, with their relaxed strength, underlying tension beneath a studied looseness, was familiar to me. I knew this man clad in shiny-lapelled tuxedo and black tie, was aware of the raw, even coarse, nature that the fine apparel disguised.

And from the expression in those roguish yet brooding eyes, I was aware that this person also knew me.

I think I swooned from shock just then, or else the room itself spun around me, and it was only the strange, extraneous sound of the doorbell that stopped me from passing out completely.

10

Whoever it was at the front door wouldn't go away. There was I, holding on to the bathroom sink, now with both hands, my eye shut again – I didn't want to see that handsome image in front of me any more – and my body still swaying, my legs enfeebled, while that persistent bellringer kept their finger against the button, releasing the pressure every now and again before starting all over, the shrill sound travelling down the short hallway and driving me crazy with its insistence.

'Go 'way,' I mumbled, not sure myself if I were talking to the visitor outside or the phantom in the mirror. '*Go away!*' I hissed, and then I opened my eye, very slowly, afraid of what I might see again.

Even as I did so, a vague recollection of having observed or perceived that handsome countenance in the past came to me, vague, peripheral glimpses that were always reflections, never the real thing, nebulous visions that vanished before they could be fastened on. Now relief – oddly tainted by disappointment – shuddered through me as my own unsightly features gawped back from the mirror.

I scrutinized my reflection, wondering at the hallucination of a moment before, silently asking myself what the hell was it with me and mirrors these days? Had the sudden rush of cocaine triggered the illusion? But I wasn't doped up yesterday when I stood in front of that cracked mirror in the repossessed house. The sound of the doorbell startled me again.

The bell, the bell. *The bells, the bells.* I shivered at the thought of those girl-gang jibes, my misery returning like a great grey cloud of chemical poison. Where was the heady coke glow, where had it gone? I was stone-cold sober, yet the traces of white dust were still on the glass shelf before me, evidence of what I'd sniffed only a few moments ago.

Knocking now. The person at the front door had given up the bell and was now rapping wood. And calling to me, calling my name. A woman's voice, soft but loud enough to reach me in the bathroom. I swore and screwed up my face even more. I had to open the door. Whoever it was outside was not going away.

Sluggishly I wiped powder residue from the shelf with my hand, then returned the rest of the stash in the clear plastic bag to the coffee grains, pushing down hard, burying it beneath them. Yanking the light cord so the bathroom was in darkness once more, I went to the kitchen and put the coffee jar on the working surface next to the sink. Then I drew in three long breaths, steadied myself, and limped down the hall to the front door.

She was small, smaller then me, and her face, illuminated by the light behind me, was round and concerned. Somehow I knew who she was even before she spoke.

'I'm Louise Broomfield.'

I wondered why she was swaying, gently rocking backwards and forwards, then I realized it was me who was in motion. I held on to the door and squared my feet against the hall carpet.

'Are you all right, Mr Dismas?'

She reached out a hand, but quickly withdrew it when I flinched away. The clairvoyant had been squinting at me because the light at my back obviously threw me into gloomy silhouette, but now her eyes widened as she got a closer look.

'My God . . .' she said in a whisper.

At the time I thought her reaction was due to my appearance together with the general dishevelment and marks the beating had left; later I was to discover it was because of something else entirely.

It was a few seconds before she had recovered enough to say: 'May I come in, Mr Dismas? It's important that I talk to you.'

'Uh, no. I don't think so. It's kind of late and I've had a heavy day.' Any irony wasn't intended: I just wanted to be left in peace to lick my wounds, brood over the mental hurts, consider reflections in mirrors. My voice sounded slurred to me and I wondered if she thought I was drunk; I decided I didn't care.

'Please,' she said urgently, the flat of her hand against the closing door. 'It really is very important.'

I hesitated, unable to make up my mind. I wasn't usually ill-mannered towards sweet-looking old ladies (although often they could be rude to me), but I really wasn't in the mood to discuss missing children and dishonest clients. I suppose it was her wide-eyed earnestness that persuaded me; either that or it was just plain too difficult to shut the door in her face, no matter how awful I felt right then.

'Okay, just . . . just say what you've got to say, then leave me alone.'

'Won't you invite me in? A few minutes of your time, that's all I need.'

Reluctantly – very reluctantly – and aware I was in no state to offer resistance, I stood aside so that the clairvoyant could come through.

She seized the opportunity, her feet across the threshold before I could change my mind, and she watched me all the way, her eyes never dropping from mine.

'Room on the right,' I instructed her and ran my hands over my face as she disappeared into the sitting-room. Closing the door, my shoulder brushed against the wall for support as I followed her down the hall. I paused in the doorway to switch on the sitting-room light and I lingered there awhile, appraising this little, rotund woman who'd invaded my space; the appraisal was reciprocal. She continued to gawk at me, and I was certain now that it wasn't because of my poor condition; I was used to stares, and hers was different – somehow it had more depth to it. Louise Broomfield had thoughts about me well beyond what she could plainly see.

'It had to be you,' she said quietly.

'Nice song,' I replied sourly, still wondering what had happened to the coke euphoria. 'I could sing a few bars, if you'd like.'

There was no smile, but she didn't appear to be offended. 'You must think I'm a little bit batty,' she said. 'It's the usual response.'

I could have told her all about usual responses, but I didn't. Instead I said: 'Look, I'm not feeling too good right at this moment, so can we make it short. There's nothing more I can do for Shelly Ripstone and I'm surprised she persuaded you to visit me.'

Concern glimmered in her eyes again. 'Oh no, Shelly didn't ask me to see you. She told me your enquiries had come to nothing, but she had no idea I would come to see you personally. No, that was entirely my own idea, Mr Dismas.'

She had a soft, reassuring voice, one that went with the kindness in her face. Louise Broomfield's hair was grey-white and she sported the kind of hairdo ladies of a certain age – sixty and over – seemed to wear like military helmets: neat, pulled away from the face, stiff-permed. Her dress was pale blue, her full breasts resting on a full tummy, and her shoes were a sensible brown brogue (not unlike the kind Ida usually wore), her stockings those thick sort that concealed varicose veins. A light, pink raincoat, open down the front, hung well below the dress and in her hand she carried a stubby, closed umbrella, tiny droplets of water sparkling from it like sequins. Studded through her earlobes were discreet shiny earrings that twinkled like faraway stars whenever she moved her head. She looked powdered and smelled scented, although her lipstick barely tinted her lips, and her eyes were a pallid green.

'How did you find my home address?' I didn't really care – she was here anyway – but I suppose I was stalling for time, trying to pull myself together.

'You gave your home number to Shelly when you agreed to take the case, so the address was easy to get from Directory.' Her hand stretched towards me again; she seemed to be a reach-out kind of lady. 'You've been hurt, Mr Dismas. There's blood on your face and shirt. Shouldn't you call a doctor or go to casualty?'

I was suddenly conscious of the wetness beneath my ear and under my chin, and when I touched my skin my fingers came away sticky with blood. From the throbbing pain just below the closed hole where my other eye used to be, I knew there'd be a swelling by morning. 'No, I'm all right. Just a disagreement with some . . . with some people on my way home. No real damage done.'

'Are you sure? At least let me clean it up for you.'

Clean it up? Maybe wash away the humiliation at the same time? Could she get rid of the degradation while she was at it? I didn't think so.

'Mrs Broomfield, I'm tired. And yes, I'm hurting quite a bit too. I want to lie down and rest if that's okay with you. I'm trying – believe me, I'm *trying* – not to be rude, but I want you to say what you have to say, and then leave. D'you get me?'

'Of course, I understand. Why don't you sit yourself down and let me make you a cup of tea? It'll perk you up.'

Perk me up? *Perk me up?* God save me from the kind and caring. She means well, I told myself, she doesn't realize she's a bloody nuisance, she doesn't know how close to the edge I am. Resignedly, I went over to the battered sofa and sank into its soft cushions. 'No tea,' I said to her, defiant to the last. 'A brandy might help, though. A large one.'

'I think you've drunk enough alcohol this evening, Mr Dismas.' There was no mistaking the accusation in those pale green eyes; I got the feeling she knew I'd taken something else besides a few whiskies and beers, but was choosing not to mention it. 'How about some coffee? Yes, that would be more appropriate in the circumstances. It won't take a jiffy.'

She was out the door before I could stop her. Oh hell, I thought to myself, let her get on with it. It'll give me more time to get my act together. The clairvoyant was back before I'd even had the chance to light a cigarette, bringing a dampened bathroom towel with her.

'Here, wipe the blood away with this, then hold the towel against your ear for a while.' Wordlessly, I took the wet cloth from her. 'Oh dear, I think you're going to have quite a bruised cheek. Use the end of the towel to press against it; it might help reduce the swelling.'

I did as I was told and she disappeared again. My thoughts went back to the mirror and the image I'd seen therein; I was surprised to find the shock had lessened. Maybe the coke's feel-good factor was finally kicking in again and I was mellowing out enough at least to accommodate the bizarre bathroom episode. I heard the cluttering of crockery from the other room.

'*Christ* – ' I shot off the sofa, moving as fast as my shaky legs would carry me. 'Not that one!' I shouted when I reached the kitchen.

But it was too late. The spoon was already scooping into the jar and I could see the top of the powder-filled plastic bag emerging from the coffee grains. The clairvoyant had spotted it too and I could tell by her expression she knew exactly what was inside the package.

'Not that coffee,' I said lamely, opening a cupboard door above a work surface and reaching in.

'I'm so sorry,' she apologized, quickly screwing the lid back on the jar she held in her hand.

I took it from her, handing over the legit coffee jar as I did so, both embarrassed and angry at being found out. 'It helps sometimes,' I growled defensively.

'It's none of my business, Mr Dismas.' She busied herself filling the kettle with water.

'You can't understand what it's like for me,' I said quietly, some of that anger cooling.

'I think I might have an idea.'

'No. No you don't. You have to live it to know.'

She pushed the plug into the kettle and switched it on. 'I have an imagination.'

I gave a snort of derision. 'You can imagine what it's like to be trapped inside a shell so hideous it makes you ashamed to walk the streets? What it's like to be pointed out as if you're some kind of freak? You know the kind of physical pain a twisted body gives you? The fear of losing sight in your only good eye? The refusal of your own body to do what comes so naturally to other people? You know all that, you can imagine it?' My short laugh was full of rancour and she had the decency to lower her gaze. 'You have *no* idea,' I told her.

'I'm sor –'

'Don't keep apologizing! It's not your fault, *you* didn't do this to me. Just don't patronize me. And okay, so I take a little stuff now and again. It helps get me through. For a little while I can escape who – *what* – I am. The feeling doesn't last long, but it helps me get by. Can you understand that? It makes me feel fine, and sometimes it takes me somewhere else, some place where I can see, I can sense, other things, better things.'

'No, Mr Dismas.' My anger didn't intimidate her. 'Drugs

never really work that way. They close down your sensibilities so that reality can't interfere with your delusions. It might be pleasant, it might make you feel better, at peace with the world, but it isn't the truth.'

'*Well, who the fuck needs the truth!*'

She took a step backwards, suddenly afraid of my rage, and I was immediately contrite. I hadn't meant to scare her, it was just frustration, self-pity, resentment – you name it.

The kettle bubbled steam and switched itself off. Something was thumping hard inside my head.

'You ought to go,' I said more quietly, although no more calmly. 'I'm bad company tonight.'

The clairvoyant managed a weak smile. 'You've taken more than just a beating. Please go and sit down and let me bring you a cup of coffee. Would you like something for your headache?'

I looked at her sideways. 'How did you know I had a headache?'

She laughed and there was no fear in the sound. 'After all you've been through tonight, why *wouldn't* you have one?'

I returned to the sofa in the sitting-room, puzzled, mystified, by this little old lady. My head hurt like hell and my body was a mass of aches and pains. The swelling below my absent eye provided its own special torment. But although I'd taken a lot of kicking, a lot of bruising, the worst thing going on was in my mind: the memory of that charming face in the mirror. Yesterday monsters, tonight perfection. From the grotesque to the sublime. Visions through a glass darkly.

'Here we are.' Louise Broomfield bustled in like a squat Angela Lansbury, Disney's Mrs Potts to my Beast, and carefully placed the mug of coffee on the small table next to the sofa, shifting aside one of the heavy art volumes I kept close at hand for easy browsing (the lives and works of the masters is another one of my 'things'; I guess I used wonderful images as an escape route when reality was on overload) to make room. 'It's very hot, so don't scald yourself. Now, let's see about that headache of yours.'

Before I could protest, she was behind the sofa, the palms and fingers of her hands slipping round to encircle my temples. I had to resist jerking my head away; nobody had ever touched me like this before. Almost immediately I felt a heat spreading from her hands into my temples and forehead, a warm, white, invasive seeping which, once the mild shock had passed, became a gentle soothing. Miraculously – or so it seemed to me – I felt the tension leaving my body, the throbbing pain inside my head diminishing to a dull, inconsequential ache until that too, melted away. All this happened within a minute or two and I was astounded; only a good grade hit had worked on me that fast before.

'It's . . . it's gone,' I said unbelievingly.

'I know,' the clairvoyant replied.

'How . . . ?'

'I absorbed the pain myself. Took it from you, then simply threw it away.'

I had noticed, or sensed, the flicking movements of her hands, preceded by the soft stroking of my temples and forehead; it was as if she were shedding water from her fingers.

'That's – '

'Nonsense? Yes, I know that too. Works though, doesn't it?'

I couldn't deny it and I wondered how well the treatment would work on a regular hangover. A fortune could be made if it could be packaged and marketed.

'Drink your coffee now.' She came round and sat next to me and I could feel her gaze as I picked up the mug. 'I didn't know if you took sugar, so I left it. Too much sugar isn't good for you anyway.'

'The coffee's fine.' It hurt my lips to drink and I realized I had taken more than a slap or punch in the mouth; somebody had put the boot in.

'Can I help you, Mr Dismas?'

She had put the question quietly and I stared at her, not sure of its meaning.

'I thought it was the other way round,' I said at last, turning away from her and continuing to sip the coffee. 'I thought you needed my help.'

'Shelly – Mrs Ripstone – does. She needs your help badly.'

'Yeah, right,' I scoffed, remembering Gerald Ripstone's will.

'Why the cynicism?'

I explained the complications over the inheritance and the clairvoyant expressed surprise. 'Shelly didn't tell me that.'

'Well, you're a clairvoyant, aren't you? You should've known.'

She laughed. 'I'm afraid it doesn't work that way. I only wish it did – I'd have a much clearer picture of things.' She joined her hands together on her lap and I shifted position on the sofa to observe her better. Underlying the sweet aroma of her perfume was a hint of lavender water and I noticed that beneath its thin layer of powder, her skin had a translucent quality, a waxy thinness that belied her years; bluish veins were just visible at her temples and her broad forehead was unusually smooth. It was the lines from her eyes and the corners of her mouth that bore witness to her true age, and the chin that was supported by another more fleshy swelling underneath which gave her matronly appeal. Those pale eyes were quizzical at the moment, but they held a deep compassion within them as well as a kind of knowing, an ability to see beyond the superficial. It seemed that her gaze might reach my soul.

'Tell me something,' I said, still taking in this weird/ordinary little woman beside me. 'Which of you was the first to mention Shelly Ripstone's missing son: you or her?'

'Shelly told me about the birth of her child soon after arriving at my home. She said she couldn't live with the loss of both her husband and her baby.'

'So she put the thought of the missing baby into your head?'

'No, she confirmed it, Mr Dismas – '

'Call me Nick. Or Dis – everyone calls me Dis.'

She gave a brief smile, a nod of her head. 'Sometimes we clairvoyants need some affirmation, even guidance. It can help clear our minds of extraneous matters, provide a focal point for our perceptions.'

'Sure. So she did instigate the idea of a missing son.'

'I understand your scepticism, but I believe her desire to see me was inspired by a force that we on this Earth will never quite understand. Just as I believe a hidden but no less forceful motivation led her to choose you out of all the many private investigators in this town.'

'That's ridiculous. My agency was recommended by her own solicitor, someone I've carried out a lot of work for over the years.'

'Synchronicity, Mr – Dis. You know what synchronicity is, don't you?'

'I've got a rough idea. It's when two unplanned things come together for a specific purpose.'

'Well . . . close. It's a meaningful coincidence in time of two or more similar, or even identical, events that aren't necessarily related.'

'I think I prefer my version: it's easier to make sense of.'

'Fine. It'll do. You see, I believe you were always meant to carry out this investigation.'

That knocked me back a little. I was still trembling slightly from the beating I'd taken and the shock of the vision in the mirror. I was also still wondering what had happened to the cocaine hit.

'I know it's difficult when you're a non-believer,' the clairvoyant said hurriedly, no doubt worried by the doubtful look I was giving her, 'but I'd like you to trust me.'

Trust her? Why the hell should I trust a stranger who

believed she could talk to the dead? 'D'you mind if I smoke?' was all I could find to say.

She shook her head, so I reached into my jacket for a pack and lit up. The clairvoyant frowned but made no comment as smoke drifted over her.

After two slow draws, I said: 'Can you give me one good reason why I *should* trust you?'

'Because I know more about you than you think,' she responded immediately.

It was my turn to be amused, albeit represented by a very crooked, maybe even sardonic, smile. 'You know nothing about me. We've never met before and as far as I'm aware I'm not in *Who's Who*.'

'You weren't born with one eye. You lost it when you were a young boy, didn't you?'

I looked at her sharply. 'How could you know about that?' Unconsciously, and a little melodramatically, my hand had gone to the sealed, red-rimmed socket where my left eye used to be. Embarrassed, I let my fingertips fall away.

'A few minutes ago, when I touched your head, I sensed something horrible had happened to you many years ago. An accident of some kind – no, worse than an accident. It was done deliberately, wasn't it? The shock of it is still present in your aura.' She touched my shoulder as she asked the question: 'You understand what your aura is, don't you?'

She waited until I'd given a nod of my head.

Truth was, I didn't know much about so-called auras except what I'd read in various magazines and newspaper articles. Apparently a person's body radiates a kind of energy field that can be 'picked up' by certain people – psychics, clairvoyants, and the like. They generally describe it as a halo of light, usually multi-coloured, that shimmers around people, or even animals, and that your state of health or mind can be diagnosed by its glow. I'd also heard that nowadays there's a technique by which it can be photo-graphed.

'Well, yours is very odd,' she informed me.

Yes, wouldn't you know it, I thought. Odd body, odd aura. Seemed natural that the two would go together.

'It's very weak, Mr Dis – '

'Just Dis,' I insisted.

'– I sensed it even before I came in. It's somehow depleted.'

'Could be I'm just unwell. A beating tends to leave me below par.' Not to mention a shock or two. I held up a finger when she started to speak. 'And anyway, I'm not sure how this aura thing works, but if it's some kind of reflection of someone's inner self, then one belonging to a one-eyed semi-crippled hunchback is bound to be somewhat off-colour, you know?'

'You said it yourself: "Inner self". There's nothing to say that your inner self should reflect your outer self.'

'Inner self, outer self – who the hell cares which it is? I'm not happy inside, can you believe that?' I was growing annoyed again; why was this woman wasting my time like this? 'Being . . .' I indicated my own body '. . . this way doesn't make me happy. In fact, it pisses me off.'

'Please don't be angry.'

'Angry? Why shouldn't I be? My mother, whoever *she* was, gave birth to a monster. Me. I'm that monster. I was so grotesque she abandoned me when I was only a few hours old. Left me among the dustbins at the back of a nun's convent, not caring if I froze to death, or some urban fox had me for breakfast. And maybe that would have been the best thing for me – a few minutes of pain, or a quick death from hypothermia, that would have been a kinder fate. Instead, the convent's caretaker found me and took me inside. His name was Nick – Nicholas – so that became my name too. And the surname – know why the nuns called me that?'

I carried on before she could speak.

'I learned about the name years later when I went back to the convent, when I was trying to trace my origins, trying to find out if they had any idea of who left me there in the cold. And one of them told me about my name, first about the caretaker Nick, then why they'd chosen Dismas as a surname. She told me quite eagerly, as though the knowledge somehow would help me in my future life. She said Dismas was one of the two criminals crucified alongside Christ, the Good Thief, the one who repented before he died and was promised paradise because of it. I was so ugly, you see, those nuns thought I was being punished for some terrible thing I would do later in life. You get that? Not for some past sin in another life, because nuns don't believe in reincarnation, but for some crime yet to be committed. So they prayed for my soul every day I was with them and long after I'd left. Not for me, the person, the poor thing they'd found among their garbage, but for my invisible *soul*. They hoped I'd repent before I even sinned and Dismas was their way of wishing me luck!'

I was breathing heavily by now, the bitterness of years beginning to spill out.

'Living as a freak of nature was bad enough, but it had to get worse. At least when I was young I could see with both eyes, but it seemed that was too good for me, I wasn't suffering enough.'

'How did you lose your eye, Dis?' Her voice was soft, encouraging, as though she were urging me to shed some of that bitterness through the words. 'Someone hurt you, didn't they? Tell me how it happened.'

'I was put in a home for boys, not a bad place in some ways. You were fed, looked after: You couldn't ask for much more, not for love and affection, at any rate. When I was eleven years old, one of the male carers tried to make me do something I didn't want to do. A big, puffy man with slobbery lips and squinty eyes, someone who should never have been left in charge of pigs, let alone young boys. He was a pervert who wanted sex with a freak.'

I shivered at the memory. I could still see him now,

towering over me, his pants down, his lips and member drooling slime.

'I resisted. I hated this man, and I feared him more than anything else in my young life. I hated his foul breath, his scratchy chin, the blackheads that covered his fat nose, and I was terrified when he nuzzled his face against my cheek and tried to reach inside my clothes. I fought against his advances and I think he was surprised by my strength, strength he couldn't understand was from fear and disgust. And the scissors I picked up were meant for his throat, but instead, in the struggle, they stabbed my own eye. While he ran off yelling there'd been an accident, I was left screaming on the ground, the scissors still in my eye socket.'

The cigarette was half burnt down and I flicked ash on to the floor, not caring where it landed, not worrying if it scorched the carpet. Louise Broomfield brushed it away with her fingers.

'Others came, adults, other kids, but no one could pull those scissors out. They were stuck there, embedded, and I was kicking too much for anyone to get a firm hold. They took me to hospital like that, the scissors sticking out like some weird attachment to my head, the blood from the wound soaking me through.'

The clairvoyant closed her own eyes for a moment, either out of pity for me, or to picture the scene, who knows which?

'And he got away with it. That big, perverted slob was never charged, never arrested.' The words came in a rush, gathering pace until I was almost spitting them out. 'No, they didn't believe him when he said it was an accident, because they knew what he was like, they'd always known he was a pervert, but they didn't want it made public, and now the worst had happened, he'd nearly killed a disabled boy in his care, they didn't want the facts to get out, didn't want more investigations because they might uncover other, secret things that had gone on inside that place and they'd all lose their jobs. So they kept it quiet, bided their time before taking action against the perve. Nobody would believe the freak-boy anyway, because Christ-in-Hell, who in their right mind would molest such an ugly piece of shit? Besides the boy was so delirious with pain and shock he couldn't speak anyway, and when he was on the mend, when what was left of his mutilated eye was removed, they would speak quietly to him, confuse him so that even he wouldn't remember the truth of it all. *Convince him it was all his own fault.'*

Spittle moistened my lips, my hands shook with old hatreds; the clairvoyant sat quietly.

'And later I paid for defending myself. Even when the confusion went away and I remembered exactly how it had happened, nobody would listen. I was just a disturbed child, a kid with too many hang-ups who was traumatized by the loss of an eye. No one listened, and the truth is, no one cared. Freaks like me, too hideous even to kiss, to hold, to cuddle, we never had real understanding. Pity maybe, and sometimes sympathy, but nobody in that place really cared enough to hear me.'

I was finally running down, exhausted before I started on this trip down nightmare alley, now racked out completely. My voice had lowered and the words were more measured. 'Every day I wake and I live with this . . .' I indicated my own body again, the crooked shell I'd been forced to inhabit, no choice required or given '. . . and I take the taunts and the stares, the jokes and the abuse, and I learn to accommodate it, even though inside it shames me, and tonight I get the hell kicked out of me by a group of girls, most of them pretty under the junk they wore and the shit they smeared their faces with – and *you* wonder why my fucking aura is not up to strength!'

And get this – this is just how pitiful I'd become that night – I began to weep again, silently though, no blubbering this time, the tears oozing from my good eye to slip down my cheek and well along the jawline.

'I'm so sorry,' I heard Louise Broomfield say before

feeling her hand rest over mine. 'Please forgive me, Dis, I didn't mean to be so insensitive.'

The insensitive sensitive. If my misery hadn't been so enormous I might have smiled at that. Instead I pulled my hand away and snuffled against the knuckle.

'Okay,' I murmured. Not, 'It's okay,' because it wasn't; just okay, leave it there. I revived the half-dead cigarette in my other hand with a long draw and its glow wavered in my trembling fingers. My tears dried and surprisingly, I felt a little better, as though the emotional release had somehow lightened my load, or at least shifted it so that it was less uncomfortable. The mood wouldn't last, I knew that, but it was a reprieve, short though it might be. I blew my nose and stuffed the crumpled handkerchief back into my trouser pocket.

'Can we talk some more?' The clairvoyant was cautious. 'Would that be all right?'

'I'm tired,' I told her, and it was no exaggeration. I could have added that I'd emptied out, there was nothing left in me that night. Events will do that to you.

'A few more minutes.' She was pleading, not insisting.

'One more minute. Then please . . . leave.' I could have cursed again, but I just didn't have it in me.

'I've shown you I have the gift . . .'

'Sorry, lady, but you haven't proved a thing to me.'

'I took your pain away.'

'The headache . . . ?'

'Your pain. You were badly hurt when I first arrived: are you in physical pain now?'

I blinked. My mind probed my body, my fingers touched my bruised ribs; I looked at my hands, examined the marks and grazes where they'd been trodden on; I thought of my battered head and hump. I blinked again, turned to the clairvoyant, the healer.

'It won't last, the pain will come back,' she said apologetically. 'But right now you're not feeling any discomfort, are you? Perhaps some stiffness, and I'm sure you're quite numb in places; but there isn't enough pain to cause distress, is there?'

'How . . . ?' It was never going to be a fully completed question, but the situation at least required an attempt.

'I explained before. I took the pain from you and discarded it. It will probably return the moment your scepticism over-whelms the idea it could really happen. Only surprise is preventing that from occurring right now.'

She'd got that right: disbelief was already setting in and the first twinges were already starting.

'I've been very disturbed since Shelly Ripstone first came to see me,' the clairvoyant said without wasting a second more of her minute. 'I could tell she was deeply troubled the moment I opened my door to her and I sensed it wasn't just because she'd recently lost her husband.'

'How could you tell?' I really was curious to know.

'I'd been prepared beforehand.'

I suppose I regarded her quizzically.

'I had been hearing strange voices for a few days, jumbled voices, confused, distraught. I could make little sense of them until Shelly came to my home. They had first begun when she rang me to book an appointment, and once she was there with me, they became clearer, one of them more distinct than the others. This voice was that of a young man who told me he was Shelly Teasdale's son. Shelly only confirmed what I suddenly knew.'

I couldn't stop myself from interrupting – all this was getting too silly. 'Wait a minute. You're telling me you actually heard a voice telling you this? A voice from out of nowhere?' I didn't bother to hide my incredulity.

'It isn't quite like that. They aren't voices as such. In fact I only hear voices when those talking to me are dead.'

I brought her to a halt with a raised hand; I needed time to let all this sink in.

Louise Broomfield sighed. 'I'm sorry it's so difficult to

accept, but there it is, this is what happens when I'm contacted by outside entities. I can't explain why the deceased appear to have proper voices and others communicate with thoughts and visions.'

'Then why did you tell me you *heard* the voice of Shelly Teasdale's son along with these other voices.'

'To make it less confusing for you. It isn't important, Dis; messages have their own way of reaching me. In this case I was sent thoughts and images. The main one, the one who claimed to be Shelly's son, said there were others with him, but it was all so distorted. In my mind I could see vague shapes, figures that appeared to be in pain, or in great anguish, I'm not sure which. I had the feeling that they were trapped somewhere. I saw walls without windows, and doors, lots of doors with strong locks. And everywhere was so dark; these people were just shapes moving in darkness.'

Perspiration beaded her forehead and she dabbed it away with a tiny handkerchief that smelled of lavender. She fixed me with those pale green eyes.

'I saw you, Dis. Amongst all those contorted images I saw you.'

'What? You've never met me before tonight.'

'Yours was the clearest image of all, although it didn't make sense to me at the time. It was only later when Shelly had hired you that it took on any significance.'

'She told you the private investigator handling her case was a hunchback and then it all made sense to you. Yeah, it had to be me you saw in those visions.'

'They revealed to me that this particular person had also lost an eye in an accident when he was a boy. When I came here I was still in doubt, but as soon as I touched your forehead I knew you were the one. It came to me as surely as if you had told me yourself. That's why I'm begging you to help Shelly find her son, Dis. That's the key to all this; finding him will lead us to them all.'

'Even if there was some sense to this, how do you propose I find the boy? There is no record of Shelly Teasdale's son ever being born, let alone having died, and the hospital where she claims to have given birth burned down years ago. The trail – if there ever was one – is stone cold dead.'

'I can only tell you you've got to try.' The clairvoyant's eyes searched my face as though she might find some sympathy there. She seemed desperate when she added: 'I think they're counting on you. I think they know you're the only one who *can* help them.'

'Why? Why me?'

She shook her head slowly, almost as confused as I was. 'I . . . I can't see that. It just isn't clear to me. But I know I'm right, Dis, I can *feel* the truth of what I'm telling you.'

'Okay, okay. Let's just say you are right. I'm not saying I'm going along with this, but just for a moment, let's say your feeling is correct. How do I go about finding Shelly Teasdale's lost son – assuming he really is alive?'

'Why should Shelly pretend she had a baby all that time ago?'

'Let's not get into that right now. I can only say I've dealt with crazy people before. But if it is all true, how can I find him if there's no record of him ever having existed? I'm an investigator, not a magician.'

'Because the voices, the visions, have provided us with a clue.'

That startled me. 'You didn't tell me.'

'You never gave me the chance.'

'So tell me now. What kind of clue?' Yes, I was full of scepticism right then, and when Louise Broomfield revealed exactly what that clue was, I nearly threw my hands in the air in exasperation.

'Sometimes we see things in dreams that appear to make no sense at all,' she proceeded with hardly any embarrassment, 'until later you realize they were there to represent something important to you. It might be something very ordinary, mundane even, or it might be something that's highly significant.'

She fumbled with the tiny, lavender-scented handkerchief, twisting it in her fingers while I waited impatiently.

'I saw wings,' she said. 'Hundreds upon hundreds of wings. They were of all colours and they flapped madly, as if agitated or frightened, and they made a terrible, thunderous roar. It was as if . . . as if they were trapped too.'

And as she spoke, I saw those wings in my mind. The odd thing was, my own image was among them. I saw myself in the midst of thousands of fluttering wings.

Only I did not hear their flurry: I heard their screams.

11

For the second night I fell into a dreamless sleep, which was not only unusual given the events of that evening, but extraordinary, because I'd always suffered – and I mean *suffered* – from full-Technicolor, Dolby sound, Senserama dreams and nightmares since I could remember. You'd have thought that the past two nights would have made things worse.

As it was, I slept soundly and awoke around 8.45am, which was pretty late for me. I felt a little hungover and my limbs were stiff, but apart from that and a few bruises (the worst was the discoloured swelling below the absent eye) I was fine. I think mentally I had absorbed the bad things – the humiliation, the fear, and the self-pity – while I slumbered. I was instantly awake and just as quickly out of bed, heading for the bathroom; only when I was in mid-flow did thoughts of the previous night steal into my consciousness. I pondered them long after concluding my daybreak liability, finally flushing the loo and returning to my bed where, pyjama-clad (I rarely slept naked), I reflected further, oblivious to cold feet and parched throat.

What the hell was going on in my life? Beggars, beaches, bitches and batty old ladies – the images spun round my mind like a carousel filled with harpies. And then there were the hallucinations to contend with, the monsters in mirrors, the face that stared back at me in the bathroom. What did *they* mean?

When my feet eventually became too cold – even in

summer it took a while for my basement flat to warm up in the mornings – and my throat too parched to bear, I wandered into the kitchen and made a brew. A cup of tea rather than coffee, a couple of paracetamols for the general pain, which had nothing to do with the beating I'd taken, and my head began to settle so that I could think more clearly. Taking the mug of tea and collecting my cigarettes on the way, I went into the sitting-room.

After my third cigarette and second mug of tea I reached for the phone and made three calls.

The Ripstones' residence was one of those big but not quite grand homes set back from the broad road that runs from the top of the South Downs, through Brighton's suburbia and down to the sea itself. The area up there is quiet and expensive, just a little dull, and in winter the wind tears up from the English Channel to rattle windows and worry rooftops. Apart from the quietness – if you liked quietness, that is – the other advantage was that within minutes you could be in the centre of a town large enough to be a city, with all the amenities that come with it, or, moving in the opposite direction and in even less time, you could be among the meadows and valley woodlands of the Downs themselves. From the tops of the rises you could see as far as the hills around London itself, although on this particular day, because there was still too much moisture left in the air after yesterday's showers, this now warmed by the morning sun, mists ran across the valley floors, veiling green pastures and wooded areas, and the distance was lost in white haze.

I'd taken a slight detour before arriving at Shelly Ripstone's place, driving to a favourite spot on the Downs that overlooked a huge rent in the hills known as Devil's Dyke, and I'd sat a while in my car, windows down so that the breeze could waft through. I'd watched the shifting mists below as they rolled lazily across the landscape, sunshine catching open patches, turning green pastures to shimmering gold, but my thoughts were of my own life and the apprehension that had suddenly filled me even before I had made the phone calls. In my heart, if not in my head, was the feeling of something momentous about to happen to me, something as inexplicable as it was certain, an eerie sense of impending . . . what? I had no idea. But with it there also came a feeling of excitement, which was just as unaccountable.

Sitting there in my car, the soft wind up there breezing through my lank hair, I tried to analyse the sensation, tried to understand its cause, but answers came there none. There was only confusion – and wonder. Yes, a deep, disturbing wonder. And it scared the hell out of me.

I drove from the parking area and headed towards Shelly Ripstone's place, doing my best to calm this inner turmoil by concentrating on the road. The pragmatist in me would not allow those vague yet potent thoughts to hold sway: I was a PI doing a job, at that moment employed to help a grieving widow find her missing son, real or imaginary, and there were procedures to follow, rules of the game that would keep me on line and eliminate fanciful notions that might only get in the way.

But if it really was as straightforward as that, I wondered, why had I asked the clairvoyant to meet me at my client's address?

Within four minutes I was driving through a set of open double gates to park in the semi-circular, paved drive. By then I was composed, those irrational thoughts tucked away in some dim corner of my psyche, perhaps to be taken out and examined at leisure later on, for now my innate professionalism fully in charge. Climbing from my car – a nondescript Ford Fiesta, beige in colour, elderly in years, its only special feature a hidden isolation switch wired in series with the coil so that with the switch in the 'off' position, no one other than me could start the engine. It prevented the car from being stolen and while on surveillance I could always claim my vehicle had broken down (neither the pushiest policeman, nor the best mechanic could get it to move once it was in that mode) – I took a moment to look up at the house. Two storeyed, white painted, red-tiled roof, I guessed it had been built around the 1920s, with extensions added and picture windows replacing former, more traditional windows over the years, the whole building much larger than originally planned. It was a wealthy man's – or in this case, a wealthy widow's – abode, but by no means a palace. Gerald Ripstone had lived well, but I guessed he'd never been part of the jet-set.

A small blue Renault was parked in front of the mock-pillared porch (one of the later additions, I surmised) and I wondered if it belonged to Louise Broomfield. The clairvoyant had left her number with me the previous night, and after first speaking to my client, I'd rung her to say perhaps I'd changed my mind about the case and would she meet me here? My third call had been to Henry at the office, letting him know my plans for the morning.

Lumbering awkwardly up the porch's two steps, I rang the doorbell and waited. It took a couple of seconds for the door to swing open and for Shelly Ripstone to smile out at me. Along with bright make-up she wore a look of expectancy on her face, and she was dressed in loose-fitting black slacks, gold and black sandals on her manicured feet, and a tight pale yellow sweater which seemed to be moulded over her ample breasts. Her ash-blonde hair was held back from her cheeks by a black velvet bow at the nape of her neck and, although her eyes initially betrayed the slightest revulsion at what stood before her, they swiftly recovered again and lit up in welcome.

'Thank you, Mr Dismas,' she said in a breathless, Marilyn Monroe way. 'I'm so glad you changed your mind.'

'I'm not sure that I have yet,' I said, stepping inside the hall as she made way for me. 'It depends on what information you can give me today.'

Her frown, I think, was a reaction to the bruises and cuts on my face, particularly the swelling below my missing eye, rather than my reservations.

'Are you all right, Mr Dismas?' she asked, her voice full of concern or curiosity, I couldn't be sure which. 'Your poor face . . .'

'Kind of spoils my looks, doesn't it?'

She didn't catch the irony: not a flicker of a smile. 'Oh, you poor dear,' she said.

I dismissed it with: 'It's okay, really. No pain – not much, anyway. It's not as bad as it looks. Is Mrs Broomfield here?'

She was and she was waiting to greet me in a room just off the hall itself, a lounge area that boasted an awful russet-red wall-to-wall carpet, broken by a white shag-pile rug in front of a York stone fireplace and two mammoth pink settees that faced each other across a wide glass-and-chrome coffee table. Hanging over the polished teak mantelpiece was a picture of Shelly and a middle-aged man, presumably her late husband, Gerald; it was one of those photographic portraits, varnished and stippled to look like an oil painting. Although cunning lighting and obvious retouching had con-spired to bring out Gerald's finer characteristics, nothing could disguise the plumpness of his face and the plumpness of his nose and the plumpness of the flesh below his chin; nor could his hair be made to look other than sparse and his paunch other than portly; nevertheless, there was a clever-ness in his eyes, an alertness to his expression, that told you he had been nobody's fool. Standing close behind and over him, as if he had been sitting for the portrait, Shelly looked harder than she did in real life and oddly proprietary, as if she were the dominant partner, as if she were in charge of Gerald and not the other way round, which hardly related to the impression she had given in my office. Maybe it had been a trick of the flashlight, an erroneous image caught in that split second; the camera mostly lied, I told myself.

Louise Broomfield was dressed in the same clothes as the night before, although minus the pink raincoat, and as she rose from one of the settees a warm smile spread across her chubby face.

'I'm so pleased you changed your mind, Mr Dismas,' she said as a greeting.

'Dis,' I reminded her. 'Call me Dis. Even my enemies call me Dis.'

I took her proffered hand and was taken aback by her sudden change of expression. Her body swayed slightly and I felt resentment rising at what I mistakenly thought was her unguarded aversion to the contact. I'd assumed she had grown used to my looks the night before, but I guess broad daylight brought out the worst in me. I suppose I couldn't be blamed for taking her reaction the wrong way and my irritation soon broke surface.

'I'm not sure I've changed my mind,' I said brusquely, letting go of her hand. 'I still think this is a wild goose chase.'

The clairvoyant was about to reply when Shelly, who had followed me into the room, spoke up. 'It isn't, Mr Dismas,' she insisted. 'Why can't you just believe me?'

I turned to her. 'Because I deal in facts, not fancies.'

It was as if I'd slapped her face and Louise Broomfield quickly interjected. 'Yet you're here today, so you must feel there is some truth in what Shelly has told you.'

'Right now I don't know what I feel,' I replied. 'Last night you convinced me to give it another shot, but in the cold light of day . . .' I regarded her meaningfully '. . . I'm not sure if I'm wasting my time.'

'This meeting was your idea.'

'I like to think I'm a pro, as well as a businessman. I don't like disappointing my clients and I don't like turning away a good fee.' I didn't mention the wilder notions that had entered the equation. 'I'll explore all avenues to complete an assignment successfully, as long as there are avenues to be explored.'

'Why don't we all sit down and have a nice cup of tea,' said Shelly placatingly – or was it desperately? 'Then you can ask me anything you think might help.'

'That would be sensible,' agreed the clairvoyant. 'And thank you for being so frank, Dis.' The puzzlement in her eyes told me she couldn't quite understand my irritation.

'No tea for me,' I said a little huffily, because I'd expected something more of Louise Broomfield; she was supposed to be a *sensitive*, after all.

'Coffee then. I've got some already made.'

Shelly Ripstone disappeared before I could decline further. I only wanted to get this over with as quickly as possible, my mood rapidly changed since I'd arrived. I guess I was annoyed at myself for allowing Louise Broomfield to persuade me that I really could help the widow. But then I realized the clairvoyant's influence had been minimal – I, myself, had resolved to see it through only that morning; in fact, I'd awoken with the conviction that I *had* to see it through.

'Are you feeling any better today?'

I wasn't sure to what Louise was referring: my physical or my mental state. Perhaps she was only making polite conversation in Shelly's absence.

'I'm okay,' I replied curtly, still misunderstanding her reaction to me a few moments earlier.

She was giving me that weird look again, a kind of scrutiny that was searching beyond the physical, and at last I began to realize her reaction wasn't one of abhorrence.

'Have you ever had any kind of spiritual experience, Dis?' she asked out of the blue.

Surprised again, I couldn't at first think of a reply. Then, stalling, I said: 'What d'you mean exactly?'

'Have you ever had an out-of-body experience, have you ever seen a ghost, heard voices in your head?'

'You must be kidding.'

'No. No, I'm not.'

I was beginning to feel uncomfortable under her inspection. I remembered – how could I forget? – the visions in the mirrors.

'I don't think I have,' I told her. 'No, I'm sure I haven't.' Hallucinations didn't count. 'What makes you ask?'

'There's something about you . . .' she shook her head and at last dropped her gaze.

We were interrupted by Shelly returning with a tray of tea, coffee, and even chocolate biscuits. 'Coffee was made just before you arrived, so it's still fresh.' She smiled at me and I could see the hope there in her eyes. I told myself that maybe her late husband's money wasn't the important thing, that maybe she really did want her son back for himself. (Of course, if the birth *was* in her own imagination, then maybe her smile was that of a crazy woman.) 'I know you only drink tea, Louise, so I've made you a pot all to yourself. Shall I be mum?'

I smiled at the irony of her last words, wondering if it was a deep-felt but subconscious plea. I watched as she poured tea, then coffee for herself and me, the perfume she wore today – Chanel No 19, I suspected – almost as powerful as the coffee aroma. She kept up a barrage of noise-speak about the changeable weather, how difficult it was to find good housekeepers, the price of lemons and other nonsense I couldn't be bothered to take in, all of it a verbal discharge of her own nervousness. I waited for a break in the flow.

'Mrs Ripstone . . .'

'Shelly, please.'

'Shelly, can you remember the names of any of the doctors or nurses who attended you in maternity?'

Her still-pretty face took on a blank expression, then frowned in concentration.

'The midwife, maybe?' I suggested helpfully, hopefully.

'It was such a long time ago.' She closed her eyes and

after a lengthy pause, began to say slowly, 'Doctor . . . Doctor
. . . Rhanji . . . Rhamsi . . . Rham . . . ? Oh, I don't know. Was
it Djani? He was Asian, I know that. A young man, very nice
hands, I seem to remember, long fingers, almost feminine.'

'It's okay, I can probably check with NHS records. Anyone
else you can think of, perhaps not on the medical staff?' I
wanted an independent witness, someone who was around at
the time and who knew Shelly had been pregnant and had
had the child, someone over whom the medics had no
influence. Because if the baby really had 'disappeared' then
the medical authorities, for whatever reason, would want the
matter kept quiet.

Shelly was slowly shaking her head, her eyes open once
more. I sipped coffee and waited. The clairvoyant drank her
tea.

'There was someone . . .' Shelly said after a while, the
memory dredged up as if from a deep well. 'I think he was
another doctor, although he didn't wear a white coat, or
anything like that. Very . . . very distinguished looking. Like
an actor, you know? I remember thinking that at the time.
But I can't place him, I think I only saw him twice. He never
even spoke, although he did examine me. No, I don't think I
was even told his name.'

I put the coffee cup on the glass table and took out a
notepad and pen. Quickly I scribbled down the selection of
names she'd applied to the Asian obstetrician under the
heading of Royal General Hospital, Dartford. 'Try to think,
will you?' I urged. 'Just try to give me some more names. I
mean, who else did you have conversations with?'

'I was an unmarried mother in a ward full of happily
married mothers. None of them were very much bothered
about me.'

The 'good old days', I mused. How things have changed.

'Well, what about your own relatives? They must have
visited you.'

'I left home at fifteen, Mr Dismas. I haven't seen my

parents, or brothers and sister, since. For all I know, and for all I care, my mother and father could be dead.'

Groaning inwardly, I lowered the pad. At this rate I couldn't find corroboration that she had even been pregnant, let alone lost a baby. Louise Broomfield, following our exchange attentively, placed her teacup and saucer on the table close to my coffee cup. The spoon in the saucer rattled against china.

'Look,' I persisted. 'How about the midwife? You must have had plenty of contact with her.'

The spoon in the saucer clinked against the empty cup again and I saw the clairvoyant look down at it.

'Of course, yes.' Shelly had brightened a little. 'She was very kind to me. In fact, she was the one who delivered the baby, because the young doctor was out of the delivery room at the time.'

'The midwife actually made the delivery?'

'That's what midwives are for, Mr Dismas. But she needed help at the end. That's why she sent for the other doctor, the older one.'

'Why would she do that?'

'Because I was having trouble with the birth, I suppose.'

'No, I mean why didn't she call for the normal doctor?'

'I've no idea. I think the other one was more senior, or a specialist or something.'

Now Louise Broomfield's empty cup rattled along with the teaspoon in the saucer and I assumed a heavy lorry passing by on the main road outside the house had caused a vibration.

'You're sure you can't remember his name, this senior doctor?' I said.

A firm shake of the head. 'I told you, I didn't even know it then. I never saw him again after my little boy was born.'

'But he was there at the birth.'

'I already said.'

I pondered on this a moment. 'Okay, tell me more about

the midwife. You say she was kind to you and you had lots of long chats. Surely you can recall her name?'

Shelly made a grumbling-groaning sound, frustrated by her poor memory. 'I remember she had a foreign accent. She was German or something.'

'You think she was German?'

'I'm not sure. Probably.'

'Think of her name.'

'I'm trying to,' she complained. 'Why would that help anyway?'

'Because if I can trace the midwife she might verify your story.'

'You don't believe me?' She sounded mortified.

I changed tack. 'She could validate the birth when I asked for a search of the records.'

The clairvoyant interrupted. 'Surely the midwife will have brought hundreds, perhaps even thousands of babies into the world. Why should she remember Shelly giving birth, especially all that time ago?'

'You got me there. But it's all we've got.' I noticed Louise looked very pale. 'If I can find the woman and show her a photograph of Mrs Ripstone, then maybe, just maybe, she'll remember her stay at the hospital. With luck she might also remember what happened to the baby. Are you okay, Louise?'

The clairvoyant looked momentarily surprised. 'Why do you ask?'

'You've suddenly lost colour.'

Her hand went to her cheek as if she might feel the draining of blood. The teaspoon inexplicably slipped over the edge of the saucer and we all glanced at it, and then at each other.

Louise's eyelids drooped and she closed them completely. 'I can hear them,' she announced quietly.

I sighed and shrugged dismissively; I wasn't into that kind

of thing and was more interested in discovering the identity of Shelly Ripstone *née* Teasdale's midwife.

'You said she wasn't English, possibly that she was German, so did she have a foreign-sounding name?'

Shelly screwed her face up again in concentration. 'I don't . . . wait . . . it's there, I can . . . No, it's gone. I almost had it.'

My head cocked to one side as I listened, not to the widow, but to something distant, something like whispers from another room. I looked around and saw nothing unusual. I glanced towards the empty doorway leading into the hall, glimpsed parts of a dining table and chairs in the room opposite, a corner of an etched mirror, probably Venetian or facsimile of.

'They're here,' the clairvoyant said in a soft breath.

'Who's here?' Shelly was alarmed. She craned her neck, trying to see into the hall. 'I can't see anyone.'

'Can't you hear the noise?' I asked her.

Bewildered, she returned my stare. 'I can't hear anything.'

But I could, and so could Louise Broomfield. Whispers, slowly increasing in volume, a jumble of agitated murmurings, and they were not from another room: these sounds were there among us. My coffee cup, along with Shelly's and Louise's teacup, began to vibrate on the glass table and the portrait of the widow and her late husband above the mantelpiece began to tilt. Suddenly the teacup, with saucer, slid across the coffee table and fell to the floor, dregs of tea and tealeaves spotting the russet carpet.

The whispering became ever louder, the sounds swirling around the room as if borne by some fierce gale.

The clairvoyant reached across to grab my hand. 'You can hear them too.' It was a statement rather than a question.

'The voices? Yes, I can hear the voices.' I snatched my hand away – her touch had been too cold. 'Who are they? *What* are they? What do they want from us?' I think my voice cracked a little.

'I don't know,' she replied. 'I can't understand what they're trying to say. They're so frightened, too frightened to make sense.'

'*They're* frightened? They're scaring the hell out of me.'

I looked around the room, this way and that, trying to locate the source. But the voices were ever-moving, never settling, not even becoming united. The long drapes at the windows were fluttering, fresh flowers on a side table were trembling in their vase.

'Christ, make them go away, Louise,' I appealed. 'Isn't that what you do? Don't you control this sort of thing?' I was perplexed, curious, and fearful all at the same time.

'I can't. It would be wrong to make them. They're trying so hard ... so hard ... to tell me ... No. It's you they want to tell, not me. Please listen to them, Dis.'

Tiny sugar grains hopped and danced in their little China bowl. My coffee cup glided towards me over the glass, coming to rest precariously on the table's chrome lip.

'*What's happening?*' Shelly was sitting bolt upright, clutching the arms of her chair, her hands like claws over the ends. '*What's moving everything? Please make it stop, Louise.*'

It was then that the voices seemed to find entry into my own head and they began their circling in my mind, the confused cacophony almost overwhelming, the excited whisperings and mutterings becoming thunderous. I clapped my hands to my head and shook myself, trying to rid my mind of the demons, afraid they would drive me mad with their incessant babbling, but instead, I sank into them, became a captive inside my own head, joining with their mutterings as though I were part of them, that their anguish was also mine. I leapt to my feet, fingers pressed tight against my temples, and was aware that the clairvoyant was reaching up to me, trying to calm me; but the voices inside drowned her words, and she seemed a long way away from me, beyond assisting.

I rocked on my heels, afraid for my sanity, the intrusion becoming too much to bear. I called out, not a word, just a sound, anything to counteract that inner noise, but it made no difference, the voices continued their tirade.

Louise was on her feet and Shelly had pushed herself further back in her seat as if trying to get as far away from me as possible, the horror on her face frightening me even more. I twisted my body as though that might help loosen the voices from their fierce grip, but still they persisted, tormenting me with their harangue. Louise held on to me and I saw her lips moving, but couldn't hear her words, didn't *want* to hear her words, because she was to blame for all this: innocent, even matronly, though she appeared, she was the catalyst, she was the one drawing these strange forces to me. I knew it, I could feel it! She had evoked those terrible sounds of wings that had haunted us the previous night, whatever sensory powers she really did possess had induced or provoked the phenomenon! But then I remembered the reflections in the mirrors. On neither occasion had Louise Broomfield been present. Christ, I hadn't even known her!

It was the thought of those mirrors that sent me fleeing from the room and across the hall into the dining-room beyond.

On the wall opposite the door, mounted above a polished, walnut sideboard containing silver-framed photographs, candlesticks and a full fruit bowl, was the Venetian-styled mirror whose edge I had glimpsed from the lounge earlier. Fake or not, it was a magnificent piece with carved, bevelled edges, the tall oval centre framed by etched flower motifs and topped by an ornate mosaic floral design. Standing across the room from it, the long, walnut dining table between, I saw my own unpleasant image reflected in the glass.

But even as I watched, a new sound was rising not just inside my head but in the room itself. It came like approaching thunder, growing louder and louder, a low rumbling that began to drown the urgent whispered voices. Before my eyes, my reflection began to fade and in its place there appeared thousands of small fluttering creatures, birds of all kinds that flew against the glass as though trapped in the dimension on the other side. Their wings beat against the clear barrier, creating the noise: there were no screeches, no chirps, only the thrashing of those agitated feathered wings and the shifting of air.

I felt the presence of the clairvoyant and Shelly Ripstone, who had followed me into the room, felt them beside me, looking at my face and not at the mirror. Only then did they follow my gaze and look, themselves, into the chaos inside the glass.

Yet when I glanced away to see their faces, perhaps seeking assurance that I was not hallucinating, was not going insane, I realized they did not see the same as I in the mirror, for their expressions held no surprise, no wonder, but merely puzzlement. I faced the mirror again and saw that the images were fading, gradually vanishing, the noise – the flurry of wings, the turbulent air, the voices – abating.

In a few moments, the room was quiet again, and in the mirror was only the reflection of Louise, Shelly and myself.

But as Shelly Ripstone stared at herself, she was speaking, her voice almost distant as though she spoke only to herself and perhaps unconsciously.

'I remember now,' she said. 'I remember the midwife's name.'

She seemed to snap out of her distracted mood. She turned to us.

'It was Vogel. The midwife's name was Helda – no, *Hildegarde* – Vogel. God, it's clear as day now. Hildegarde Vogel.'

12

Like most big town centres nowadays, getting to a specific place in Dartford had been screwed up royally by its one-way traffic system and I was forced to use a car park some distance away from where I wanted to be. Walking long stretches was always a problem for me and after the beating I'd taken on the beach the previous night, the bruising and stiffness in my limbs didn't help much. It even hurt when I breathed too deeply, although I didn't believe I'd fractured ribs – one particular kick I'd taken while I was down had merely left its mark, a deep purple and yellow contusion over my left rib cage. The afternoon was hot too, which had a draining effect on my energy as I walked.

Grumbling to myself all the way, I eventually reached my destination, the road where the Dartford General had once stood. It was a broad, busy thoroughfare with metal railings on either side to prevent idiots, children and dogs from running out into the traffic. On the spot where apparently the hospital in which Shelly Ripstone/Teasdale claimed to have given birth had stood was a massive, granite and glass office block, an insurance company's name and logo over the main doors. I lingered outside awhile, leaning against the pavement rail, catching my breath and resting my legs, inspecting the territory at the same time.

On this side of the main road were mainly other offices, these broken up by a couple of estate agents, a betting shop and a bank, all of which looked comparatively new – at least built within the last ten years, that is. On the opposite side of the road, though, I saw what I had hoped to find. It was a longshot, but all I had.

That morning, my client had been quite certain of the midwife's name. Hildegarde Vogel, a little, thin woman, not at all robust as you might expect one of her profession to be. And very kind. Shelly had impressed that on me: she recalled that Hildegarde had been very kind to her.

Both Louise Broomfield and the widow had been shaken by the mysterious storm that had erupted inside the Ripstone house, and further worried by my actions during it. Why had I fled to the dining-room to gawp into an ordinary if fancy mirror on the wall there? I told them both of the tiny birds I had seen trapped inside the glass and although Shelly had stared at me as if I were mad, the clairvoyant had merely nodded her head, not in comprehension, but in belief. The message was becoming stronger, she informed me. Somehow it would eventually make sense to us.

Shelly Ripstone was pouring herself a large gin and tonic when I left the house, while the clairvoyant tried to assure her that all would be well, that while the phenomenon might be unusual, there was no evil intent to it. I wondered how she could be so sure.

When I got back to the office, I had spent some time on the phone, checking out the midwife's identity with the NHS, and after being transferred from one office to another, finally learned that yes, there had been someone on the Dartford General's staff who went by that name. The records said she had been transfered from the Prince Albert Hospital in Hackney, in fact, their records did not go back beyond ten years, so she was only just on their list. Did I know that the Dartford General had burnt down? Ms Vogel certainly wasn't on the NHS list any more, so if she had left the service there would be no record of her current address. Great. Another dead-end.

However, there are certain processes you can go through to trace an adult missing person: checking the electoral roll of the area where the person was last known to have resided is one, scouring through the local telephone directories is another. Or you can use specialist computer tracing companies, which are linked into data bases all over the country. Unfortunately, their services are very expensive. Speaking for myself, I liked to use the method that had rarely let me down: local enquiries, visiting the missing person's old neighbourhood and asking around. It's surprising what you can dig up by personal contact, which is why I found myself in Dartford on that hot summer's afternoon.

I had to walk further along the road to reach a break in the pavement barrier where a pedestrian crossing would get me over the lively main road, my limp quite pronounced by now. I hobbled across, feeling the glares of drivers forced to stop – not their impatience, but their curiosity – then retraced my steps to a spot almost opposite the insurance block. The shop I sought out was a tobacconist/newsagent/confectioner and although it had obviously been modernized some time within the last decade, I was hoping the shop itself had been around for a lot longer. A lottery ticket sign was on the window and through the plate-glass I could see magazine displays and stacked shelves full of sweets and chocolate. Just the kind of place that would be frequented by staff and visitors alike from the hospital that had once stood opposite, particularly if there had been no railings to prevent easy access.

There were few customers inside: a couple of little kids by the ice-cream treasure trove, an elderly man with a stick browsing the magazine shelves. The kids, a boy of seven or eight years old, a girl a year or so younger, regarded me with large, solemn, dark and beautiful eyes, and the boy slyly nudged the girl. She nudged him back, a little harder, so that he tottered.

'Shabir! Farida! Behave yourselves or go into the back room.'

The youth who had admonished them had the same

exquisite looks, but was considerably older, somewhere in his late teens. He stood behind the counter at the far end of the shop and his eyes revealed nothing as he watched my approach.

'Can I 'elp you, sir?' His accent was a peculiar mix of Hindi and Estuary.

'Uh, yes, you might be able to.'

The boy giggled.

'Shabir!' The youth said sternly and the two kids wandered off towards the shop's entrance.

I showed the young shopkeeper my calling card – it meant nothing in itself, but many people assumed (mistakenly) that it carried some authority.

'I'm from the Dismas Investigations agency and I'm trying to locate someone who used to work in the hospital over the road there . . .' I indicated with a thumb '. . . before it burnt down.'

'Oh, I'm very sorry, but I don't think – '

'There's a chance she used to shop here.'

'I know nothing of any 'ospital.'

'It was destroyed about ten years ago.'

'We – ' spoken as '*Ve*' ' – were not here then. But wait – ' '*Vait*' ' – a moment. Perhaps my father . . .'

He called through the open doorway behind him. 'Father, I have someone here who is enquiring about an 'ospital.'

I heard the stirring from the room beyond and a middle-aged man appeared, a copy of the *Sun* newspaper in his hand, a curved yellow pipe with a large foul-smelling bowl drooping from his lips. What little hair he had stretched over his brown scalp was a contrasting mixture of black and white; his whiskers and the hair at the back of his neck were more abundant, bushy even, the white amongst it more dominant. Despite the heat of the day, he wore a threadbare green cardigan over a collarless shirt, and weary-looking slippers peered from beneath the folds of his baggy trouser legs.

He regarded me without expression before removing the pipe with his free hand and saying: 'Yis, there used to be a hospital.' No southern-sprawl accent here, although his English appeared to be good. 'But that was – ' again, the *v*as ' – long time ago, before we came here.'

Bugger, I thought. 'I don't suppose anyone who *used* to work there still comes in?' I ventured without much hope.

'Oh no, I do not think so. Why do you want such a person?' *Vy do you vont such a person?*

'Just making enquiries for a client. No problems involved, but it is important that we contact this person or anyone who knew her.' I thought quickly as father and son watched me, neither one saying a word. 'How long have you been running this place?' I asked.

'My father has owned the shop for eight years,' replied the youth.

'Nine years,' the older man corrected. 'You were ten years old, Rajiv, and the little ones had not even been born yet.'

'Ah,' said the son.

I rested a hand on the counter between us and shifted my weight to my good leg. 'So the people you took over from would have been here at the time of the fire and presumably for some time before.'

'The man and his good lady-wife owned the shop for many, many years. I am told the business was passed on from generation to generation, but the couple had no children of their own to keep it in the family.'

My heart sank a little. 'They were elderly?'

'They were of near retirement age and the closing of the hospital affected custom considerably. I think they had had enough of life's hard toil so they were very pleased to sell to me at a good price.' He was watching me shrewdly, sucking on the pipe between replies. Scented smoke drifted my way.

'D'you know if they're still alive?' I asked hopefully.

'That I do not know, sir. We kept in touch for a while – they advised me on supplies and stock requirements, that sort of thing – but I have not spoken to Mr and Mrs Vilkins for many years now. So my answer is that I do not know if they are still among the living.'

'But you still have their next address?'

'Oh yis, I believe so. It would be in the book.' He turned to his son. 'Rajiv, go and fetch my big red address book to me. Hurry for the gentleman – you'll find it in the cupboard under the television set.'

He gave a little bow in my direction as his son disappeared into the back room. Then he took the pipe from his mouth and gave me a benevolent smile.

'Thank you, Mr . . . ?' I said gratefully.

'Dahib Sahab is my name and I am most pleased to be of assistance.' Without any embarrassment, he studied my crooked form as if wondering how it could possibly function. Then he nodded as if satisfied that he had figured it all out. 'Very unlucky this time, no?' he said to me.

'What?'

He pointed the stem of his pipe at me and was about to say more when his son returned carrying a battered red-covered book, many of its pages loose and threatening to spill on to the floor. The shopkeeper took the address book and opened it out on the counter.

'Let us see,' he murmured to himself as he leafed through. I noticed that the little girl had wandered back down the shop and was leaning against the counter, her wonderful dark eyes peeping up at me. I did my best to give her a friendly smile and was relieved when she smiled back, not at all afraid.

'Vilkins, Vilkin . . .' the father was muttering as his stubby finger slid down the pages. 'Ah yis. George and Emma Vilkins.' He turned the book around so that I could see the name and address he was pointing at.

'Wilkins,' I said.

'Yis, Vilkins,' he agreed.

'May I write it down? The address and phone number?'

'Please.' *Pliz.*

I took out the small notepad I always carried with me and jotted down the information I needed. 'Ramble Avenue,' I said as I scribbled. 'Is that far from here?'

'Not very.' It was the son who spoke, his eyes slightly suspicious, as they had been throughout the exchange. 'On the other side of the motorway, going towards Swanscombe.'

'Great,' I said, studying my note. 'And you say you haven't spoken to Mr and Mrs Vilk . . . Wilkins . . . for some time?'

The shopkeeper shook his head mournfully, as though the lapse made him sad. 'I did not like to bother Mr Vilkins too much in his retirement. In any case, the business is not difficult, so there was no need.'

The girl, Farida, was touching my arm as if to feel if I were real. I gave her another smile, which she returned again, continuing to run her fingers along the sleeve of my jacket.

'Uh, thank you very much,' I said to the shopkeeper and his son. 'You've been very helpful.'

The older man accorded me another small nod of his head, but the son merely walked away and began tidying newspapers further along the counter. I turned to leave, then glanced around at the shopkeeper again.

'What did you mean when you said I was unlucky this time?' I asked him.

For a few moments he said nothing. Then, his gaze going beyond me, focusing on something in the middle-distance, he replied: 'If you do not know yourself, my friend, then it is not for me to say.'

Gathering up his ragged, loose-leaved address book, he retired to the backroom.

The sun was hard on me as I traipsed back to the car park, its harsh rays pounding my head without respite. I peeked longingly into the open doorways of pubs that I passed, but bravely resisted the urge to drop in for a cold beer and shade every time. In my line of work, it presented a bad image to make enquiries with alcohol on your breath.

I was still puzzled by the Asian shopkeeper's last remark, wondering what was behind it, precisely what was he getting at? He had said it so sagely and with such inscrutability, as though he were the Keeper of Hidden Knowledge and I was the poor sap who didn't have a clue. I remembered that the Hindu religion subscribed to reincarnation, so maybe that was what he was getting at: I'd come back this time in a less than lovely form. Shit, what nonsense! What would have been the point in that? Yes, I really was clueless.

When I finally got to my car I collapsed on to the front seat, leaving the door open wide to get rid of the build-up of heat inside. Giving myself a minute or so to get my breath back and to rest my aching legs, I struggled out of my jacket and threw it on to the passenger seat, first taking my cellphone from a pocket. I wiped my face with my shirtsleeve before tapping out the Wilkinses' phone number with my thumb.

There was no reply, but at least the line was still in service. I sat and pondered awhile, enjoying the comfort of the car. Okay, I was down in this neck of the woods so I might as well drive to the Wilkinses' last known address; even if they had moved away, or passed on in the terminal sense, the neighbours would be able to tell me either way. Stretching over to the back seat I picked up the Greater London Street Atlas I always kept in the car – it covered all the streets in the suburbs as well as the city itself and was invaluable in my line of work – and consulted the index before flicking through the pages to find the area I wanted. Ramble Avenue wasn't far away, a couple of miles at most. I closed the car door, flicked the isolation switch (yes, even in a car park I still took precautions, out of habit, I suppose) and started the engine, turning the cooler on to full blast.

It didn't take long to locate the tree-lined road and I

slowed the Ford as I drove along it, noting the house numbers on the gates of small, tidy front gardens. The homes were mostly bungalows, ideal for people of a certain age for whom climbing the stairs was an unnecessary grind. I drew up to the kerb when I saw the one I was looking for and, as I wound up the window, leaving a narrow gap at the top for air to circulate, a face appeared over the hedge of the garden across the pavement. The face belonged to an elderly man wearing a checked flat-cap, his creases and wrinkles deepening as he eyed me through horn-rimmed bifocals.

'Mr George Wilkins?' I called out, winding the window down again.

'Who wants to know?' came the reply.

'Nick Dismas,' I told him, satisfied that this was the person I'd come in search of. I pushed open the car door. 'I'm with Dismas Investigations.'

I reached back inside for my jacket and slipped it on before approaching the gate (whatever the weather, I always felt more comfortable fully clothed, something to do with concealment, I suppose). He watched me without saying a word.

'May I come in?' I asked, pausing at the entrance to his God's little half-acre.

'Depends,' he responded noncommittally.

The tiny lawns on either side of the stone path leading up to the bungalow's front door were parched and brownish, despite yesterday's showers, but the flowerbeds that edged them were well-maintained and full of begonias, petunias and geraniums, their reds and oranges slightly past their best, the recent hot weather having sapped their vibrancy.

'Ain't been usin the 'osepipe, if that's what yer've come about,' the old boy insisted gruffly.

I rested my hand on top of the gate. 'Didn't know there was a hosepipe ban in force.'

'There's always one down 'ere, every bleedin summer. Always been the same, ever since water was privatized.'

'Profits before services,' I agreed amiably.

'Bleedin right.' He eyed me up and down again and moved closer to the gate on his side.

He was a spry little guy, the paunch beneath his faded NEVER MIND THE BOLLOCKS T-shirt (I hadn't seen one of those in many a year) belying the thinness of his arms and exposed lower legs. He wore scuffed sneakers (imitation Nikes), no socks, and long shorts (below his knees) and I was mildly disappointed that he'd chosen an old-fashioned flat-cap rather than a back-to-front baseball cap to cover his silver hair (which protruded enough to top large stick-out ears). Dirty green pads covered his knees and in his hand he held a short hoe.

'So what d'you want?' he asked suspiciously.

I showed him my card and he squinted at it through the lower half of his bifocals. 'You are Mr Wilkins, aren't you? You once owned the newsagents' and confectionery shop opposite what used to be Dartford General?'

'That was a long time ago.' He pointed at the bruised swelling above my cheek. 'Get that bein nosy, did yer?'

'Walked into a door,' I lied.

'Oh yeah?'

I don't think he cared one way or the other.

'So what you after? I been retired years since.'

'Yes, I know. But you and your wife ran the shop for quite a number of years, didn't you?'

'Too bloody long. Weren't a bad business, though. Emma liked it, God bless her.'

'Emma's your wife?'

'She was. Dead now. Passed on six years ago.' He shook his head as though still mourning his loss. 'Never had much of a retirement, shoulda sold up long before we did. You gotta get the most out of yer life, son, all work's no good to no one. You want some lemonade?'

Maybe the mention of his late wife had softened him now.

He suddenly seemed pleased to have company, someone to chat to for a while, and that was fine by me.

'I'd love some, Mr Wilkins. It's a little too hot today, isn't it?'

'Never complain about that, son – it's a bloody long cold winter.' He lifted the latch and opened the gate. 'Come on through. You can sit on the doorstep while I fetch us both a nice drink.'

I followed him up the path and waited as he placed the short-handled hoe against the step.

'Take a pew and get rid of your jacket – you'll roast in this heat.'

I did as I was told and the old boy disappeared into the house. I lowered myself awkwardly on to the scrubbed stone doorstep and draped the coat over my knees. Squinting around with my good eye, I took in this little piece of suburbia heaven, the neatly-kept dwellings, the immaculate miniature front gardens, all under a vast, clear blue sky. It held an ambience far removed from the drama and aberrations of my last couple of nights in Brighton, the eerie whisperings of only that morning, the very normalcy surrounding me, although probably boring to some, offering a pleasant kind of comfort.

'There y'are, boy, get that down yer neck.'

Wilkins was back with two still-bubbling glasses of lemonade in his gnarled old hands, one of which he gave to me. I shuffled my bottom along the step but, instead of sitting next to me, he reached back inside the door and dragged out a foldaway canvas chair. Wrestling it open with one hand and one leg, he placed it on the pathway in front of me and sank into it. His grimy kneepads stared me in the face, the thin legs beneath them bristling generously with white hair.

'Your very good health,' he said tilting his glass and taking a long, glugging swallow.

I sipped more moderately, although I relished the cool taste as much as my companion apparently did.

'Ah,' he sighed, wiping his mouth with the back of his hand. 'Nothing better than a nice cold lemonade after a couple of hours' gardening. Beats all the booze, or tea and coffee. Now then, Mr . . . what's your name again, son?'

'Dismas.'

'Mr Dismas. The good thief, eh? Yer don't look too dishonest.'

At another time I'd have wondered what he thought I did look like, but at that moment I was too surprised he had caught the religious connotation to my name. Not many people did.

'Now then, Mr Dismas, what's this all about? Why d'yer want to know about the old shop? Yer not from the VAT, are yer? Finally caught up with me, eh?' He chortled to himself, fully aware that I was from no government department.

I grinned back at him. 'Nothing like that. As I said, I'm from an enquiry agency and I'm trying to trace someone who worked at the Dartford General eighteen years ago.'

He studied me seriously, pinching his grizzled chin with thumb and index finger. 'Eighteen years, yer say? We had a lot of them doctors and nurses comin in buyin their fags and newspapers and all that. Lot of 'ospital visitors used to pop in for sweets and chocolates for sick relatives and friends, too. No shop in the 'ospital itself, yer see, not like nowadays. Oh yeah, we had a good turnover in them days. Even had my boy workin for us full-time. Afore he went off into the music business, that is. He loved all that punk – we had him late, yer see, so regular rock 'n' roll, which we could've stood, wasn't good enough for him. No, he had to go potty with all them earrings and face studs and things.' His eyes rolled behind the glasses. 'The rows we had.'

As he shook his head I caught the connection with the Sex Pistols T-shirt. Anxious to get back on track, I prompted him: 'So would you remember any of your customers?'

'Don't see much of him any more. Lives in Newcastle. Come down for his mum's funeral, that was the last time.' His attention was still a long way off.

'You must have got to know some of them quite well, didn't you?'

'What's that? Oh yeah, sorry, son. Driftin, yer see? Comes to us all.' He took another swig of lemonade and smacked his lips. 'Yeah, we were busy, but we did make friends with a lot of 'em. Blowed if I can remember their names, though.'

'The person I'm looking for was a midwife. She went by the name of Hylda Vogel. A foreign lady, German.'

'Why didn't you say? *Hildegarde* Vogel, not Hylda,' he corrected.

'You remember her?'

My eye must have lit up, because he gave me a broad, pleased grin.

'We were good pals of Hildegarde's. My old girl and her used to go to the pictures together. Lovely little woman, very kind, very generous. Mind you, she might've been a midwife, but she looked like a strong fart would knock her flat. Tough as old boots, though, really; couldna' done the work otherwise. Very good to kids, she was, always buyin the little mites in the wards sweets and comics. Spent a lot of her 'ard-earned wages on that.'

He was silent for a while and I didn't press him. He gazed over my shoulder, eyes distant, as though recalling his old friend.

I waited an appropriate time before asking hopefully: 'D'you happen to know where she lives currently?'

'I don't even know if she's still alive, son.' He took off his cap and wiped perspiration from his forehead with it.

My heart sinking, I said, 'You lost contact with her?'

'Oh, we stayed friends long after we retired. Hildegarde was always poppin round to see my Emma until she took ill.'

'Until your wife became ill?'

'No, son, it was Hildegarde who took ill first. She was

never the same after the 'ospital caught fire and they was all left out of work. Most of the staff either moved away or got took on by other local 'ospitals, but Hildegarde decided to call it a day. Some of the kiddies died in the fire, yer see? Down to the smoke, not the fire itself. If y'ask me, I think that done her in a bit. Loved the kids, didn't she? Anyhows, she was past retirin age, so it was no bad thing in that respect: she'd worked long and hard enough. She was terrible upset at the time, though. Loved her job, she did.'

'She moved away from the area?'

'Had to in the end. Stayed hereabouts for a while, but when her health got too bad, they took her into an old people's home. She was gettin on a bit, y'know.'

'This home – is it local?'

He shook his head gravely. 'No. That's the pity of it. Meant Emma couldn't visit her as often as she'd have liked. Somewhere on the other side of London, near Windsor I think it was. Never went there meself – don't like them places – and my old lady only managed a coupla times. Too fur, y'see? And anyway, accordin to Emma, it was a bit snooty and they didn't seem to like too many visitors. Hard place to get to, enall. When Emma became poorly she couldn't travel that fur any more.'

'So you really don't know if Hildegarde Vogel is still alive?'

'Told yer, didn't I? I suppose I shoulda tried to keep in touch meself, but after Emma went ... well, I didn't have much heart for anythin. Kept meself to meself, got on with the gardenin in spring and summer, played indoor bowls down the club in winter, and looked after me canaries all year round.' He nodded towards the front door just to let me know where he kept his pet birds. 'Mind you,' he went on, 'I shouldn't be surprised if the old girl was still around. Had bags of energy, did Sparrer, even when she retired. Always flappin around!'

'But you still have the address of the home, don't you?' I was leaning towards him, my elbows resting on the jacket over my knees, knuckles almost touching his dirty green kneepads.

'Got it somewhere, phone number enall. Emma always used to ring her after she packed up visitin.'

'Would you mind finding it for me?'

He lounged back in the seat, the almost empty lemonade glass resting in both hands on his lap. 'What's this all about, Mr Dismas? What d'yer want with Hildegarde? I don't want to be causin her any trouble if she is alive and kickin.'

'Oh no, no,' I assured him. 'There's no trouble at all. She might just have some information that's important for a client of mine. I promise you, I won't bother her in any way.'

'What sort of information?'

'I'm afraid I can't tell you. Client confidentiality.'

He weighed me up, undecided.

'It really would be helpful,' I said.

He appeared to make up his mind – maybe he thought I could do with any small break life would give me.

Placing the glass on the stone path, he hauled himself out of the canvas chair and went into the house. 'I'll do my best to find it, son,' I heard him say as he disappeared out of sight.

It was a good ten minutes before he returned and I was pleased to see he carried a scrap of paper in his hand. I stood and on the doorstep he towered over me; NEVER MIND THE BOLLOCKS was at eye level.

Holding up the piece of paper, he fixed me with his gaze. 'I'm trustin yer not to pester Sparrer too much, mind.'

'I promise. No pressure whatsoever.' I held out a hand for the address.

With one last moment of reservation, he gave it to me.

I examined the scrawled writing, then looked back at the old man. 'Tell me something,' I said.

'Go on.'

'Why did you call her Sparrer?'

'Spar*row*, son. Like the bird. Sparrer. She was always

flappin her arms around when she was excited or busy. Just like scrawny little wings. Went with her name, too. That's why I started callin her that.'

'I don't get it.'

'I spent some time in Germany just after the war, picked up some of the lingo. A bit of National Service wouldn't do some of the yobboes 'angin around the street corners and muggin' old ladies nowadays any 'arm, either. Soon straighten that lot out. Would've done my own boy a bit of good too.'

'I still don't understand. Why Sparrow?'

'Because of her name, Vogel. Don't you know what it means in German?'

'I don't know *any* German.'

'Means "bird". Vogel's German for bird.'

I suddenly had an image of hundreds – thousands – of flapping wings beating at the glass of a mirror.

'That's what she was like, yer see? A little bird with flappin wings. A little sparrer.'

13

I was still in a mild daze as I closed the car door behind me. Old man Wilkins had gone back inside his house for his 'usual afternoon's kip', leaving me to find my own way out of the gate. I sat and stared out the Ford's dusty windscreen.

Wings . . . birds . . . Sparrow . . . Vogel – what the hell was that all about?

Merely a coincidence? Or was I truly being sent some kind of message through the clairvoyant and mirrors? Before I had left Shelly Ripstone's home earlier that morning, Louise had claimed it was the disturbances that had jogged the widow's memory, helped her think of the old midwife's name. Even though neither Louise nor Shelly had witnessed the phenomena in the dining-room mirror, those thousands of tiny wings, they had both heard the sounds before the whisperings in the lounge. Although more subliminal than the vision itself, had the effect been the same? It still begged the question why I had been the only one to 'see' the wings, but Louise had suggested that the full power of the communication was directed at me and that she, herself, was only some kind of conduit for it.

I gripped the hot plastic steering-wheel in both hands and watched as a small bird – a sparrow, no less – landed on the car bonnet. It eyed me with beady detachment, cocking its head to one side and issuing a throaty little chirrup. If I had been more fanciful, I might have assumed its arrival was of some special significance: but I wasn't – as yet – that far down the road. No, it was just a sparrow taking a breather.

As if in agreement – although, in truth, displaying no such interest – it chirruped again and flew off.

Better to be like that bird, I told myself. Okay, things that I didn't understand were happening and, it seemed, with increasing frequency. And the clairvoyant insisted I was a key player in all this. So go with it. You don't *have* to understand, just let it roll. Maybe then the answers will find their way through. The feeling I'd had up on the Downs that morning, that something momentous, perhaps even portentous, was about to happen? Well, everybody got that same kind of feeling at least once in a lifetime, and it didn't necessarily signify anything, it was only chemicals in the brain overloading or mixing in the wrong way. No big deal. Not necessarily so, anyway. The thing of it is, there's nothing you can do except ride it. Go along with it and see what happens. Feel a little better? No, not at all.

Resignedly, as if my own free will was no longer playing a part, I reached for my mobile and tapped numbers, glancing at the scrap of paper old Mr Wilkins had given me.

The number rang at least eight times before: 'PERFECT REST, how can I help you?'

It was a woman's voice, more brisk and efficient than the time it had taken to pick up the phone might have suggested. It was also totally cold.

'Ah, yeah, um, I wanted to visit one of your residents today, if that's possible.' I had deliberately chosen not to enquire if Hildegarde Vogel was still living – I didn't want to appear to be a stranger to her if she was, because some of these residential care places could sometimes be fussy about visitors and private enquiry agents in particular.

'We do usually require at least twenty-four hours' notice for visits,' came the curt reply. 'Whom did you wish to see?'

'Uh, Hildegarde Vogel. She's been with you for several years.'

'Of course she has.'

I breathed a quiet sigh of relief. So the midwife was still around.

'Unfortunately,' the voice on the other end continued, 'Ms Vogel is quite unwell at the moment.'

'Yes, I know,' I improvised. 'That's why I wanted to come and see her.'

'Are you a relative?' Same cold tone.

'Not exactly. I knew her some time ago and I've only just learned of her illness. I'm a friend.' If the ex-midwife was poorly, all the more reason for the care home to be reluctant to allow a 'snooper' to bother their charge.

'Oh, just a friend? That's a pity. Ms Vogel doesn't appear to have any relatives – at least, not in England.'

I wondered just how ill the old lady was. 'Well, I am a kind of *special* friend. I know she'd be very pleased to see me, so can I come along?'

'I'm afraid I can't say. Let me put you through to someone who might be able to make that decision.'

Before I could say another word I heard distant clicks down the line. Within seconds, another voice came on.

'Hello. I understand from our receptionist you wish to see one of our residents?'

This new voice also belonged to a woman, but oh, the difference. It was soft, almost gentle, with none of the aloofness of the first speaker.

'Yes,' I replied. 'I'm an acquaintance of Hildegarde Vogel.'

'I'm afraid she's very ill these days.'

That voice. My response might seem ridiculous, I know, but over the years as a PI I'd learned to tell a lot from disembodied voices at the other end of telephones. This woman – girl? She sounded quite young – had a sweetness of tone that threatened to turn my natural, in-built cynicism to mush.

'Is she getting worse?' I had to keep my mind on the job in hand.

'I'm afraid there *is* no cure for emphysema, Mr . . . ?'

'Nick – Nicholas – Dismas.'

'. . . Mr Dismas. And of course, she is very elderly. We can only keep her as comfortable as possible and protect her from infection. Then, of course, there is the other problem we have to deal with.'

I guess I was too distracted by the sound of her lovely voice to pay full attention to what she was actually saying, so I failed to follow up this last remark. It was probably just as well though – I didn't want to appear too ignorant of the old lady's condition.

'You say you're an acquaintance? Our receptionist informed me you were a friend.'

I had to think fast. 'Yes, I am a friend. A special one. Hildegarde delivered me into the world.' I tried to put some lightness into my own voice. 'You know, when she was a midwife? That was a long time ago, of course.' I gave a little laugh. 'Too long, in fact. The years have gone by so fast.' Why did I feel so guilty deceiving this woman? 'She always kept in touch and was very kind to me when I was growing up. Haven't seen Hildegarde for a long, long time though.' Despite the guilt, how easily the lies came.

'How did you find out Hildegarde was here?' She didn't sound suspicious, only interested.

'A mutual friend, George Wilkins. His late wife used to visit Hildegarde at PERFECT REST.'

'Yes, I remember her. I think we can make an exception with you, Mr Dismas. You're obviously very anxious about Hildegarde. But we will have to see how she is when you arrive, so I can make no promises. Are you sure you want to make the journey? I'd hate you to waste your time.'

It'd be worth it just to put a face to your beautiful voice, I thought. 'No, that's fine,' I said. 'I'll take the chance.'

With a sweet goodbye, she rang off.

*

I had checked the road atlas before setting off on the long hike around the M25, feeling both apprehensive and strangely drawn. To break the tedium of the drive I hummed bars of old songs – Twenties and Thirties stuff, the sophisticated, romantic ones that came out of that era – but I was constantly distracted by the memory of her voice. I chastised myself for not having got her name, irritated that I didn't even know her position at the home – nurse, supervisor, carer, administrator? I tried to put a face to those sweet, almost soothing, tones, an overall image of her, visualizing an elegant yet soft-featured girl/woman, graceful in movement and manner as the voice suggested. I was sure she was beautiful and, as such, way out of my reach. *What the hell was I thinking of?* I'd had one brief conversation with this person and I was already thinking in terms of a relationship. Was that how desperate my fantasies had become? And anyway, she didn't have to be beautiful to be out of my reach – she could be ugly and still be beyond me. When *was* your last love affair, Dismas? Oh, never? Yes, that's right, you've never had someone fall in love with you, have you? So quit dreaming and just do your job. Be who and what you are, that way you won't get hurt. Not too much, anyway. All right, not as much as you would be by entertaining notions of romance.

Angry at myself, I took my own advice and rang the office, a diversion that might just get me back on track. Henry, as ever, was heavily involved in paperwork, but took time to inform me that Ida was at that moment swearing affidavits on papers she had successfully served, while he, himself, was writing a 'letter of appointment' to some scallywag who was never at home (or pretended not to be) whenever legal documents had to be served on him. If he failed to answer the door or was 'out' next time, despite the appointment having been made through the letterbox, then the matter would go to court anyway. Philo had nothing special to do, so Henry had set him the chore of cleaning the insides of the office windows (which, apparently, our apprentice was none too happy about). Henry wanted the okay from me to contact a computer data agency for information on a particularly elusive debtor whose personal and business affairs appeared to be uncommonly complicated and I expressed doubts about the expense of doing so.

'Well, it's the client who pays, Dis,' was his unconcerned reply, 'and I honestly believe it's the only way we're going to get this joker.'

'Get the client's agreement first, then.'

'Will do. Hey, I've got a good one for you. Who played the bombshell in the 1933 film *Bombshell*?'

'Come on, Henry, you can do better than that. Jean Harlow.'

'Right, right. It was based on a true story about a movie star who was abused by her studio and family. So who was the real star it was based on?'

'Clara Bow, Henry. Clara Bow.'

I heard a curse from the other end – he had expected me to say Jean Harlow – so just to cheer him up, I added: 'Did you know she once slept with the entire USC Trojans football team?'

'Clara Bow did?' His voice had brightened.

'Yup.'

'How do you *know* these things?'

'Just love the old movies.'

'Yeah, but that's not the kind of thing you find in old movie mags.'

'Well, I picked it up somewhere.'

'Sometimes I suspect you make up half these little tidbits. Hard for us to know, isn't it?'

'Just trust me.'

'Wish I could, Dis. But I know how despicable you can be.'

We both laughed and I said, 'Okay, gotta go. I think I've got a date with a beautiful lady.' Briefly I told him of the new lead in tracing Shelly Ripstone's 'alleged' missing son and of my destination that afternoon.

Henry wished me good luck. 'But I'm not sure all this is worth it, Dis,' he said. 'We're spending a lot of time and effort on something that might turn out to be a wild goose chase.'

'Like you say, Henry, it's the client who pays the bill. I'm going to hang up now before the patrol cops stop me for using the mobile while driving. I'll call back later, let you know how I got on with old Sparrow Vogel.'

'Who? Did you say "Sparrow"?'

'I'll explain later. So long.'

It would have been too complicated and would have sounded too foolish to explain to Henry about wings and birds and German names over the phone. Then again, it was going to sound just as foolish face to face.

PERFECT REST wasn't an easy place to find. According to the map book, it appeared to lie directly under the flight path to Heathrow airport, just a few miles away, which was surprising as it was supposed to be a *rest* home. I'd come off the great circular motorway around London at Exit 13, then driven along B roads towards Windsor, passing vast half-empty water reservoirs along the way, until I reached a long, winding main road that had many inconspicuous lanes along its length. In fact, so unnoticeable were some of these that I had to turn back and drive more slowly to locate the one I was looking for.

A sign of some kind giving a clue to the home's where-abouts would have been helpful, but there was none. Aware that the River Thames, on whose north bank PERFECT REST was situated, was nearby I began trying each lane one by one, heading in the general direction of the river. Most of the properties I passed looked pretty expensive, and the area itself, with fields and woodlands lending a rural setting, would have been an estate agent's dream had not the constant drone of aircraft disturbed the natural peace and quiet. After a while, though, the sound of those engines high overhead became almost subliminal and I realized that was how the locals here must cope: the noise was no more than a background hum if you paid it no mind. Only when Concorde flew over did the noise become an intrusion, one that lasted minutes after the hook-nosed jet was out of sight.

I came across no pedestrians along these lanes and, although tempted to knock at one of the houses to ask directions, I decided against it: it was sometimes a shock for people to find me unforewarned on their doorstep, an embarrassment I tried to avoid whenever I could. I'd try one more lane at least before I took that risk.

Fortunately, I had at last found the right one. It was a long, narrow lane of hardened mud, with a few twists and turns and mostly fields and hedges on either side. It was difficult to believe it might lead to the kind of establishment I was looking for, but I knew PERFECT REST had to be somewhere in the area, so I persisted. I passed very few houses and these were mainly gathered near the lane's beginning, although I did eventually come to one that appeared deserted, its lower windows boarded up, front door heavily padlocked. The further I travelled down the winding lane, the more I had the feeling of being miles from anywhere, of venturing into a remote part of the countryside, even though I was aware that the city itself was no more than thirty or forty minutes away. Even the steady stream of air traffic high above failed to convince me I wasn't in some distant hinterland.

Soon, however, and just when I was considering turning back, I spied rooftops and chimney stacks rising above the trees ahead. Judging from what I could see, it was a large, tall building, at least three storeys high, its roof and gables topped with aged, red slates, a multitude of television aerials attached to the chimneys. Relieved, I drove on and soon came to a wide entrance, its large iron gates closed. The sign on one of the stone pillars on either side of the entrance was discreet and in faded gold script on a deep brown background declared:

PERFECT REST

Residential & Nursing
Home for the Elderly

Dir: Leonard K. Wisbeech, MD, FRCS, FRCOG, FRCP, DCH

I'd had to press a button and speak into an intercom mounted below the sign on the pillar to get someone to open the gates for me, and as I drove through I noted my surroundings, a mental exercise I invariably performed in my role of private investigator. In this case it wasn't necessary, it wouldn't answer any questions, but it was a habit that was hard to break. The lawns on either side of the lengthy driveway were scorched brown by the summer's sun, the grass itself cut too short for middle season, and flowerbeds strived to cheer the approach to the house, although their colours had passed their best and were not varied enough anyway to raise the spirits. To my left, almost by the gate itself, was another drive, this one overshadowed by trees so that it looked more like a tunnel than a roadway. I gave it scarce attention, for the home itself loomed up soon after I was through the entrance, a big white building, beyond it the great wide River Thames, swift-flowing and muddy-brown. Across the water and through the trees there, I glimpsed fast-moving traffic, and I assumed this was the main Windsor road that I'd noticed in the map book. The broad river formed a natural moat, the trees on the opposite bank a partial screen that afforded the home all the privacy and peacefulness it could desire as well as a barrier against a busy world that had little time for the elderly; on this side, the long twisting lane through fields and woodland provided another buffer against the outside intrusion, and I wondered if this was the purpose of PERFECT REST's location. It certainly seemed to be the perfect half-way-house towards oblivion.

The building had projecting wings on either side, hence the gables, and was, as I'd guessed, comprised of three storeys, the windows on the ground floor high and elegantly framed. The white stonework was cracked in places and a fresh coat of paint would not have been amiss, yet it was still a grand structure and it was easy to imagine its former glory. At one time, perhaps in another century, it had obviously belonged to a wealthy landowner or nobleman, a private mansion house now given over to commerce, and it occurred to me that present residency in such a place would come expensive, too expensive, I would have thought, for an ex-NHS midwife. Maybe she had a rich family back there in Germany, relatives who could afford to pay for her care here. But then why wouldn't they take her home again, so that she could be close to them? And George Wilkins hadn't mentioned any rich relatives. I shrugged my shoulders. What did it matter? The case I was working on concerned a missing baby, not the financial affairs of an ailing elderly ex-midwife.

I pulled up outside the main entrance, an incongruously modern addition to the original structure with its plate-glass doors and side windows, framed in mahogany, seemingly 'stuck on' to the main building itself as if the architect or builder had no concept of architectural harmony. A gentle wheelchair ramp led up to the doorway and inside potted plants brushed against the glass on either side. Craning my neck to get a better view I saw that beyond this conservatory-type vestibule was a long, wide hallway stretching towards the back of the building, a screened receptionist's desk positioned a little way along its length.

Climbing awkwardly from the car, I made my way up the ramp and pushed open one side of the clear doors. A head popped up from behind the white panel screen and I felt myself scrutinized as I hobbled towards the desk. The pale cream walls were hung with wonderfully reproduced gilt-framed prints, the glorious works of Ingres, Reynolds, Renoir, Cassatt, all depicting beautiful women, perhaps chosen to cheer the home's elderly residents (although I would have thought such reminders of youthful loveliness might depress the more age-sensitive among them). A particular favourite of mine, although scorned by many present-day élitist critics for its elegance and ideality (which made it, of course, too 'populist' for them), caught my eye: it was Alma-Tadema's painting of women bathers in a Pompeiian bathhouse, and it wasn't just the incredible feel for texture and surfaces that got to me – no, it was also the understanding the artist had for the human form, its grace, its vulnerability. Its perfection.

Even though my pocket would only allow me to indulge my love of art through galleries and artbooks (even my reproductions were minimal), art stirred the imagination – my God, it *allowed* the imagination! – in a way that reality rarely does. Through art I could yearn without bitterness, fantasize beyond restraint, the picture itself was the dream and my own mind the observer, the visionary; my thoughts could go anywhere without hindrance from truth. The brushstrokes here proclaimed the natural symmetry between the figures and their environment, shape and substance extolling a harmony that would always elude me because of my own *dis*symmetry (unless, of course, I were to stand amidst clamour and distortion); yet rather than be reminded of my flaws, I was persuaded to become part of this fabulous insight (those piss-poor critics might label it 'visual fallacy') and this kind of *escape* never ceased to please me. I had paused in front of the print, momentarily captured by its delicate power, and the receptionist's voice rudely reclaimed me.

'Can I help you, sir?'

Her screened desk was positioned on the other side of a junction, narrower corridors leading off from the main hallway, left and right, and I crossed over to it, avoiding a white-haired, crook-backed gentleman in pyjamas and dressing-gown and supported by a Zimmer frame shuffling by as I did so. I noticed a Titian print on the wall to the receptionist's left, the print depicting a naked woman reclining while a dark figure seated before her showered her with gold dust. Again, the nude's form was beautifully defined, the colours rich and adding to the sexual lustre.

'My name's Dismas. I rang earlier – about visiting Hildegarde Vogel?' Resting my elbows on the screen's shelf, I watched her smile adjust to my closeness. It withered slowly. A visitors' book lay open by my left arm and I noticed there were very few sign-ins for that particular day. Only one, in fact.

'Sorry, your name again . . . ?'

Her smile was almost rictus by now. The name-tag pinned to her cream buttoned-to-the-neck blouse declared her to be 'Hazel'.

'Nicholas Dismas.'

The receptionist was plump and on the other side of forty, the circles of her mottled-blue-framed spectacles almost usurping her face, so big and statement-intended were they. She tapped my name into a computer hidden beneath the screen's shelf, stopped to consult her wristwatch, then continued tapping. Bare details registered, she returned her attention to me.

'You spoke to Ms Bell, didn't you?'

'I'm not sure. I spoke to *someone* about Hildegarde.' My use of the ex-midwife's Christian name might indicate familiarity.

'Yes, I put you through to Constance. Just one moment, I'll see if I can contact her for you.'

'I only need to see Hildegarde Vogel,' I insisted.

Her voice became frosty. 'Just one moment . . .' She picked up the receiver of a grey telephone next to her computer and with an imperious gesture of her other hand she indicated a row of brown-fabric armchairs against a wall back towards the entrance vestibule, a low, blond-wood magazine table in front of them. 'If you'll just sign the visitors' book, then take a seat . . .'

Picking up the pen that was attached by a thin ball-chain to a black base fixed to the shelf, I scribbled my name, but where it said 'Address or company', I put in the agency address without its title. At this delicate stage I wanted neither to reveal my profession, nor to give away my flat's location (I was always reluctant to divulge my home address in case anyone with a grudge decided to pay me a visit at home – some debtors or errant members of the public I'd had dealings with seemed to regard me as their personal persecutor). That was why I carried two calling cards with me, one with both addresses (for clients only), the other with only the agency's (for witnesses, informants, debtors, anyone who had no real cause to contact me at home). I replaced the pen and as I retreated to the visitors' chairs by the vestibule I heard the receptionist tapping again, this time digits on the telephone base. As I sank into a seat, my eye immediately going to the two prints opposite, the Cassatt and the Ingres (the latter another exquisite female nude), I heard her say: 'Constance? I have a Mr Dismas here to see Hildegarde Vogel. You said you'd want to have a word first? Right. I'll ask him to wait.' She replaced the receiver and once more those owlish eyes regarded me over the top of the screen. 'Ms Bell will be along shortly,' she informed me before lowering her head again so that all I saw was a grey-streaked bush apparently resting on the shelf.

Constance Bell, I mused. A nice name to go with the beautiful voice I had heard over my mobile. My expectations rose.

An ambivalent odour of staleness and sterility pervaded the air, my nasal passages, with their keen sense of smell, irritated by the mixture. Distant noises came to me – a clank of metal, the squeaky wheels of a trolley, a soft crash somewhere, followed by a muted burst of laughter – none harsh enough to disturb the general serenity of the place. The elderly man who had crossed my path minutes before escorted his Zimmer frame back across the reception area again, looking neither left nor right, or even ahead, his attention exclusively concentrated on the marble floor two feet in front of him. His breath seemed to rattle as it escaped his lungs. I heard the almost entirely invisible receptionist shuffling papers on her desk, then all became still and quiet again.

Ignoring the back-dated yet still gleamingly new-looking copies of *Punch, House & Garden, Tatler* and the like spread over the squat table before me, I studied the paintings on the wall opposite once more, wondering at the choice for such a place as PERFECT REST.

The sound of footsteps approaching along one of the corridors, a clatter on marble that oddly was without a regular rhythm, drew me from my musing, and I looked towards the open area where the hallways met. The person was still out of my sight as the receptionist, her position allowing a good view of all approaches, glanced up and said, 'Hello, Constance,' before nodding in my direction.

The footsteps grew louder and I straightened my body as much as I was able (not much, unfortunately), surprised by my own growing expectancy. The sound of her lovely voice, heard only over the phone, was still fresh in my mind.

Oh my God, I said silently as Constance Bell came into view.

14

Her face was beautiful. Her face was perfect. With those deep brown, liquid eyes, that slightly tilted nose and chin so softly drawn, her face was exquisite. Her medium-brown hair was pulled back from her face revealing the elegant curves of her cheeks and neck, and her gentle smile was as perfect as a smile could be.

But Constance Bell's body was like mine. Only in some ways it was worse.

It was twisted and small – not dwarfish by any means, but little (had it been normal, it would have been described as *petite*). Her body had been deformed by spina bifida, her limbs twisted, her spine misshapen by the *sac* it carried, her walk, assisted by metal elbow-crutches, ungainly. But even so she was beautiful and I wanted to weep for her.

She hesitated when she saw me, her clumsy steps faltering for a moment; her expression – her so-sweet expression – was a mixture of surprise, curiosity, and something more, something I could not define. It was as though a veil were drawn across her innermost thoughts, the hint of darkness around her eyes the subtle manifestation of sleepless nights, a secret kept. Still, her smile did not vanish completely.

'Mr Dismas?' She had quickly recovered her composure and was walking towards me again.

'Yes . . .' My response was almost as hesitant as her own initial reaction.

'I'm Constance Bell. I'm a care-supervisor at PERFECT REST.' She held out a small, delicate hand, the crutch on that

153

side perfectly balanced by her elbow, and I felt a shiver run through me, not one of aversion – God forbid that *I* should feel such an emotion – but a kind of *frisson* that seemed to run between us. I'm perhaps ashamed that I also took pleasure in being able to look *down* into a woman's eyes, an all too infrequent occasion for one of my stature.

'I spoke to you earlier . . .' I said for the sake of saying something. 'On the phone.'

The fullness of her smile returned and again I was lost in her beauty. 'Of course,' she replied and it occurred to me that she might misinterpret my unease. I rushed my words.

'Uh, Hildegarde Vogel. I asked you if it would be all right. To see her, I mean. I'm a friend . . . I know her. Used to know her.'

'Yes, I checked on Hildegarde after your call.' Her eyes were serious, searching mine, looking for . . . ? Looking for what? Dishonesty, subterfuge? No, I didn't think so: her gaze was too sincere, too gentle. Perhaps she was just wondering how I'd acquired the bruises and swelling on my face. 'It's one of her relatively good days,' she went on, 'so I'm sure she'll be pleased to see you, even if she doesn't recognize you at first. I'm afraid it will have to be a brief visit though – Hildegarde tires very quickly.'

Her voice was as alluring as it had been over the phone, a voice that matched her face but held no alliance with the irregularities of her body. I let its sound sink into me, just as I allowed her gaze to search mine.

I pulled myself together, remembering something Constance Bell had hinted at during our telephone conversation. 'You said Hildegarde had another problem as well as emphysema . . . ?'

'You weren't aware? Mr Wilkins didn't mention it?'

I shook my head and hoped those penetrating eyes wouldn't detect my guile.

'Well, I suppose it has been a few years since Mrs Wilkins'

last visit, and Hildegarde's decline into senile dementia has been more rapid recently.'

'Senile dementia?' I could feel my hopes sinking.

'I'm afraid so. Hildegarde rarely even remembers her own name now, although recently she's been referring to herself as "Sparrow".'

'That was her nickname.'

'I know. We learned that even before she arrived here.'

It was something else I let go for the moment, this time distracted by the closeness to Constance Bell herself. I remained unsettled by the sight of her, my inner thoughts in a strangely pleasant turmoil, my emotions turning cartwheels. I'd never been quite so captivated by anyone in this way before. She wore a pale blue, short-sleeved tunic with lapels, a buttoned front and a plastic name tag above her left breast, the home's nursing uniform, I guessed, which had obviously been tailored to her awkward shape. I noticed that her hair was tied into a neat little tail at the back, unusual for a girl who appeared to be in her mid-twenties, but all the more beguiling for it.

'Now if you'll come along with me, we'll see how she is,' the cause of my distraction was saying. 'I can't let you stay too long though, Mr Dismas – Hildegarde is very frail these days and, as I said, tires easily. I'm afraid conversation with her might be difficult because of her deteriorated mental condition anyway – unfortunately brain atrophy isn't something that can be reversed. Just lately we've found her wandering the corridors late at night as if searching for someone. When we question her she can never remember who.'

Constance Bell led me past the reception desk towards a broad staircase further along the hallway and I realized, as Hazel, the frosty receptionist, twisted in her chair to watch, we must have made an odd sight, both of us hobbling along, in some ways twinned by our appearance. I noticed more superbly reproduced prints of old masterpieces adorning the walls on the way, but these were subtly changed. They still portrayed beautiful women – a Klimt to my right, a Mucha to my left – but they were more stylized, less realistic, impressions of beauty rather than exact representations, and they were both incorporated into symbolic or swirling designs. There was also another aspect to them that might have been considered out of place in an old people's home: both bore suggestions of eroticism. As we drew nearer to the staircase and further into the innards of the home itself, the artwork appeared to take on yet another aspect. These reproductions were by the likes of Cézanne and Munch, the themes as before, but now ill-drawn, as if the artist cared little for the qualities of the physical form but chose to describe them – in my view, at least – in more exaggerated and sinister terms. Perhaps the fault lay with me; perhaps because of my own physical distortions I idealized the per-ceived perfection too much and felt only disdain for its corruption. Foolish, maybe, philistine to some, no doubt; but there it was. Possibly a shrink could convince me to lighten up, not to take these things so personally.

Now my thoughts centred on Constance Bell once more. How did she cope with her disability? I wondered. My heart suddenly ached for her and not *just* out of pity. It was cruel enough to be born such as I, ugly both in features and shape, for at least it was a *corporate* image, a bitter unification; but this woman bore the extra torment of having the face of an angel shackled to an impaired body. Perhaps this was the inner turmoil I thought I had recognized in her earlier, the dealing with the dichotomy of her own identity. All these reflections of mine were fleeting as most thoughts are, and soon we had reached the broad stairway.

The care-supervisor, this lovely creature Constance Bell, turned to me. 'Are the stairs all right? We could take the lift if you'd prefer, although it's only one flight.' One of her hands rested on the post of the thick, oak stair-rail.

'No problem.' I gave her a smile, more concerned for her than myself: I didn't need crutches to get about on.

'We like to keep the lift free for our more elderly and infirm residents. And those in wheelchairs, of course. Besides, the exercise is good for me.'

I wondered if she simply refused to give in to her condition.

'How long have you worked at PERFECT REST?' I asked as we began to climb. I was curious about this extraordinary woman, wanting to ask much, much more.

She smiled. 'Oh my goodness, for more years than I can remember. Dr Wisbeech brought me here when I was a teenager.'

Another print mounted over the stairway caught my eye. I couldn't be sure, but I thought it was a Modigliani, a portrait of a girl's face, the shapes distorted, elongated, yet the expression revealing grace and vulnerability.

'You said Hildegarde was the midwife who delivered you into the world,' Constance said, a slight breathlessness to her voice now that we were half-way up the stairs. She used her crutches expertly, but I sensed the climb was harder for her than she pretended. She added, with a hint of playfulness: 'I bet you gave her a shock.'

I almost missed a step and she laughed, the sound as pleasing as her voice.

'I'm sorry.' She was smiling again, enjoying the tease. 'You just looked so . . . well, so concerned with yourself.'

'Is that how I come across?'

'To me you do.'

My turn to smile. And to apologize. 'Some days it just gets you down, y'know?'

'Oh, I know, Mr Dismas, believe me, I know. Try to remember there are others even worse off.'

'You think so?' I meant it lightly, but in a flash her humour was gone.

'I know so,' she said.

We began the next flight of stairs and until we reached the landing there was no more communication between us. I'd observed the stark cleanliness of the place before, the freshly painted pale cream walls, polished woodwork and doors, the crystal chandelier hanging over the main hall; now I noticed the change in smell, from chemicals and senility to the mixture of boiled cabbages, decay, disinfectant, the general malodour of such places, when the old mingled with the old-sick. I supposed nothing on earth could ever truly disguise the resident scent, not even in the grandest of old folks' homes.

Two ladies of late years and dressed in nightwear shambled past us, supporting each other, their heads close as if sharing a secret. They broke their journey to look back at us, their imperious expressions rather spoilt by their obvious curiosity. To them I guess the care-supervisor and I were the odd couple exemplified.

Constance greeted them with that wonderful smile. 'Good afternoon, ladies. Hildegarde has a visitor today, isn't that nice?'

One of the ladies sniffed, while the other muttered something I couldn't quite catch. But at least they each faked a quick smile before turning and shuffling on their way.

'I'm not sure they even know who Hildegarde is,' Constance confided to me in a low voice.

'It's got to cost quite a bit to be a guest in this place,' I commented as we began walking again.

'It is quite expensive,' she replied, 'particularly as PERFECT REST is completely privately run without any funds at all from the government or local council.'

'I hadn't realized Hildegarde Vogel was wealthy,' I said, bemused.

'She isn't,' Constance replied.

'Then how – ?'

'Hildegarde is a special case.'

Before I could follow up this new piece of information, we

were interrupted by someone leaving a room – from the glimpse I caught, it appeared to be an office of some kind – we had drawn level with. She was a tall woman, five-nine at least, and her build, while not hefty exactly, was substantial. She looked as if she had more than average female strength and knew how to use it. Her red hair was a little faded, as though it had lost much of its original vibrancy, and it was curled back over her ears in sensible fashion. I guessed her to be in her early forties. The uniform she wore was similar to the care-supervisor's, except a wide black belt drew in her waist and the long sleeves ended in white cuffs. Her eyes were small and puffy, and they seemed to regard me with suspicion.

She shifted her attention to Constance, a question in her cool expression.

'Rachel, this is Mr Dismas,' the care-supervisor responded quickly. 'He's here to see Hildegarde Vogel.'

The look I now received from this tall woman could have frozen chili. 'On whose authority?' she demanded, continuing to look down on me.

Constance was flustered. 'Hildegarde is much better today – I was sure it would be all right.'

'You should have checked with me first,' came the rebuke. 'You know Hildegarde becomes very confused.'

I thought it was about time that I spoke. 'I've come a long way and I'd really like to see her.' Not if she's *that* confused though, I thought to myself. How would I get answers from someone who didn't know what day it was?

Her piggy eyes glared and her fleshy throat appeared to quiver, but just as she was about to speak the door behind her opened again. A big bruiser of a man clutching a document of some kind stepped out to join us. His uniform was obviously the male equivalent of the supervisor's: pale blue, short sleeves (revealing well-muscled, hairy arms), but reaching just below the waist and with a buttoned Nehru-type collar; he wore joggers rather than trousers, the same shade of pale-blue as the tunic, and casual, white Nikes rather than formal shoes. His dark hair was cut short, brushed forward, speckles of white adding texture, and I imagined he modelled himself on *ER*'s George Clooney, although he looked more like Stallone – Stallone gone wrong, if you can imagine *that*; even his chin was heavily shadowed as if he'd neglected to shave that morning (although he was probably the type who had to shave twice a day). A hooked nose and a curled-lipped mouth completed the presentation. Oh, and the sorry smell of Blue Strata.

'Rachel,' he began, 'they want us to confirm the order for –' He broke off when he saw me. He glanced at the tall woman, his eyebrows raised.

'A visitor for Hildegarde Vogel,' he was told curtly.

His eyes came back to me. 'That's not a good idea, is it?' he said. 'Has Dr Wisbeech been informed?'

I was becoming a little annoyed at people staring at me while speaking to someone else.

'I only want to spend a couple of minutes with her just to, y'know, just to let her know someone out there cares,' I said, appealing to the tall woman.

'I doubt she'll even know you,' was her chilly response.

The man – orderly, nurse, I didn't know what he was – nodded in agreement. 'Some days she doesn't even remember who I am and I've dealt with her for nearly ten years.'

He may have been around six-foot-two, but I didn't like the way he said 'dealt with her'. What was wrong with 'cared' or 'helped'? 'I think she'd like to see a friendly face,' I said, not caring what they made of that remark. 'And I gather she doesn't get many visitors.'

'None at all, actually,' Constance chimed in helpfully.

'So I might just cheer her up a little bit. And besides, for my own personal satisfaction I'd like to thank her for all she did for me years ago, even if she can't remember me.' I said all this in a firm, no-nonsense voice that sometimes worked for me. By then, I'd realized that Hildegarde's senility might, in fact, run in my favour – when she failed to recognize me it would be blamed on her condition.

'All right,' said the woman called Rachel, irritation on her face and in her tone. 'Dr Wisbeech is away today but, Constance, you'll have to let him know of Mr Dismas' visit this evening when he returns. And next time I'd like you to check with me first.'

'Of course,' Constance agreed meekly. 'It was such short notice and I know how busy you are . . .' She let her words trail away.

Without further comment, although disapproval was still evident in her body language, the heavy-set woman turned on her heels and marched off down the hallway, the big guy following, holding the paper he clutched towards her. 'I need your signature and then it can be faxed through,' we heard him say before they disappeared from sight round a corner.

'Nice lady,' I remarked as their footsteps faded.

'Rachel Fletcher. She's both senior nurse and chief administrator.'

'I can see why she's busy then.'

'I hope you won't be too disappointed if Hildegarde doesn't remember you,' my companion said, moving on towards the same turn in the hallway that the senior nurse and orderly had taken.

I'm counting on it, I thought to myself, although hoping her memory wouldn't be completely wiped: I needed the ex-midwife to tell me about Shelly Ripstone's long-lost baby. I groaned inwardly, realizing how slim the chances were.

'Tell me something,' I said. 'With senile dementia, does the victim forget everything?'

'Good gracious, no.'

Good gracious? I loved it. I hadn't heard that kind of exclamation in many a year. A curse or blasphemy usually did the job nowadays.

The victim might be unable to think clearly or understand complex ideas, and they will forget people's names, even the names of relatives or close friends. They might also forget recent events, even what they had for breakfast, but some can remember what happened in the distant past as if it were yesterday. They could tell you what they did fifty years ago, yet be unable to tell you what they did that morning. It's one of the mysteries of the illness.'

By now we had reached the corridor leading off from the main hallway and we turned into it. It must have run along the centre of the building, for there were doors on either side, some open, others shut. I heard the muted rumbling of a large aircraft passing overhead.

'Isn't it a bit noisy for your patients?' I asked as we went on. 'You know, with the airport so near?'

That coaxed a smile again. 'Most of our *guests*,' she corrected, 'are hard of hearing anyway, and the windows here are double-glazed, so the noise doesn't bother them much. Sometimes the vibration might, especially when a plane is too low or Concorde is passing over, but it isn't often and you soon get used to it.'

'It's in an odd location, though. It was pretty hard to find.'

'Dr Wisbeech likes it that way – it's more private for our residents. Besides, the house belonged to the Wisbeech family long before the doctor turned it into a nursing home for the elderly. He completely renovated the place to make it suitable.'

'He must have come from a wealthy family.'

A plump, blue-uniformed figure appeared from a doorway further along the corridor and gave Constance a wave. Her hands occupied with the crutches, Constance gave a nod of her head in response. I peeked into open doorways as we passed by, catching glimpses of sparse but comfortable-looking rooms: iron-framed beds with multi-pillows, bright bedcovers, fresh flowers on small cabinets, a wardrobe here and there, small, portable televisions on sideboards, all cosy and well kept. Occasionally, an old face returned my curiosity, but mainly the residents I saw seemed preoccupied with their newspapers, their little television sets, or the empty air in front of them. Some had tubes attached to their bodies, while others lay still in their beds as if already dead. Through the windows in the rooms to my left I could see fields and sparse woodlands, distant houses dotted here and there, yet on my right, from where the views of the River Thames and beyond would have been glorious, there were only blank walls.

I had no time to ponder this, for the nurse who had waved to Constance was strolling towards us.

''Lo, there. A new friend, is it, Constance?' There was a nice Irish lilt to the plump nurse's voice.

'Just someone to see Hildegarde, Theresa,' Constance replied, showing no strain at having to repeat the familiar line.

Theresa – pronounced Ther*ai*sa – was a pleasant-faced girl, with a chubby, freckled face and an easy manner. 'Is that right, now?' she said. 'That's a good thing. Hildegarde will enjoy that.' She seemed genuinely unfazed by my appearance and I wondered if that was because of her daily contact with Constance. 'I've just left the poor old' – *auld* – 'thing an she's as quiet as a mouse. Not sleeping, though, so you won't be disturbin her.'

As the plump young nurse stepped aside to allow us by, she gave me a little wink, then grinned at Constance.

'There's a fine feller,' she said, and you know, I think she meant it.

When I peeked a sideways look at Constance, I was amazed to see she was blushing. I almost laughed.

'I'll be seein youse later, Constance,' Theresa called as she went on her way. 'An see youse both behave yerselves, mind.'

We heard her chuckle to herself and Constance gave me a sheepish glance.

'Don't mind Theresa,' she said. 'She's always jolly.'

Jolly? Oh yes, I loved the words Constance used. 'I bet

she's a good worker, too,' I replied trying to help her out of her embarrassment.

'She certainly is.'

'How many medical staff or carers work here?' I asked, waiting for the redness in her cheeks to fade.

'Eight in this unit, five in our other section. Then there's Rachel Fletcher, our chief administrator-supervisor/senior nurse, and her secretary, and our main lobby receptionist, of course.'

'The guy with Nurse Fletcher – he's a nurse, too?'

'Bruce is a general orderly, but also a kind of assistant to Rachel.'

'What is this other section you mentioned?'

For some reason she seemed almost relieved that we had reached the doorway from where Theresa had waved. Was I asking too many questions? If so, I still didn't understand why that should make her uncomfortable. Then again, why was I asking so many questions anyway? Too many years as a professional snooper. I thought at the time it was my natural – some might say *un*natural – instinct, the one I relied on so much in my line of work, needling me, sending little vibes to pester me; little did I realize it was so much more than that.

'If you'll just wait a moment I'll check on Hildegarde first,' Constance said, ignoring my last question.

She disappeared into the room and I heard her say in a voice that was louder than normal: 'Hildegarde, your visitor is here. Remember I told you someone was coming to see you? Are you feeling well enough?'

There was a throaty sound that might have been assent or just a cough.

Constance returned to the doorway and dropped the pitch of her voice. 'She'll be fine. But please don't make your visit too long, will you? There's a buzzer by the bed should you need any assistance.'

With that, she looked directly into my eye again, as if

searching for something there. Perhaps it was the truth
behind the lie.

'Th-thank you.' Yes, I actually stuttered and it was my turn
to feel sheepish. There was a sudden warmth to her gaze,
and then she was gone, moving awkwardly around me and
heading back towards the main stairway. With one last look
at her hunched back, I entered the room.

It was like all the others we had passed, the walls painted
the same peaceful cream colour, the woodwork white. The
large sash window overlooked the drive and lawns, the light
from the north subdued. In one corner was a small sink, a
rectangular mirror with a strip light over it. A free-standing
screen stood close by, the edge of what looked like a
commode just visible behind it. A picture of Christ hung on
the wall opposite a narrow iron-framed bed, a deep red heart
burning from His chest, golden rays bursting from it like
brilliant shafts of sunlight. The compassionate eyes seemed
to watch me as I crossed the room, and one of His hands
was raised in benediction.

The thin, frail figure of Hildegarde Vogel, 'Sparrow', was
raised by pillows at her back, a nebulizer and other apparatus
close at hand on a bedside cabinet. Like the Christ image,
she watched me as I drew near.

Her trembling, skeletal, blue-veined hands reached out to
greet me.

In a voice so tearful and weary that the last word fell away
in a moan, she uttered: 'My . . . poor . . . baby . . .'

15

Pale and watery though those aged eyes were, they seemed to burn with an inner fever. I was dismayed at the pity and deep sadness I saw in them.

'My ... poor ...' Hildegarde repeated, but this time the last word eluded her.

I flinched at the thin, claw-like hands that reached for me, somehow afraid to let them touch, fighting the revulsion I felt for this cadaverous old lady lying there propped up by pillows, her long dry white hair, the scrawny chicken's neck, the yellowish skin, with its deep creases and rampant liver-spots – and most of all the fetid smell that came from her, musty-sweet and tainted by the odour of degenerating flesh. I despised myself for giving in to the very emotion I reviled in others, those people who cast eyes upon my own shape for the first time and who, either because of surprise or ignorance, were unable to disguise their reactions. I quickly pulled myself together and managed to smile.

'Sparrow,' I said, and her expression changed as she remembered the nickname. Her mouth widened into a thin, toothless grin.

But as I drew even closer, her weak eyes narrowed and the grin shrivelled to a glower. She cocked her head to one side, eyeing me suspiciously.

'You're not one of my ...' Although the words she spoke were more crisp, the sentence trailed away again. Her hands dropped to the sheets covering her skinny old body and now there was consternation on her face. So cavernous were her cheeks that they were shadowed, and although she was slight, some of her flesh hung loose, as though the bone inside had shrunk. I hated to admit it, but the only bird she reminded me of was a vulture.

'Miss Vogel . . . er, Sparrow, I'm a friend,' I forced myself to say, angry at myself for giving into such prejudices. There was a hardbacked chair against the wall and I pulled it nearer to the bed. My hump pushed me forward when I sat and I rested my wrists on the edge of the narrow bed. Her head slumped back on the pillows and she watched me with distrustful eyes.

'You are not, you are not a friend.'

The German accent was still evident in her weary voice, although it was slight, an intonation rather than a pronunciation.

'George Wilkins told me about you.'

Her wizened face formed a thousand more wrinkles as she frowned in concentration. 'George?' It sounded like *Chorge*. 'I don't know anyone . . .'

'Sure, you remember. He and his wife used to run a shop opposite the hospital you worked in.' Shit, what was the wife's name? I'm supposed to be a pro, I should have made a note of it. 'The Dartford General. You were a good friend of George and his wife. You used their shop all the time.'

'Emma. Where is Emma? Has she come to see me?' She craned her neck to look at the open doorway as if expecting her old friend to enter. 'Where is . . . ?'

Her hand gripped my wrist on the bed.

'Yes, Emma. See, you do remember. Emma Wilkins.'

A toothless smile again. Heavy lids closed over her eyes as she recalled her friend. I hoped other memories would come back to her this afternoon.

'I worked in many hospitals,' she muttered and I could hear the wheezy rattle of her breath as it settled into her leaking lungs.

I had no idea that she had, but I prompted her. 'Yes, you did. But you remember Dartford General, don't you?'

Her breath now made a whistling sound as it left her mouth. 'Is ... is Em ...' the name almost escaped her '... Emma coming to see me today?'

'No, not today.' I didn't want to upset her, so I lied again. 'Emma's not very well, but she sends her love.'

Another thin smile and she opened her eyes once more. 'And tell me, why are you here? I'm sure ... I'm sure I do not know you. Or are you just someone else I've forgotten? I do forget things these days. I do not mean to ...' Her hand unclasped itself from my wrist and her eyes began to close once more.

Afraid she might fall asleep, I hastened my approach. 'Another friend sends her love, too. Shelly Teasdale. You do remember her, don't you?'

Hildegarde gave a feeble shake of her head. 'No, I do not ...'

'You helped deliver her baby in Dartford General. It was a long time ago, eighteen years ...'

'Baby? Oh, the poor babies.'

She lifted her head and began to look around, this way and that, searching for something. In frustration, she slumped back and turned to me. I saw a sharpness in her eyes then, a clarity that had not been there before. It was as if the wasting of brain cells had been held in check for a moment.

'Where are the babies?' she demanded to know.

I probed as gently as I could. 'What babies do you mean, Sparrow?'

'The poor little ones. The unfortunates. He said they would always be cared for.'

'Who said? Was it one of the doctors you worked with in Dartford?'

'All over. Other places. We always worked together. The Doctor has always been ... good ... to ... me ... to ...

others . . .' She drew in a long quivering breath. 'Ever since . . .'

I was losing her and I gave her arm a gentle little shake. 'Ever since when, Hildegarde? Tell me what happened.'

Her eyelids sprang open and I saw an excitement there, as though the memories had suddenly become clear, pleasing her, giving her back some vigour. She looked up at the ceiling as though it were a screen on which those recollections were being played out.

'I was young then. Not like this, not old and useless.' A wheezy sigh, and then a short struggle to regain the breath she had lost. I waited impatiently, ready to grab the nebulizer mask should it be needed.

'Oh dear Heavenly Father, I remember that night so clearly.' She smiled and I couldn't tell if it was because of the visions she saw, or because of the sudden lucidity of her mind.

I leaned closer, ignoring the smell that had so stupidly offended me earlier. 'Tell me about it, Sparrow,' I whispered. I didn't know why, but I wanted to share in her reverie. Perhaps I thought she was referring to the time when she had been midwife to Shelly Ripstone *née* Teasdale.

'The hospital was in London. It was . . . no, I can no longer remember its name.' Her voice was querulous, but it had an underlying strength to it now, the visions helping the telling. 'The hospital was in a bad part of the city, where the bombs had done so much harm.'

I guessed she was talking about London's East End, or the docklands, which had been so badly battered by German planes during the Second World War.

'Wilhelm was gone. Oh my darling Wilhelm . . . killed by the enemies who were to become my friends. Seven years after the end of the war there was nothing for me in Berlin and our conquerors were begging skilled people to come to their shores. In Germany we were trying to rebuild, but there was nothing there for me, no close relations, not many companions, not enough food, and the money paid for labour was a pittance. It was little wonder I saw England as a land of opportunity.'

Although her eyes remained open, some of the fresh lustre had faded from them.

'Tell me about the hospital, Hildegarde,' I urged quietly.

'Ach, the hospital. So drab, so grey. Yet I thought it was wonderful, even though I was treated as an outcast. The people found it so hard to forgive and who could blame them for that? But I worked . . . my God, how I worked. Both night and day – it made no difference to me, I had nothing else to do . . .'

I was disappointed. Hildegarde was going back more than fifty years, long before the time I was interested in. Yet now, having urged her to remember, there was no diverting that train of thought.

'I was on night duty, very tired – I'd helped deliver three little ones that afternoon. I think it was midnight. Yes, I'm sure it was . . . I took my break about that time. I had no one to talk to – the people were still suspicious of us Germans even after all that time, and besides, my English was still very bad.'

A silence followed and I had to prompt her again. 'What happened that night, Hildegarde? In the hospital, it was around twelve o'clock at night . . . ?'

Her head slowly turned so that she could look into my eyes.

'*You* do not know?'

It sounded like an accusation.

She spoke in a harsh whisper. 'Are you not one of them? Is that not why you are here?'

'I'm not sure what you mean, Hildegarde. Why don't you just tell me about that night?' I was perplexed, but put her confusion down to the disease in her brain.

'That night . . . ? Oh yes, that night. I decided I would explore the hospital . . . *mein Gott*, what was it called . . . ?'

'It doesn't matter, Hildegarde. Just tell me your story.'

'Yes, my story. The one you already know. Are you trying to trick me, do you think I am insane? Is it that you wish to find out how much I still know, how much I have forgotten?'

'No, Sparrow.' I persisted in using both her Christian name and nickname in the hope it would make me sound more familiar to her. 'I'm interested, that's all. I'm not trying to trick you.'

'How do I know that? The doctor tells me I should forget. But I do not *want to forget!*'

Her voice had risen in pitch and I patted her hand reassuringly, afraid she might alert one of the staff. 'It's okay. Take your time. Don't upset yourself.'

'Are you a friend?'

'Yes, I'm a friend.'

'Like Emma?'

I nodded my head.

Tears formed in the corners of her eyes. 'The doctor isn't my friend any more.'

'I'm sure he is.' I wondered who this doctor was. Could she have meant the proprietor of the home himself, this Dr Leonard K. Wisbeech?

Her chest, which had began to rise and fall rapidly, became calmer.

'Nobody told me there were places in the hospital where I should not go. But I was young, and curious, and I had nothing else to do that night. I wandered through the wards and corridors, getting to know the place, introducing myself to the other duty nurses. I was a stranger and I wanted to be accepted, I wanted to know my way around. It was such a huge building, but eventually I found myself on the top floor.'

She started to cough, at first softly, but then the exertion sending spasms through her whole body. I became anxious, unsure of what I should do: help her use the nebulizer, or press the call button so that a trained nurse could deal with the situation? But even as I fretted, the spasms grew less

171

violent, the coughing less harsh, until eventually the seizure passed. Her cheeks were damp with forced tears and spittle drooled on to her chin.

I took tissues from a box on the bedside cabinet and gently wiped her face. She appeared not to notice.

'The corridors were dark up there,' she went on as though nothing had occurred, the rise and fall of her thin little chest assuming a regular rhythm once more, 'so very, very dark. I did not realize this was *verboten*, that I should not be there. I thought perhaps that this part of the hospital was unused and I wondered why. I found the doors to a ward that had no name, no markings or numbers, nothing at all. I was too nervous to go inside, afraid I would get into trouble.'

Her voice descended to a whisper and she leaned my way, as if to confide in me. 'I looked though. Oh yes, I peeked inside. And that was the beginning for me, you see, that was the moment it all started. That was when I became involved.'

I tensed. I didn't know why, but my body, my mind, became suddenly alert. I tried to control my impatience. 'What was in that ward, Hildegarde? What did you find?'

Those grey, watery eyes fixed on me. 'I found the infants,' she said. 'The poor little ones whose only offence was how they looked.'

A peculiar sensation ran through me, a kind of rush that heightened my senses and set my nerves on edge. I *knew* the answer even before I put the question.

'What was wrong with them, Hildegarde?'

She spoke as if from a distance, her eyes looking ceiling-wards, its whiteness a screen once more.

'They were like you,' she said. 'But worse. Harmless little babies born so hideous that they had to be locked away in darkness so that the world would never know its shame. Infants whose mothers did not know they were alive.'

Her eyelids closed like curtains to the ceiling's screen, shutting out the images, bringing an end to the spectacle. But it seemed that the pictures in her mind were far stronger than those conjured on the ceiling, for now she was closed in with them, the impressions bolder and more disconcerting because they were even more intimate. She began to twist her head from side to side.

'They . . . they are calling me . . .'

With horror, I realized that for her, the past had become the present. Her enfeebled brain had brought the memories to her, so that she was reliving the moments of many years before. I reached for her wrist and made soothing sounds in an attempt to bring her back to reality. It was no use though: her mind was in another place.

'The older ones . . . they are . . . their poor little stunted arms . . . they are reaching out towards me . . . "Mama", they call . . . "Mama" . . . and I take them in my arms . . . I comfort them . . . and they love me as I love them . . .'

She was thrashing around in the bed and I stood, my hands going to her shoulders, all the time trying to calm her, to soothe her with words I knew she could not hear.

'And he . . . and he finds me there . . . but it is too late . . . I know the secret . . .'

She was rambling, her words beginning to make no sense, her voice rising in pitch.

'Who found you, Sparrow?' I said close to her ear.

'God, help them . . . please help them . . . I cannot . . . any more . . .'

'What on earth is going on here?'

The harsh, new voice came from the doorway and I turned in surprise. The senior nurse and administrator, the one whose wrath Constance had incurred in the hallway earlier, was standing there, a look of pure rage blazing from her broad face. I hardly knew what to say. Shit, I hardly knew what to *do*.

Hildegarde was wriggling in the bed, the sheets becoming entangled with her stick-thin legs; she was making terrible sounds as she fought for breath, her desperate inhalations dry-raw, her wheezing alarming to hear. Her bony, blue-veined hands beat at the air and her lipless mouth was like a black hole at the centre of her face.

Nurse Fletcher hurried in, brushing me aside to get to her patient. 'It's all right, Hildegarde, please calm down,' she said as she tried to smooth the little woman's brow with the palm of her hand.

To me she shouted: 'Why have you been upsetting her? Just what do you think you're doing?' Ignoring my pleas of innocence she stabbed at the call button by the side of the bed. A red light above it blinked on.

'I really didn't do anything,' I tried to explain.

'I heard her shouts from the other end of the corridor,' the nurse said through gritted teeth. 'You must have done something.'

I have to admit, I found this woman daunting. There was too much icy fury in her, too much barely-restrained power in her stance. I backed towards the door.

Hurried footsteps pounded the corridor outside and then the male nurse, the big guy Constance had called Bruce, was in the doorway. His handsome-but-flawed face looked dumb in its incomprehension as he glanced from me to the action on the bed.

Nurse Fletcher yelled at him: 'Help me pin her down so I can get the mask on her!'

Again I was rudely pushed aside as he ran to help the nurse.

'Just push her down and hold her there for me. We'll use the nebulizer to help her breathe, then I'll give her something to sedate her.'

By now the old lady was screaming between gasps for air and, as the orderly placed his beefy hands on her scrawny little shoulders to press her down on to the bed, I decided to leave the room – I didn't want to witness any more of this. Outside, I leaned back against the wall and closed my eyes; still I could hear the struggles from inside, the torturous inhalations now muted by the nebulizer mask but heart-rending all the same.

'Oh shit,' I said to no one but myself.

I'd pushed the old lady too hard, and I regretted that, but unfortunately that was sometimes what a PI's job was all about: probing, delving, winkling out the truth even when it meant upsetting people. This time though, I wondered if I hadn't gone too far.

Time to leave, I told myself. No point in hanging round just to take another harangue from Head Nurse. Besides, I wasn't going to learn any more from Hildegarde Vogel that day. As I headed for the main stairs, pale, time-worn faces appeared in doorways, some shrinking away as I passed by, others bold in their curiosity, wondering what the fuss was all about. These latter residents either glared at me, annoyed by the interruption, or looked askance, perhaps hoping I would linger awhile to explain the disruption to their daily tedium. A bald-headed man with rheumy eyes and a complexion that was slightly less healthy than a cadaver's shook his walking-stick at me as I went by his room. He stepped into the corridor behind me, snarling and warning me to keep my distance. I not only kept it, I increased it also, hurrying to get away from there as fast as I could. More grey heads peered round doorways to disappear as soon as I drew close and I began to feel like some kind of pariah, an untouchable, spreading disease in my wake. I avoided their gazes, casting my own eye downwards so that all I glimpsed was slippered feet, the hems of dressing-gowns and nightdresses, the wheels of invalid chairs, and all I heard was mumblings and mutterings and the occasional intake of breath and the odd slamming of a door or two. My breathing had become laboured, my steps more lumbering, and I had broken out into a sweat, all because of the fear and hostility directed at me. It was funny, but the corridor seemed longer than before.

At last, I turned the corner into the main hallway and landing, and there was Constance Bell coming towards me, her own breathing a little ragged after her climb up the stairs.

'What is it?' she asked, her lovely face filled with concern. 'Hildegarde's call bell – '

'I'm sorry,' I blurted out. 'I really am sorry.' I was still walking, heading for the staircase.

She put one of her sticks across my path to stop me. 'What did you do, Mr Dismas?' There was no anger, only dismay in her voice.

'I didn't mean to upset her,' I replied, coming to a halt. 'I only asked her a few questions.'

'What kind of questions? I thought you were a friend of Hildegarde's.'

She frowned at my silence.

'You'd better come along with me,' she said abruptly, like a schoolteacher at the end of her tether with a disruptive pupil. She turned back to the stairs and began to descend. Meekly I followed.

Yet even though contrite and not a little embarrassed, my natural inclination as an investigator soon edged discomfort aside as we clumped our way down the broad staircase. I had remembered something the care-supervisor had mentioned earlier. 'Er, Ms Bell, you said that you already knew Hildegarde Vogel's nickname was Sparrow before she even came to PERFECT REST. Can I ask you how you knew?'

We had reached the small landing at the turn of the stairway and the care-supervisor wheeled round to face me.

'Just who are you, Mr Dismas?' she said, suspicion now causing her to frown. 'What is it that you want here?'

'You also implied that she had connections. Is someone paying for Hildegarde's stay here? She doesn't have any relations in this country, does she? And even if she gets a state pension, it could never cover the cost of care in this place.'

Constance stared back at me and in her silence I thought I could sense . . . well, it felt like fear. But why should she be afraid of my questions? Why should she be afraid of *me*? My God, that was the last thing I wanted.

She didn't answer. She turned away and resumed the descent. Again, I meekly followed.

Only when we reached the ground floor hall did she address me.

'I want you to leave immediately,' she said, and I noticed that her hands were trembling.

A conversation further down the hall between the receptionist and the young Irish nurse who had joked with us earlier came to a halt mid-flow as they both turned in our direction.

'Look, I really am sorry,' I said to Constance and it came out more like a plea than an apology. 'I want to be honest with you if you'll take a moment to listen.'

'So you admit you've been dishonest?' she came back.

'Well, yes. But only because I didn't know how you'd react if I played it straight.' I could tell by her expression that this hadn't helped my case much. 'Look, I'm a private investigator and I thought Hildegarde Vogel might be able to help me with some information.'

It was as if I had slapped her face.

'I thought it would make things easier for me, you see,' I added hurriedly. 'I thought I wouldn't be allowed to talk to her if I wasn't a relative or at least an acquaintance.'

'What kind of place do you think this is? Our residents have visitors all the time.'

I didn't think it was worth mentioning that the visitors' book at reception only had one other name on it that day. 'Hildegarde is old and unwell,' I said, 'and private investigators don't always have the best of reputations . . .'

'And you wonder why?'

'. . . so I thought you might be reluctant to grant me access.'

'I've already asked you to leave, Mr Dismas, so please do so before I call Security.'

Security, in an old folks' home? Well, I supposed it was necessary these days in most establishments. 'Look, if I could just see her once more, maybe when she's feeling better?'

'Please, Mr Dismas . . .' Her face was set and she had half-turned towards the desk as if about to issue instructions to the receptionist.

'Okay, okay.' I knew when to give up. 'Let me give you my card though, in case you change your mind. I'm just trying to trace a missing person for a client, that's all.' I reached inside my top pocket and presented my card.

It was with some reluctance that she took the card, and she did not even give it a glance before tucking it away in a pocket.

I half-raised both hands as if in mock surrender. 'Right. I'm leaving now.' Then I felt abashed once more – no, I felt low, I felt miserable, and I wished the ground would swallow me up. I'd played it all wrong and I was never going to forgive myself. I really didn't want this person to despise me.

'I, uh, I really am sorry,' I said in a quiet voice and walked towards the main entrance. I'd almost reached the reception desk when she called out.

'What has this missing person got to do with Hildegarde?'

I stopped, shuffled around. 'She was midwife to my client. It's the child that's missing.' Even as I spoke, I realized how ridiculous it sounded. But Constance Bell neither scoffed nor frowned. She merely said:

'You don't seriously believe Hildegarde can help you?'

I shrugged. 'Maybe not. It's kind of complicated anyway. But the midwife is all I've got.'

'Then I really am sorry, Mr Dismas,' Constance said, and I had the feeling she honestly meant it. 'But you must have seen for yourself that Hildegarde is in no condition to offer any information.'

I knew she was right.

'Good-day, Mr Dismas.'

At least some of her anger seemed to have dissipated. 'Ms Bell . . . ?' I began.

'Good-day.' It was a *firm* farewell this time.

'Yeah . . .' I said, and left.

16

With early evening rush hour traffic already stacking up on the motorways it took almost two hours to get back to the office, and I was in a low mood by the time I arrived. The thing that was bugging me even more than the pointless exercise of tracking down Hildegarde Vogel was my alter-cation with Constance Bell. I'd had plenty of time to mull it over during the long drive back to Brighton and I kept asking myself why I was so bothered. She was a stranger to me, yet I felt I knew her. Yes, I felt I knew her intimately. Crazy? Of course. But I thought I understood why. We were the same, Constance and I, two people saddened by our own Calvaries, the lifetime's purgatory to which we had been born. I had caught the loneliness in her lovely eyes, the disquiet that shadowed their gaze; and I had sensed the yearning that lay hidden in that same shadow, a constant longing which, on another occasion, in different circum-stances, might have bonded us, for it was something else we both shared. Was I fooling myself, was it merely wishful thinking on my part, or had something intangible – a mutual reaching out, a fusion of emotions – passed between us as we had faced each other in the grand hallway at PERFECT REST?

But even if I were right, it no longer mattered anyway. I had blown it, my deceit had ruined whatever might have been.

The self-torture continued. Might have been? *What* might have been? Did I honestly think I stood a chance with the beautiful girl? Just because she had a crippled body like mine, did that make me a contender? I was kidding myself. She, at least, had a wonderful face and fine, delicate hands while I had no redeeming features at all. I was a freak: she was stunning. Stupid, stupid, stupid! Yes – I was stupid!

By the time I'd climbed the creaky stairs to the agency and lumbered through the door, my mood had changed from anger – anger at myself – to almost lachrymal self-pity.

Ida and Philo had left for the day, but Henry was still there, going over his precious books, looking as prim and self-satisfied as he always did. He peered over his bifocals at me as I slunk into my office.

'Any luck?' he enquired.

'Nothing useful,' I replied distractedly.

'Mrs Ripstone called while you were out. Wanted to know if there were any developments. You only saw her this morning, so I don't know what she was expecting.'

I groaned. 'I've got to tell her again, haven't I?'

'That it's still a no-go? Dis, we did our best for her. Some cases just don't work out, and we've plenty more to be cracking on with.'

How could I explain to him that this one was special, that something inside me – something *deep* inside me – was telling me not to let go, that something extraordinary was happening and I was part of it? How did you explain such a 'sensing' to someone like Henry who, despite his occasional flamboyance, was an accountant, a facts and figures man who relied on profit margins and balance sheets to steer him through life's little minefields? How the hell did I explain it to myself?

'Yeah, you're right, Henry. We're not exactly starved for work right now. I'd better call her back and tell her the bad news.'

'At least she's getting used to it.' He gave me a grin, still peering over his spectacles. Abruptly – and this was typical of Henry – he changed the subject. Maybe he could tell I was a little bit down and wanted to cheer me up. 'Why don't you come over tonight, Dis, watch a film with mother and me?'

Henry's mother was the archetypal Jewish widow who doted on her 'boy', often sending him to work with chicken sandwiches and flasks of soup when the agency was on overload, aware that he would skip lunch altogether rather than leave his books for an hour. Evie Solomon had been a feisty little woman in her time – she looked as if she were made from three obese globes of unequal sizes, all balanced one on top of the other, a fat little head, a fatter little torso, and a very fat stomach and butt, these component parts balanced on two short legs and tiny feet – until failing health (which apparently no doctor had ever been able to diagnose, but which became extreme every time Henry made plans to leave home) had rendered her a little more temperate. Henry's father had walked out when Henry was a small boy and the stepfather who had taken his place had suffered a fatal heart attack years ago and that, I suspected, was when Evie's emotional blackmail had truly begun, her various maladies increasing in number and severity as the years progressed and her son's natural instinct for independence had come to the fore. We'd never discussed it, Henry and I, but we both knew he was irrevocably stuck with his situation – until, of course, Evie passed on (which, truth be told, would have a devastating effect on him).

'I don't think so, Henry,' I said in reply to his invitation.

'Hey, I've got a good vid. You'll like it. Gene Kelly and Cyd Charisse. Such legs! Cyd's, I mean. Up to her neck, those legs, the longest in showbiz in the Fifties. It's a musical.'

'I didn't think it'd be a Tarantino. What is it – *Brigadoon?*'

'Hah, gotcha! *It's Always Fair Weather*, actually.'

I turned away from his gloating: it could just as easily have been *Singin' in the Rain*, although the Charisse role was minor in that one. 'Yeah, you got me, Henry. But I'll pass on it tonight, if you don't mind.'

He must have caught the dejection in my voice. 'Are you okay, Dis?' he asked. 'This case got you down? You know, it's hardly make or break.'

I gave a huffing kind of sigh. He was right, of course. But then Henry wasn't aware of all the peculiar things that had happened since Shelly Ripstone had visited my office three days ago, nightmarish incidents that seemed to give the search for our client's allegedly missing son some special, although for the moment obscure, significance. I was tempted to confide in Henry right there and then, but I was sure he would only scoff at the idea of strange 'forces' at work and the ragging I'd take over the next week or two would be unbearable.

'I'm all right,' was all I said. 'Maybe I'm just tired of telling Shelly Ripstone that all bets are off again.'

I went into my office, slumped into the chair behind the desk, and reached for the phone.

The call from Constance Bell came through on my other line while I was talking on the phone to Louise Broomfield. I had already spoken to Shelly Ripstone and was now explaining to the clairvoyant just why there was little point in continuing with the case, that this time we really had reached a dead-end. Henry had lifted the receiver in the outer office and he had come to my door to let me know the call was for me.

'Someone by the name of Bell?' he said as I raised my eyebrows at him while covering the mouthpiece of the phone I was using. 'A lady. Sounds very nice. Needs to speak with you.'

I waved an okay and said to Louise: 'I've got to take another call and it might just be relevant to our discussion. Can I phone you later?'

The clairvoyant agreed and I replaced the receiver, immediately grabbing at the other phone on my desk.

'Ms Bell?' I said.

That sweet voice again. 'Mr Dismas? I hope you don't mind my calling you.'

Mind? My foolish heart was thumping. 'No problem,' I said. 'What can I do for you?'

'Our proprietor at PERFECT REST heard of your interest in Hildegarde Vogel today and he would like to see you. He thinks that perhaps he might be of some help.'

'Your proprietor . . . ?'

'Proprietor, director, senior doctor – he goes under all those titles. Dr Wisbeech.'

Ah. I remembered the name from the board outside the gates of the old people's home. Dr Leonard K. Wisbeech. 'Did he mention how he could help me?'

'I'm afraid not, Mr Dismas. He just asked me to get in touch with you.'

'Could I come over tomorrow?'

'Dr Wisbeech said some time in the morning.'

'Around 10.30? Would that be all right?'

'I'm sure it would.'

'And, er, will I see you again?'

There was a pause at the other end. You can read so much into a short pause, and probably all wrong.

'I'll be here,' she said.

'Um . . .' For some reason I needed to clear my throat. 'Uh, fine. Tomorrow, then.'

'Yes.' She said goodbye and I held the receiver to my ear even after I heard the distant *click*.

A night of dreams and constant awakenings.

Images of wings, white-feathered wings.

Which did not belong to birds; they belonged to angels.

Eyes snapping open, instant wakefulness, body in a sweat.

Sleep again. Disturbed, troubled sleep.

Dream: Cyd Charisse dancing with me, both of us naked, the top of my head only reaching the top of her legs, so that I looked at thick black pubic hair sprinkled with sequins. Those lovely long beautiful legs, leading me in the dance, the scent of her womanness strong in my nostrils. I weave with her rumba rhythm, but I'm not so happy: I *know* I'm taller than that, that my head should at least reach her shoulders. I begin to weep at the unfairness. And then she changes and I'm dancing with Constance, our bodies perfectly – *im*perfectly – matched, her arm over my crooked shoulder, my eye looking *down* into hers, her face upturned, her lips lifted towards mine, and the music is changed, it's slower, more dreamy, and we glide and we twirl and our lips draw even closer ... And Gene Kelly is tapping me on the shoulder, on my *crooked* shoulder, and as I turn at the interruption the great dancer shimmers and he fades and he morphs into someone else, someone whose face I recognize, because it's so familiar, so well-known, so famous ... A tall and elegantly handsome man whose name I can't recall ... his smile is a leer and I hate him, I fucking hate him ... But there's nothing I can do as he takes her away from me and although I protest, although I try to hold on to her, they are gliding away from me, so light on their feet, so heavenly graceful ... And he is holding Constance aloft like a beautiful prize and he winks at me ... so handsome, so diabolically handsome ... and they are fading into the night while the melody ... and his fucking laughter ... lingers on ...

Again I wake.

But I resist the drugs that I know will alter my mind-state, will help me slip back into a more happy slumber. I resist and already I regret the resistance ...

Because now the dream is *truly* horrible ...

I am in darkness, but I am not alone. I cannot see the others, but I can hear their tortured cries. Clumsy hands snatch at me, voices whisper pleas in my ears. I reach out and I touch someone . . . something . . . and I feel a form that is as twisted as mine. It pulls away, but another takes its place and this time I feel its face, as a blind man might feel the contours of a companion, fingertips substituting for eyes. But there is no face. Only a deep, glutinous hole where there should have been features, a great yawning, toothless mouth that seeps liquids and expels foul fumes. As I recoil, other, stronger hands grab at me and arms snake around my neck and my waist and squeeze and crush, so that I scream . . .

And my own scream wakes me for the third time.

I am already sitting up in bed, my neck stretched, my mouth open wide.

This time I am weak: I *have* to take something, anything that might soothe my nerves, something that would help me drift into sweet oblivion. But instead I think of Constance and it's her image, her voice, the precious touch of her hand in mine, that soothes me.

I wipe my brow with the bedsheet and sink back against the pillows, and my mind is calmer, my trembling beginning to settle. I am more tired than I know, for I am immediately sliding into troubled sleep again.

I find myself drawn into a phantasmagoria of shapes, sounds, and impressions, a soft-focus variegation of shifting images, all distantly calling to me, invocations that I cannot understand. Even *he* is there, so charming, so sublimely perfect, yet still imperceptible, ill-defined . . . until . . . until he begins to come towards me, freeing himself of the chaos around him, advancing and raising a hand . . . and I can see it's a well-manicured hand, for his shape is becoming sharp, focused . . . and I can *see* his face, discern his features, and I begin to recognize him, recognize him because I know him so well . . . and, like the others who have almost faded to invisibility, he is pleading with me. He tells me we are the same, he and I, and I can only return a bitter laugh as I look into his deep brown eyes . . . but he is adamant . . . asks me to find it in my heart – in my *soul* – to save him – to save us *both*, for we really *are* the same – from eternal misery . . . and as he begs his face crumples and his spiritual tears flow . . . and he is drawn away from me, paling into the oblivion . . .

And yet again I am conscious, this time awakened by the dawn light stealing through the breach in the curtains.

I push myself up and look around me as if to make sure I really am here in my gloomy bedroom, here where I should be, and I'm relieved that morning has finally come. And in that very instant, I forget all the dreams of the night.

17

Only snatches of those dreams came back to me (I was to remember them in their entirety eventually) during the long return trip to PERFECT REST, and because they presented themselves as short jumbled images, they made no sense to me at all.

When the spectre of the dark Adonis, the deity of good looks, appeared in my mind's eye I almost steered my car into the side of an overtaking XJS. The sharp and repeated tooting of the other driver's horn quickly brought me to my senses, and as I pulled back over into the proper lane, I waved an apology, while he held up a middle finger for my delectation. I slowed down to a speed that was accommodating to introspection.

You see, now I recognized this tuxedoed charmer and I began to understand the reason for those recurring visions and last night's dreams a little (at least, this was how daylight logic aspired to provide me with a rationale). With my knowledge of old movies I should have identified him before, because he was a famous matinée idol of the late Thirties and early Forties, a screen star famous the world over for his gay (in the *old* sense) repartee and rugged prowess, a celluloid adventurer who could play swashbuckler or sophisticate, hero or roguish charmer, priest or gunman. He was everything I yearned to be – tall, athletic, debonair, and devishly and devastatingly handsome – and this was where the first gleaning submitted itself for consideration. The images of him that I saw in mirrors were not *reflections* but were *projections*, mere, yet deep, wishful-thinking on my part, a fantasy stoked by drugs present but mainly past (as you know, I no longer did the hard stuff), those chemical residuals still floating around in my system – *and in my psyche*. For me, flashbacks had become drawbacks and I was becoming haunted by them.

I thought my illusions had ended with childhood, but now I realized they were only repressed. I still wanted to be something other than I was, and who could blame me for that? So when I looked into mirrors these days, I sometimes saw, aided by those chemical imbalances, that which I desired to be rather than what really was. The other hallucinations? Perhaps they were nothing more than psychological manifestations of my own tortured soul (and by now you'll know just how tortured my soul was).

And yet . . . and yet there was still one thing that bothered me: I could not remember this old-time film star's name. Every time I thought I had it, it eluded me. Every time it was on the tip of my tongue, it tripped off again. And I was supposed to be good at that sort of thing.

The XJS I'd almost side-whacked earlier was stuck in a long line of held-up traffic in the fast lane and I gave him a friendly toot and wave as I sailed by; he glared back, but there was no swivel-finger in evidence this time. I did notice, however, that a fantastic-looking blonde babe occupied the passenger seat and I wondered how obnoxious pigs like him managed to pull women like her. The shiny bright Jag provided my jealousy with an easy and probably quite erroneous answer, but it led my thoughts to Constance Bell. I realized I had become foolishly besotted with her and it was one of the reasons I was so eager to visit PERFECT REST again: I was fairly sure a meeting with the home's proprietor would not advance the search for Shelly's absent child one bit further, but the chance to meet Constance once more was too good to miss.

Why would I fall for her so rapidly and so easily? The

answer to this one was also easy – only this time there was
nothing false about the judgement. You see, Constance Bell
was like me: we both bore afflictions that made us unattrac-
tive to the majority of normal society (unfortunate, but it was
an unpalatable truth that no amount of politically correct
well-meaning propaganda would change). And because she
was like me – except, of course, for her beautiful face and
hands – she might just be attainable. Sad? Pathetic? You
really wouldn't know.

The weather had been overcast since early morning and
when I turned off the motorway, heading for Windsor, the
heavens opened and it began to pour with rain. I switched
on the Ford's sidelights and grumbled to myself about
the usual changeable patterns of the English summer. By the
time I turned into the rutted lane that would lead me to
the Thames riverbank and PERFECT REST, the rain had
ceased and the sun was making its first proper appearance
of the day.

The car splashed through puddles and its suspension did
little to prevent my body being jolted as it progressed
through dips and over bumps, giving me further pause to
wonder at the home's difficult location. Maybe death's
waiting-room was meant to be isolated from worldly distrac-
tions. Even the jets passing overhead every few minutes
scarcely intruded upon the calm. I took the bends in the lane
carefully, occasionally taking time to peep through the gaps
in the hedgerows on either side. I caught glimpses of flat
grasslands where no animals seemed to graze, untidy clumps
of woodland beyond. Here and there I spotted single houses,
these almost as remote as the rest home itself. The square
top of a pump station in the far distance, a church spire even
further away. But I passed no other vehicle, nor any walkers,
on this lonely track that purported to be a lane. I knew from
the map book that the area was abundant with water reservoirs, some small, others as huge as lakes and even used by
sailing clubs and water-skiers; there were also sewage works

and sludge beds in the vicinity, as well as the remains of ancient monasteries and nunneries. Across the broad river was the very meadow in which the Magna Carta was allegedly signed. So it was a strange landscape, so close to the city itself and Heathrow airport, yet almost a hinterland whose pocket villages and hamlets appeared all the more forsaken because of the emptiness of the regions between them.

Not long after I'd passed the old abandoned house I'd noticed on my previous journey down the lane, with its boarded windows and overgrown frontage, I saw the rooftops and chimneys, then the gates of the home up ahead. I slowed the car almost to walking pace so that I could study my surrounds in more detail than before. If not for the sign declaring what lay beyond the gates and high walls, with high trees and foliage both before and behind the walls adding to the screening, a person this close (I was almost at the entrance now) might never guess that such an expansive dwelling lay just out of sight. The place was obviously visible from the other side of the Thames, the river itself providing a broad natural boundary. Through the bars of the iron gates I could see the tree-shadowed secondary drive, this much narrower than the one leading to the front of the house, and I assumed it was used by tradesmen and for deliveries, a route to the side or rear of the big building. It looked neglected and unfriendly, prohibited to the casual visitor.

I used the intercom on one of the stone pillars to announce my arrival and the gates duly swung open. I drove through and as soon as I rounded a gentle bend and cleared the trees, the great house that was PERFECT REST spread across my windscreen, quickly filling my view although I approached slowly, looming over me when I finally brought the car to a halt.

Out of habit I set the engine's isolation switch before climbing out of the car and making my way up the wheelchair ramp's slight incline. Maybe it was due to the long drive I'd just had, but if anything, my limbs and body were even more stiff than the previous day, the beating I'd taken on Brighton beach continuing to take its toll. I pushed through the vestibule doors and immediately saw Constance Bell standing by the reception desk as if waiting just for me.

There was a nervousness to her smile as I walked towards her, and I wondered why; then I realized I was nervous as well. Okay, don't misinterpret things here, I warned myself. The reason for her jitters was probably different from mine: maybe she just didn't like private investigators.

'Mr Dismas,' she greeted, using her elbow-crutches with practised ease as she moved forward.

'I'm a little early,' I apologized.

We shook hands, a mere touching of fingers, and I relished her softness. She stared at my face and I wanted her to examine my soul.

'That looks as if it's still very painful.' She indicated the bruised swelling on my cheek.

'Uh? Oh, it's not so bad now.'

'It must have been *some* door you walked into.'

I managed a sheepish grin and that did hurt.

'Let me show you to the visitors' room. Dr Wisbeech won't be long.' She broke away, moving back to the reception desk and pointing to the book on its shelf. 'If you'll just sign in.'

I followed the house rule, feeling like a schoolboy because of the height of the desk front. Hazel, the receptionist, barely gave me a glance before Constance led me towards the broad staircase leading to the upper floors, but we passed it by, heading towards the rear of the building. Along the way I studied yet more paintings on white walls, their style becoming increasingly bizarre the further we went.

Constance stopped at a large oak door on our left and paused with her hand on the doorknob. 'If you'll wait inside I'll let Dr Wisbeech know you're here.' She opened the door and stepped aside to allow me through.

'Miss Bell . . .' I began to say.

'Yes?' She looked at me expectantly.

'I . . . I just wanted you to know I'm grateful.' And that I think you're the loveliest creature I've ever met, I wanted to add.

'Grateful for what?' She gave a little, perplexed shake of her head.

'Uh, for getting Dr Wisbeech to see me.'

'But I didn't. I merely told him of your interest in Hildegarde and he decided he'd like to meet you himself.'

'Really? He didn't say why?'

'I can only assume he didn't want you to feel we were being uncooperative.'

I suppose I was disappointed that she hadn't engineered the meeting herself as a means of getting to see me again. Within the space of a few minutes I was left feeling like a schoolboy again, one who had a crush on the prettiest girl in the class and so mistakenly imagined motivations that were favourable to me. What a chump, I chided myself and the only excuse I allowed was that I was sure a *frisson* of excitement, pleasure – of *knowing*? – had passed between us at our first meeting. I couldn't believe it had all been in my own imagination.

'Mr Dismas?' She was still waiting for me to enter the room and as I went by her, she said: 'I hope we can. Help you, I mean.'

My spirits rose at that perfect smile and the warmth that emanated from it. Despite the faraway sadness that seemed perpetually to haunt her eyes – a sadness I understood only too well – I could *feel* there was a kind of union between us, that she could see beyond my physical shackles and she knew that I could see beyond hers. She closed the door and I listened to the sound of her irregular footsteps as they faded down the hallway.

I stood there for several long moments, gazing at the door, thinking only of this woman who had suddenly entered my life. Don't expect too much, Dismas, I told myself. Don't expect too much and then you won't be disappointed. I had looked for and found no wedding ring on her finger, no rings of any kind, in fact; but that didn't mean she wasn't in a long-term relationship. With wonderful features like hers I would not have been surprised to learn she was romantically attached to some super-hunk, a tall, handsome guy with chiselled features and a kind disposition, all the things I didn't have. Oh Jesus, if that were true, I didn't stand a chance; no matter how much I might kid myself otherwise, I could never compete. My natural if cynical pragmatism brought me back to the real world and with an inward sigh, I studied the room around me.

Apart from two incongruities, it was strictly functional: two hard-looking couches, colour grey, a wooden coffee table between them, this one without magazines for visitors to browse through; an unhealthy palm planted in a terracotta pot in one corner and a tall hat and coat stand in another. The two incongruities? On one plain white wall was a large copy of Hieronymus Bosch's *The Garden of Earthly Delights*, the centre panel only and easily recognizable to me because one of Brighton's seedier private members' clubs I had cause to frequent (strictly in the line of business, you understand) had the same print behind its bar. The picture depicted a wild sexual orgy in a detailed landscape, bizarre beasts involved with distorted humans, its theme lust as the reason for mankind's downfall. I had to admit it was a fascinating piece of art and I might have taken time to study it more closely had I not taken an interest in the room's other inappropriate feature.

The horizontal mirror was on the wall opposite the door and it seemed too long for a room of this moderate size. It was black-framed and actually set into the wall itself, and if its purpose was to give visitors the opportunity to tidy themselves up before greeting whoever they had come to see, to me it seemed extravagant both in cost and dimensions. My natural suspicion was aroused.

Watching my own shambling reflection, I walked towards the glass and when I was only two feet away, I stopped. From my inside jacket pocket I drew out the pencil I always carried for rough sketches or diagrams, or for whenever my pen ran out of ink, and pointed it at the mirror. The lead tip touched the glass.

Now with normal mirrors there was always a double reflection, the stronger image at least an eighth of an inch away from the real pencil tip. This was because an ordinary mirror is always silvered at the back. In this case, the lead tips, original and reflection, actually touched, indicating that the glass was front-silvered. Which meant that this was a two-way mirror, the kind used for surveillance or voyeurism.

There had to be a darkened room next door, where someone could covertly observe the waiting visitors. Now why the hell would an old people's nursing home need such a set-up?

I moved away, wondering if someone was watching me from the other side at that very moment. Taking a seat and offering a profile to the mirror, I stared at the Hieronymus Bosch before me, relieved that I hadn't taken a closer interest in its nude figures before and now further wondering if this was not one of the reasons for its placement, the hidden observer watching the visitor's reaction to the picture. It might be just one of the ways a potential resident was judged suitable or otherwise, some kind of psychological test for the applicant. Maybe they were even questioned about the painting's subject matter afterwards, responses deemed unhealthy a negative consideration. Or perhaps it was a pre-interview test prospective staff unknowingly went through. Oh, come on! I was fantasizing. No establishment – particularly one of this nature – would use such a pointless procedure. But then, why the mirror? As I pondered, I heard the door open.

A tall trim man, over six feet in height, entered and raised a hand to bid me keep my seat. I was half-way up anyway, so I continued, proffering a hand towards him.

'Mr Dismas.'

His grip was firm rather than strong.

'Dr Wisbeech?'

I supposed I'd expected him to be wearing a white coat, stethoscope draped around his neck (or, as in the new fashion for young doctors, around his shoulders), but no, he wore a dark grey suit, finely-cut, mohair weaved into the material so that it seemed to have a subtle sheen to it.

He nodded to me. 'Won't you please be seated?'

His manner was extremely cordial, his light blue eyes keen with interest. He glanced at the bruising on my face, but made no comment; those eyes were taking in *all* of me.

The doctor was a handsome man and I judged him to be in his low sixties, possibly a bit younger. His well-groomed hair was dark grey, lighter-grey-to-white at the temples and over his ears, and he sported a neat beard, shot with white, not quite a goatee, but stylish all the same. He had a strong, almost patrician face, with a sharp, high-bridged nose that went well with his defined cheekbones. His pale blue tie and cream breast-pocket handkerchief were silk and the cuffs of his white shirt fell precisely three-quarters of an inch below the sleeves of his jacket. Even his black shoes had the right kind of dull shine and I was willing to bet his socks were black or matched the grey of his suit. I was trying to think of the movie star he resembled and it had come by the time he took the seat opposite. It was one of the old crowd, long since dead, but a major player in his time.

Michael Rennie. Remember him? Harry Lime in the black and white TV series, an alien in the film *The Day the Earth Stood Still*. Tall, gaunt, cold – and the perfect gentleman.

'I understand you are a private detective,' he said. (Incidentally, I'd have won my bet – his socks were charcoal grey.)

'Private investigator, actually,' I replied.

'I'm sorry, I didn't know there was a difference.'

He smiled as he spoke and I saw his teeth were something of a disappointment; not that they were unsightly, but they were yellowish, stained here and there by too much tea or coffee, a blemish on an otherwise impeccable presentation. It gave me some satisfaction.

'Well, an investigator is less glamorous,' I explained, immediately aware of the irony in my statement. 'Our work is usually pretty mundane,' I added.

'I see. And you are interested in one of our guests.'

Not 'patient', nor 'resident', but 'guest'.

'Hildegarde Vogel,' I said unnecessarily.

'Yes, so I believe. Can you tell me why?'

As we spoke, his eyes were constantly studying me as if interested in my misformed physique.

'She acted as midwife for a client of mine some eighteen years ago. My client claims the baby was taken away from her only seconds after the birth and she never saw it again.'

'Then presumably the baby died.'

'She says it didn't.'

'Was it a difficult birth, do you know?'

'She didn't say it was,' I lied.

'I merely wondered if she had been overwrought at the time. Sometimes the labour is a terrible ordeal for the woman, especially if it's a long-drawn-out experience. The mother might imagine all sorts of dreadful things, none of which have any basis in reality. Does she say the baby was healthy?'

'No. They told her that there was something wrong with the boy, that he died within minutes.'

'Then I really don't understand . . .'

'Neither birth nor death was registered.'

'You checked this for yourself. You went through the normal agencies?'

I nodded.

'And you contacted the hospital in question? I assume the infant was born in hospital and not at home.'

I nodded again. 'Unfortunately the hospital – it was the Dartford General – burned down some years ago.'

'And all records were destroyed?'

'Apparently so. That doesn't explain why the birth and death wasn't registered elsewhere, though.'

'Such things happen in any bureaucracy, especially one the size of the NHS. Incompetence, neglect, sheer laziness – it's rather common in the public services. I think we all know that the National Health Service is undermanned and under-funded, at least where medical matters are concerned. Mistakes and omissions happen all the time. And eighteen years ago, before computers were truly regarded as tools of the trade, the system was in an even worse state.' He still watched me keenly, now looking straight into my eye – or, I should say, the puckered hole where an eye had once been. 'I'm surprised you didn't relate this to your client,' he continued. 'Perhaps you needed the work?'

I ignored the implied sneer (his face was passive, not even the hint of a smile beneath that finely clipped moustache). I suppose I could have explained about the whispering voices, the mirror images, the illusion of thousands of wings, but I had sense enough to realize how utterly crazy it would all sound.

'I did try,' I said, 'but my client was adamant that the child was born and is still alive.'

'Your client's name?' It was a brisk question, demanding an answer.

'I'm not at liberty to say. Client confidentiality, and all that.'

'Very well. Yet you expect me to let you bother one of my clients.'

'Hildegarde Vogel might be of some help.'

His manner hadn't changed since he'd entered the room:

interested, detached, brusque, polite – yes, these were differences in tone, but his expression and attitude hardly varied.

'You witnessed Hildegarde's condition yesterday. Indeed, I've been told it deteriorated even further while you were with her. She is unwell, Mr Dismas, and very confused.'

'She was okay when I first spoke to her. Quite rational, in fact. It was only later, when she began to remember certain things, that she became upset.'

It was *then* that I noticed a change in him, a stiffening of body, an even greater sharpness in those cold, blue eyes. It was barely perceptible, but alterations in moods is another thing I'm good at recognizing – or *sensing*.

He scarcely missed a beat. 'And what was it that the poor woman remembered?'

'Deformed babies,' I replied.

It hung in the air between us, a statement so stark that we were both quiet for a moment or two.

Then the doctor said: 'I'm not sure what you want.'

'My client's intuition – a *mother's* intuition – tells her that her son is still alive. My guess is that the baby was so sick and malformed that they did not want to show him to her, and that he died soon after the birth. But my client will not accept that. Now if I were to bring her here to talk to Hildegarde herself, she might be convinced. Maybe the meeting might nudge something in the ex-midwife's memory, she might even recall my client – I understand that at the time Hildegarde was a great comfort to her. My client might listen to her and finally accept that her son is not alive.'

I was leaning towards him now, my one eye as intense as both of his, I'm sure, my humped back no doubt even more unsightly because of my crouched position, my gnarled hands clenched between my knees. He appraised me carefully, as glacial as ever, undisturbed by my proximity.

'What was your diagnosis in your infancy, Mr Dismas?'

'What?' I was taken aback. Indeed, reflexively, I even sat back a little.

'Cerebral palsy, spina bifida, osteogenis imperfecta – no, no sign of blue sclerotics in your eye. Marjous Syndrome, then? No, I doubt that's the cause of your deformities. Perhaps you had rheumatoid arthritis as a child? Poliomyelitis? Spondylitis? No, you seem active enough. So which was it, Mr Dismas? What did they tell your parents was wrong with you?'

'I've no idea and it isn't relevant.'

'Sometimes babies are born so badly deformed that not even their parents wish to keep them.'

'I didn't know my parents,' I told him, beginning to burn inside.

'Ah. Then not even your mother wanted you.'

'I don't see what –'

'Of course not. I don't expect you to. But I want you to understand. You see, even in this day and age, when treatment is so extensive and accessible, when the foetus can be studied in the womb and abortion is virtually on demand, malformed babies that are so grotesque that their mothers do not even wish to hold them are still being born. These poor unfortunates are taken away and left to die naturally. If there is pain involved, an injection might help them on their way. It's harsh, yes, I know, but the grief is soon over and the parents recover, perhaps to go on and have other normal, healthy children. Who knows what terrible tribulations they would have to endure if their disabled child had been allowed to live?'

'Everyone's entitled to a life,' I commented flatly.

'An anti-abortionist?'

'Just *for* life. Hardship and nuisance-value is no excuse for preventing life. It may be difficult, it might mean a lifetime of misery for the child, but he or she deserves the chance to live and experience things in their own way. It doesn't always have to be a bad existence. Consider your own care-supervisor.'

'Constance?'

'She's obviously devoted a large part of her life to caring for the sick and elderly. She's helped others just by her presence.'

The smile was in his eyes, but not on his lips. Was I so transparent? Could he sense my emotions towards her?

'And of course, your own time here on Earth has proved helpful to others,' he said, and I wasn't sure if the smile in his eyes was not mockery.

'Maybe it has. The point is, I was given the chance and so was Constance Bell. Think of all those others who weren't.'

'Well, there lies a huge moral dilemma: to give life and with it, great hardship, or to take it away as an ultimate kindness.'

I understood his meaning. There were many times in my own life when I wished I hadn't been born, and yes, I'd cursed the person who had allowed me to live after the moment of birth. Perhaps the one who had dumped me outside the convent in the dead of winter – I had always assumed that it had been my mother who had left me there – had taken the easy option, unable to smother me to death themself, so leaving me there in the cold to let fate play its own hand.

'As far as I'm concerned,' I said, 'it's every mother's own decision. I only wish some would give it more consideration. But I don't understand your interest in me. I'm here to discuss Hildegarde Vogel.'

'Life, in any form, has always been of concern to me. It's why I joined the medical profession in the first place.'

There was something about his eyes that was almost mesmeric. They made me feel uncomfortable yet, perversely, they seemed to draw me in. Purposely, I looked away.

Directly to the point, I asked: 'Will I be allowed to see Hildegarde again?'

He thought for a moment, then appeared to soften his stance (I say 'appeared' because I had no idea of what was going through his mind). 'Let's see how she is tomorrow, or perhaps the next day. I'm afraid the excitement yesterday affected her adversely: she really is quite unwell this morning.'

'You'll let me talk to her, though?' I was unable to conceal my surprise.

'If or when she's well enough. Why don't I get Constance to phone you tomorrow with a final decision?'

'That's fine by me.' It was more than I'd expected.

'Of course, if Hildegarde becomes upset again you must promise me you'll desist immediately. You will leave and not bother my patient again.'

'It's a deal. Believe me, I don't want to make her any worse than she is.'

He rose from the couch, a hand extended towards me, and I, too, got to my feet, gratefully taking that hand. As we shook he continued to observe me, his interest unconcealed. Dr Wisbeech towered over me and I could feel his power – not the kind that has to do with physical strength but the kind that has to do with the mind, the persona, stemming from an individual's very psyche, a faculty that enables them to intimidate/dominate others, sometimes without the other person even being aware. It was hard to ignore, but then I'd been fighting that sort of thing all my life – my stature (or status, if you like) made it a regular conflict. I grinned as I released my hand from his, and I think we both knew right then that an engagement (in the sense of battle) had been postponed. It occurred to me to wonder why I was thinking in these terms as I made my way towards the door, my grin fading to an inner wry smile. I had always been quite perceptive as far as the feelings of others were concerned, particularly if their feelings were directed towards myself, but the *animus* in this man, despite its suppression and his pleasant if condescending manner, could be felt as plainly as if he'd spat in my empty eye.

'Mr Dismas?'

I lingered in the doorway.

'Who are your friends? Are they others like yourself?' There was no apology in his question, no awkwardness.

'What do you mean by "others"?' I said stiffly.

Again, no awkwardness, no embarrassment. 'Others with similar disabilities,' he replied. 'Or have you managed to become accepted by normal people? Indeed, do you accept *yourself* as normal?'

My hand gripped the door frame. I wanted to throw myself at him, beat that handsome, patrician's face to a pulp.

'I hope I haven't offended you,' he said, but not as an afterthought: he knew exactly what he was doing.

What was his game? I asked myself. Was he deliberately riding me, playing for some kind of reaction? Or . . . was it possible? . . . was he genuinely interested in how I got by? No, nobody could be that insensitive. Or that wicked?

'I'll wait to hear how Miss Vogel is,' was all I said as I turned away and stomped off down the hall. If he uttered some response to that, I didn't catch it.

Bastard, I thought as I stomped, *absolute-bloody-bastard*. I could feel his eyes on me and I knew if I looked back he'd be there in the doorway, watching my departure with that peculiarly cool interest. *Bastard*.

Outside, I forced myself to take in some deep breaths, expelling the stale degenerative air of the home from my lungs and sucking in the purer stuff. The day had suddenly become overcast again, clouds with bulging, charcoal-grey bottoms milling low in the sky, each piled, cumulonimbus heap trying to gain elbow room, pushing against its neighbour and creating deep-growling rumbles, occasional flares of pure energy. The rain soon began, great heavy dollops of it, bursting, splatting, against the driveway, drumming an escalating beat on the roof and bonnet of my car. Turning up my coat collar, I made a clumsy dash for the Ford, my head and the hump of my back soaked before I could drag open the driver's door and bundle myself inside.

'Bastard!' I said aloud in the solitude of my metal capsule.

When you're as I am, you rarely completely forget your condition, your own oddity is always present in your mind (usually right at the front) and you never need reminding of how different you are to normals. You never ask to be reminded, either. You might have thought that Wisbeech, in light of his profession and lettered qualifications, would have understood that; as a learned and obviously civilized human being he might even have appreciated the insult his remarks might have dealt me. My guess was that he cared little about my sensitivities and nothing about the question itself: my belief was that he had been testing me. What that test meant, I had no idea; I just had the feeling that I'd failed.

Switching the isolation switch off and the engine on, I angrily shoved the gear stick into first, pulling away from the home's front entrance a little too fast, a little too powerfully, the tyres throwing up stones from the drive. I violently twisted the steering wheel to head towards the high gates, giving one last disgusted glance back at the building as I did so. My foot almost slipped from the accelerator in my surprise, for the dark upper windows of PERFECT REST were now filled with pallid faces.

It was as if most of the elderly residents had come to their windows to watch me leave. I only caught a glimpse, for the turn completed itself of its own accord and the car was set straight for the gates, but the image of those grey-white blobs against the glass, the rooms leaden behind them, stayed in my mind as I changed gear and controlled direction. A quick look in the rear-view mirror presented a receding reflection of the building itself and it seemed suddenly ominous in the sullen, rain-dulled light, a semi-Gothic mansion that was full of secrets rather than a restful haven. A raindrop had dripped into the crevice between my neck and shirt collar, running sideways around my hump and down my back, causing me to shiver. I gripped the wheel more tightly, straightening the car, and wondered at the home's sudden lack of charm. Now I could feel a hundred or more sets of eyes watching my retreat, every pair hostile. *Idiot*, I berated myself. *Imagination*, I tried to convince myself. They were just sick old people with nothing better to do, curious about strangers, bored inside death's waiting-room. There was no antagonism towards me on their minds; they prob-ably watched every new coming and going in the same way. Visiting hours – if they had had set visiting hours – would have been a riot.

That's when I realized that on neither visit to PERFECT REST had I seen any other visitor. Nor anybody else who looked like an outsider, for that matter. This place really was private.

I kept the car in second all the way down the drive and when I entered the short, wooded area the gloom forced me to switch on my headlights. I passed through the gates that had already opened for me and pulled up outside. Taking out my small notepad and pen from my inside pocket, I leaned across the passenger seat, wound down the window on that side, and peered out at the sign on one of the stone pillars. I wrote down: MD, FRCS, FRCOG, FRCP, DCH. Then I drove on, quickly reaching third, sticking with it while the car splashed through instant puddles and lurched into existing dips. The landscape began to open up again and the rain pelted the windscreen with some force; the wipers struggled to keep vision clear, but I was soon forced to lean even closer than my usual position to the glass in order to see my way ahead. The turns seemed to come up too fast even though I was still only in third, and it was a while before I realized the engine was labouring, desperate for a shift upwards; uncon-sciously I had been trying to speed away from the home and the sinister – yes, I admitted to myself, that was the word, he *was* sinister – Dr Wisbeech. I eased off the accelerator, slowing to a more appropriate speed.

High and far ahead I noticed bright blue patches in the otherwise troubled skies that told me the storm would not last too long. In fact, the further south-east I went, the clearer it would become. But that was for later – right now it was cats and dogs out there.

I was approaching the now familiar abandoned house by the side of the lane when I saw the tiny figure sheltering hunched-up under a tree. Elbow-crutch resting against her hip, Constance Bell waved a hand at me to stop.

18

She was soaked, the tree she cowered under affording scant protection. As I drew up alongside her she took a couple of faltering steps towards the car.

'Get in before you drown,' I called out, pushing open the passenger door.

Constance put a hand on top of the door frame and peered in at me, her lovely eyes blinking away raindrops; she did not have to duck to see me. She looked like a child, a very troubled child.

'I can't,' she shouted over the pounding of the rain. 'I have to get back before they miss me.'

'You sound as if you've made a jailbreak.' I tried to ease her obvious tension with a grin.

'No, I mean it, I don't have long.'

'Then at least sit in the car so we can talk without hollering.'

She took a quick look around her, first back down the lane towards the home, then in the opposite direction. She pointed towards the abandoned house and the overgrown track that led towards the rear.

'If I do, will you drive us out of sight?'

I'm sure I registered disbelief, but I nodded anyway. 'Sure. Just get in out of the wet.'

She eased herself into the seat backwards, resting the elbow crutches against the door as she did so, then swivelled round so that her legs were also inside the car. Retrieving the crutches, she closed the door.

'Terrific,' I said and steered the Ford off the lane on to the bumpy track. Apart from the odd untidy heaps of timber and rubble, there was little else behind the house: a half-collapsed shed stood some distance away and beyond that there was only long grass and shrubbery, woodland their backdrop. I brought the car to a halt beside the building's battered rear door.

'What are you afraid of?' I asked my passenger as I switched off the engine and shifted round in my seat so that I could take her in more easily.

She was dabbing raindrops from her face with a tiny handkerchief, bedraggled locks of hair loosened from the tie at the nape of her neck to stick against her cheeks. I wanted to reach forward and brush the strands away, to push them gently behind her ears, an excuse to touch her, to feel her soft skin beneath my fingertips. Naturally, I sat there and did nothing.

'Why . . . why do you think I'm afraid?'

Her poor imperfect body rested awkwardly in the passenger seat; her gaze on me was intense.

'You obviously don't want to be seen talking to me,' I replied to her question.

'It's just that . . .' She gave a little shake of her head. 'Mr Dismas – '

'Please. People who know me call me Dis. Or Nick – my friends call me Nick.' (In fact, even my friends called me Dis, but I wanted Constance to use my proper Christian name.)

'I don't think you should come back to the home.'

'Hey, I'm not going to upset Hildegarde again. Besides, I only get to see her if your boss decides she's well enough. I promise I'll treat her gently.'

'You don't understand. It's the doctor I don't want you to upset.'

'Wisbeech? Why should I upset him? I only need the answers to a few questions, none of which have anything to do with him.'

'Please listen to me.' My hand was resting on the hand-brake between us and she touched the top of my fingers with her own. 'Dr Wisbeech is not someone you should anger. He's a very powerful person.'

I found it difficult to get my thoughts back on line despite the gravity of her tone. Her flesh against mine: dear God, was this how teenagers felt when first crush led to first touch? I wasn't experienced in these things, so I had no way of knowing (I guess that same lack of experience also accounted for my over-reaction right then).

'Did you hear me?' she asked, leaning a little closer, her puzzled eyes examining mine in the gloomy interior of the car. 'Mr – Nick, please understand what I'm trying to tell you.'

Her hand left mine and I managed to pull myself together enough to say: 'Why are you going to so much trouble to warn me?'

She seemed to withdraw into herself; certainly she moved away from me.

'I'm not going to any trouble. I nearly always take a walk along the lane some time during the day, usually in the late afternoon.'

'In the pouring rain?'

'It wasn't raining when I left.'

'But you are concerned.' I almost added 'about me', but that would have been foolish – and probably wishful thinking. 'What exactly do you think the doctor can do to me?'

'I have to go.' She began to turn, to reach for the door release.

'Wait a minute!' I caught her arm. 'Please. Talk to me a little while longer, okay?'

She was facing the door and I studied the long curve of her neck through the damp, loosened hair, a graceful line that led to her cruelly stunted body. Slowly her head came round and she rested back in the seat.

'I can't tell you any more than I already have,' she said quietly.

'You haven't told me anything.'

She remained silent.

'How could I anger Dr Wisbeech, Constance?' Just speaking her name for the first time sent a shiver through me. 'How is he powerful, in what way? He's only the manager of an old people's nursing home – '

'He *owns* PERFECT REST.'

'Okay, he owns it. How does that make him powerful? Are you telling me he has connections in high places and if so, why should my enquiries put any noses out of joint?'

'I used the wrong word. I simply meant he is very wealthy.'

'Wealthy enough to pay someone to discourage me?'

'You've got it all wrong . . .'

But I was on a roll, my PI instincts coming to the fore. 'Dr Wisbeech has an awful lot of letters behind his name. They look pretty fancy for someone who only runs an old folks' home. Why should he be paranoid about a few questions to one of his residents? And tell me this: why does he keep a two-way mirror in the visitors' room?'

That gave her a start.

'Those kind of mirrors are easy to spot,' I went on, pushing for an answer.

'Dr Wisbeech likes to study people before meeting them, particularly those applying for residency.'

'Odd way to vet future clients.'

'He prefers to see their real condition, not the one they put on for interviews. Dr Wisbeech is very selective of his guests.'

'But why should he want to observe me beforehand?'

'What makes you think he did? I told you, it's used when dealing with prospective guests.'

'Kind of weird though.'

'We have high standards.'

'So I noticed. I'm still wondering, by the way, how someone like Hildegarde Vogel could afford your services.'

'That isn't a mystery. Hildegarde is a very special guest of Dr Wisbeech. She worked with him many years ago when he was a consultant for several major hospitals.'

I allowed a moment or two for that to sink in. 'They worked together . . .' I said, more to myself than to Constance.

'Yes. The Doctor once told me that Hildegarde was invaluable to him during those years and because she's in such poor health now, with no friends or family to support her, he feels responsible himself for her wellbeing. I suppose it's his way of repaying Hildegarde for her loyal service.'

'He doesn't come across as the guardian angel type to me.'

'First impressions can be deceptive – as you, of all people, should know. Dr Wisbeech is a wonderful benefactor.'

'So why are you warning me against him?'

'To try and stop you becoming involved in something you don't understand. The Doctor doesn't tolerate disturbances to his work.'

'His work with old people? You know I'm still puzzled by his medical virtuosity. Isn't he a little over-qualified to be taking care of geriatrics, ailing or otherwise?'

'It's his choice. Perhaps he feels he can do so much more by dedicating himself to one area of medicine rather than many.'

'Yes, but *old* people?'

'What have you got against the elderly? Haven't they earned the right to live out the rest of their lives in some comfort? Haven't they paid their debt to society?'

'Some, maybe.'

'As I said, Dr Wisbeech is very discriminating. Now I really must get back.'

'Constance . . .'

It was too late: she had already pushed open the door and was sliding from the seat before I had a chance to question her further. We hadn't noticed, but the rain had lost its intensity to become a steady drizzle.

'Let me take you,' I pleaded as she braced herself with the crutches on the uneven ground.

'No. It's better that you just leave.'

As she lurched away I wondered why she didn't want to be seen with me. Was she that afraid of this wonderfully benevolent boss of hers?

'Can I phone you?' I called out.

'No!' But she paused. 'I don't know. I think it's probably better that you don't. Goodbye, Mr Dismas.'

'Dis. Call me Dis.' But she was gone. 'Or Nick,' I said to myself with a sigh.

19

When I got back to the office I sent Philo out for sandwiches and coffee while I went through paperwork that had accumulated throughout the morning. Working lunches were not unusual either for myself or for Henry – even when out on fieldwork a quick snack in a pub, or sandwiches scoffed in my car, were frequently the order of the day (the latter particularly when on surveillance). Lunchtime was also good for getting things done without being disturbed by phone calls from clients and contacts. I allowed Henry to get his daily fix with one movie question, mercifully an easy one: Which Marx Brother failed to appear in 1942's *Hellzapoppin*? Answer: All of them; the film was an Olson and Johnson starrer, who were serious rivals of the famous brothers at the time. After that, it was strictly down to catching up on boring but vital correspondence and office minutiae. There was one special phone call I wanted to make, but I had to consider the fact that others actually lunched out most days.

An hour or so later when I was readjusting a client fee that Philo had submitted for approval – he had a habit of forgetting to add ten per cent to all costs and expenses, including hours spent travelling on a case, so that the agency could realize a reasonable profit (standard practice in our business, my friend – pays for overheads, wear and tear, and all indirect costs), Etta Kaesbach appeared at my open office door.

'I thought I might catch you on my way back from lunch,' she said by way of announcing herself.

'Come in.' I laid my pen down and smiled, always pleased to see her.

She shook her dripping, half-closed umbrella out, making tiny puddles on the floor; I caught Henry's disapproving frown through the doorway.

'What a summer,' Etta complained as she took the seat on the other side of my desk. 'Glorious one minute, monsoon season the next.'

She laid the short umbrella on the floor beside her and removed the grip from her hair, pushing wayward strands back and regripping them once they were tidy. I watched, comparing her to the girl with whom I'd shared my car earlier in the day. Both had special qualities, but my feelings for them were different. Vastly different. And, of course, I thought I might stand a chance with Constance.

'My God, what's happened to your face?' Etta's own face was aghast.

Involuntarily, I touched the swelling below my absent eye. 'I took a tumble down the steps of my flat,' I lied, unwilling to revisit the humiliation of two nights ago.

'The wages of wine?' She was being lyrical, perfectly aware that I rarely touched the grape, beer and spirits my usual juice.

'Slippery stone. Sometimes the steps are tricky with this ol' leg of mine.' I tapped the offending limb under the desk, rapping on wood with my other hand at the same time.

Etta smiled as she shook her head, letting me know that she suspected booze was the cause of my 'downfall'. Then she got straight to the point: 'Why are you upsetting my client, Dis?'

Oh Lord, someone else I was upsetting today. 'Shelly Ripstone?' I asked.

The solicitor nodded. 'She called me yesterday, claiming you've dumped her twice. Shelly might be somewhat melodramatic on occasion, Dis, but she's a good client and her late husband was an even better one. Looking after her interests is a duty my firm takes very seriously. So please tell me what's going on. One minute you're on the case, albeit reluctantly, the next you're off it. Then you're back working for her again, only to give it up once more.'

I groaned wearily, resting my elbows on the desk and cupping my head in my hands. 'Would you believe me if I told you I was back on it yet again?' I said.

'Shelly doesn't appear to be aware of that.'

'I forgot to call her back when something else came up.'

'Something to do with her alleged missing son?'

'Possibly. I suppose at the back of my mind was the thought that it might be another wild goose chase – like the previous one of trying to find a record of birth and death. I didn't want to build up her hopes again.'

'Dis, I think you'd better tell me everything you've done so far, then perhaps I can pacify her.'

So I did. I went over the case from start to present moment – everything except hallucinations and visions of wings and birds and debonair men seen only in mirrors. I didn't mention whispering voices either and only spoke of Louise Broomfield in passing, implying that she was a friend of Shelly's rather than some clairvoyant mentor of mine now. But Etta was sharper than that.

'Who did you say this Broomfield woman was?' she asked, watching me suspiciously.

'She's a kind of, well, a kind of spiritualist. A clairvoyant, actually.'

'Oh Dis.' It was a reprimand.

'Hey, I didn't bring her in. That was our mutual client's idea.'

'I said Shelly was melodramatic. I hope you're not taking this Broomfield woman seriously, Dis.'

'You know me better.' Another deceit, but I really didn't want to get into all the psychic stuff right then. 'The point is, I'm hoping to see the old ex-midwife again tomorrow if she's well enough.'

'And you really think she might be helpful?'

'I seemed to hit a nerve the first time I spoke to her.'

'But she's sick and she's senile?'

I nodded. 'Yup.'

Etta rested back in her chair and shook her head despairingly. 'You should have let it go, Dis.'

'I thought you thought I had and that's why you were telling me off.'

'No. That was because you kept changing your mind so my client didn't know where she was. Now I think you should stick to your original decision. I'll explain it to Shelly, I'll tell her you've done your best but without further firm leads there's no point in going on with it. You'd only be wasting her money and your time.'

'I already mentioned that to her.'

'It'll come better from me. She might just see some sense.'

'And so lose control of a lot of money?'

'Sometimes that's the way it falls. She'll have to live with it.'

'Tough guy, huh?'

'Only when there's no alternative. It's best for all concerned.'

'I don't think she'll see it that way.'

Etta shrugged. 'That's too bad. One of my duties as her legal adviser is to make sure she doesn't throw away her money on lost causes.'

I surprised myself by pleading for a second time that day. 'Give me a little longer, another day or so. Let's see what happens tomorrow. If Hildegarde Vogel is well enough for me to visit, I may be able to wrap the whole thing up.'

'I doubt it, even if the poor lady is feeling better. There's no sense to it, Dis.'

'Only one more day then. Remember, it's Shelly Ripstone who's employing me, not your firm.'

'Tough guy, huh?' she countered.

'I won't even let Shelly know I'm back on the case and I won't charge her for my extra time if there's no result.'

'Is this the Nick Dismas I thought I knew? No charge? Come on, Dis, what's got into you? And what would Henry say?'

There was a mumbling from the outer office, but I didn't think Henry had caught the drift of our conversation, otherwise he would have been in like a shot. He must have just heard his own name mentioned.

'When I started this agency,' I said quietly to Etta across the desk, 'I promised myself I'd give every case one hundred and ten per cent's worth of effort and I've always stuck with that principle, even when the fee amounted to nothing more than the cash to buy a couple of rounds in the nearest and cheapest bar. We both know that attitude has served me well over the years, so I'm not about to break with tradition now, no matter how cynical and hard-faced I've become about the business. This extra day will just be that ten per cent over the odds.'

She held up her thin hands. 'All right, all right, you've convinced me. You're a noble person. In any case, as you've reminded me, Shelly's contract is with you, not my firm. It's up to you how far you go with it.'

'You know I wouldn't go against your wishes, Etta.'

At last she smiled. 'Yes, I do. Fine then, Dis, it's your baby.'

We both winced.

'You know what I mean.' She picked up her umbrella and rose from the chair. 'But promise me you won't give Shelly any more false hopes.'

'I didn't give her any in the first place.'

'No, but her expectations rose when you took up the case again.'

'This time she won't even know.'

'She's expecting me to call her, but I won't for a day or

two. And if she phones me in the meantime, I'll say I couldn't get hold of you, you were out every time I tried.'

'Thanks, Etta. I mean it.'

'I'm aware that you're crazy, but at least you're fairly harmless. Will you contact me if you discover anything that will help?'

'Of course. And if I do, shall we tell Shelly together?'

'Might be an idea. Then at least she'll know her solicitor is looking after her interests. Take care, Dis, and keep in touch.'

With an air-blown kiss, Etta left my office.

The rest of the afternoon was filled with more mundane agency work.

Mundane stuff, but vitally important to the business, because it meant a constant turnover of work and that was the difference between success and failure for an outfit like mine.

All the cases I entered into my day-to-day, week-to-week, month-to-month instructions book, the entries later to be filed on computer by Henry. Hard files would also be kept, these held in the current-work cabinets in my office, later, on completion, to be stored in cupboards in the outer office. Letters of acceptance would have to be typed for each new commission, fees for services included where necessary as well as requests for more information (usually unnecessary, for most of our professional clients knew the form). As neither Philo nor Ida could type, letters and reports were a task I shared with Henry, and it was part of the job I detested. I always promised myself that one day I'd hire a proper secretary.

Henry dealt with most of the incoming phone calls that afternoon, although one did come through to me when his line was busy. It was Ida and she was using an old ploy to obtain a certain telephone number (the one she was ringing from, in fact), which I'd used myself many times in the past. She was chasing down a divorced absconder who owed his ex-wife maintenance money for their kids; my instructing client, the woman's solicitor, needed the ex-husband's telephone number so that the man could be harassed for payment not just by letter, but also by verbal 'assault' (another old ploy greatly enjoyed by ex-partners). The absconder, who had gone to ground, naturally had gone ex-directory, so no BT operator was going to give out his number.

His new address was easy to find by the usual methods, and Ida, attired in her best granny clothes, had parked her car right outside his front door, claiming that it had broken down when she knocked and our target had appeared on the doorstep. He had taken pity on her (the ruse doesn't *always* work) and allowed her to use the phone inside the house to call her regular garage. While there she had done a swift and necessarily superficial inventory of the house's contents, peeking through open doorways, perhaps even asking to use the loo, so that she could sneak a look into the upstairs bedrooms. She would have already made notes on the building's exterior and surrounds, so that together with what she had learned from inside, she would be able to provide a reasonably comprehensive status report for our legal client (very handy should the ex plead poverty). However, the prime purpose was to obtain the covert telephone number, so instead of ringing a garage, Ida rang the agency using a special codeword we'd devised that indicated the phone she was calling from did not have its own number displayed. After a short dialogue with 'Harry the Mechanic' – 'Harry' being our codeword – she rang off, no doubt thanking the gullible householder profusely for the use of the line. The moment I heard the receiver replaced, I dialled 1471 and made a note of the number given by the automatic operator. Simple but effective; this runaway was going to get a lot of nasty phone calls from his ex-wife, her solicitor, and maybe even his abandoned kids. I had no sympathy for him.

Philo arrived back from a trip to Eastbourne further along the coast, where he had delivered a set of legal documents to a firm of solicitors for me, the papers too urgent to post and too important to risk a courier service; personal delivery was another of our minor but no less crucial services. I immediately sent him off to photograph a vehicle that had been involved in a road-rage incident, its headlights and windscreen not smashed in the accident itself, but by the driver of the other car wielding a tyre lever. The insurance company, who regularly used the agency when their own assessors were too busy, wanted the book thrown at the offender.

Nothing glamorous about our daily routine, rarely very exciting, and not often involving anything to fire the imagination. Despite my physical drawbacks, I was an ordinary guy conducting a fairly unexceptional line of work; flights of fancy were not the order of the day (night-time privacy was another matter). I guess I'm just trying to lay down a solid, even mundane base to emphasize just how extraordinary and unimaginable to me were the events that were to follow.

Anyway, it wasn't until towards the end of the working day that I got the chance to call the BMA, the British Medical Association.

20

Dreams again. Worse than ever. Bloody terrifying dreams.

At least, I *thought* they were dreams.

When I'd left the office that evening I'd warned Henry not to work too late; as much as I appreciated the effort, he was putting in *too* many hours, always complaining that it was the only way he could keep up with the paperwork when we were that busy. I reminded him that he had a dear old mum at home who relied on him for company, but he scoffed, saying it was good for her to get used to the idea that he had his own life to lead and working overtime was part of it. I left him to his accounts and time sheets, reluctant to tell him he was lucky to have someone to worry over him.

I went straight back to the flat without stopping for a drink on the way, and on my own that evening I smoked only straights, not even tempted to do Skunk or Rock, because I was mellowed out on something better. Constance Bell was my opiate that evening.

As cynical and streetwise that I thought myself to be – and I pretty much *was* both, life experience and my occupation seeing to that – I was still acting like a teenager in the throes of his first romantic crush. As I microwaved my frozen-pack lasagna dinner, I was even humming a medley of old love themes. Sure, I'd fallen in love before – I *thought* I had fallen in love before – and more than just once. There was a time my legs turned to jelly and my brain to mush at the mere sight of Etta, but this time it was different, this time I was on a level playing field. In my mind – and I had to keep reminding myself it was in *my* mind – our disabilities cancelled each other's out; it didn't make them go away, but it kind of *absorbed* them. I felt that for the first time in my life I stood a chance with someone I could really care for, someone who stirred me in that perfectly normal way. Our relationship, if it had a chance to flourish – God, if it had a chance to *happen*! – could be that of equals and that somehow would make it ordinary – oh Lord, how I'd longed to be *ordinary*! It's hard to explain, but my world is a different world to yours, no matter how much the well-meaning and the politically correct might have it otherwise, and the thought that I could share in the normal emotional experience made me feel like the luckiest man alive for a few hours. I was certain that something had passed between us, even on the first occasion we'd met. A mutual attraction, an understanding of each other's feelings and tribulations, a subliminal touching of senses? I had no idea what it was, but I was sure it was not one-sided on my part. I had also detected a strange trepidation in Constance's gaze, a distant haunting that I could not comprehend; its effect, though, was to make her seem even more vulnerable.

I wanted to phone her at PERFECT REST on the pretence of discussing the information I'd gleaned from the BMA earlier in the evening, the meaning of the list of credentials behind Dr Leonard K. Wisbeech's name, but in reality just to hear her voice once more, to imagine her lips so far away yet so close to mine. Common sense prevented me though: I realized she was probably off-duty by now and I didn't even know if she lived at the home itself or somewhere close by. It struck me that I knew nothing about her except that she was a care-supervisor and that life had played one of its cruel, dispassionate tricks on her.

Doubt insinuated its way into my happiness. Maybe Constance lived with a partner.

The thought froze me. She was lovely enough to gain the love and respect of anybody, regular or, like me, otherwise.

There were enough good people out there who had never worn the shackles of prejudice, who clearly could see another's inner self, their real worth, superficial physicality no barrier to true appreciation; and Constance, not *just* because of the almost mystical loveliness in those dark eyes, the beauty of her features, but because of the innate yet evident gentleness of her nature, the purity of her essence, would be easy to fall in love with.

My mood was spoilt; anxiety set me to brooding. Tormenting uncertainties accompanied me to my bed that night.

Voices screamed inside my head and wings, huge, powerful things, the wings of unseen unbirdlike behemoths, pounded my flesh. Amidst the cries were plaintive wails of despair and startled shrieks of terror, but I think it was the sound of my own protests that finally woke me.

I found myself raised from my pillow, bedsheets in disarray around me, tepid light from the hallway casting a wedge-shaped glow through the partially-open door on to the carpet. My skin was wet with perspiration and I was still yelling, my voice raspy, hoarse, as though I'd been at it for some time. My demands were for the creatures of my dreams to leave me alone, to get out of my head and my home, and there should have been some relief in waking, the nightmare should have ended, but they didn't: the screams, the anguished howls, the beating of gargantuan wings were still with me inside the room, as if joining me from my subconscious, invisible tormentors escaped from their dream base.

I thought I detected moving shadows in the darkest corners of the bedroom, but each time I endeavoured to focus upon them, they dissolved, becoming nothing once more, my eye catching movement elsewhere so that I looked away, only for the process to be repeated. I became aware of the seeping coolness of the air, a kind of icy cold that crept into the very meat of my body, slowing my blood, prickling my surface skin; yet I dripped with sweat and my head felt feverish. Even in the poor light, I could see the mists of my breath.

Pulling the sheet tangled about my legs up to my crooked chest, I retreated towards the wall behind my pillow, moving warily, cautiously, silent now with only my mind begging those persecutors to leave me; yet just as they had followed me from my nightmare they now inched after me along the bed, drawing close, sniggers and chuckles among the screams. Shadows seem to grow stronger, though still they could not be defined, and the light from the hallway seem to dim even more in their presence.

The hump of my back touched the unyielding wall and I turned to my side, drawing my legs up, hands clenching the bedsheet to my shoulder. No hero I, I began to whimper.

I would have fled, but my limbs had solidified and were of no use to me at all. Whimpers denigrated into sobs.

Horrifyingly, the shadows began to deepen, began to mass, so that they filled my vision, and I was too frightened to close my eye against them. The movements within took on forms and they seemed to convulse, to writhe, and even in that darkness I could see that they resembled no living creature that I have ever known. Unlike man and unlike beast, they squirmed before me, the light from outside fading pitifully under their weight.

I hadn't been aware, but my foot was exposed from the sheet and something intensely cold and slimy brushed against my toes. My own scream, the yowl of hysteria that so far had been locked deep within my constricted chest, finally erupted to fill the room and echo back from the four walls. It broke off, spasmed as the dark contorted shapes frenzied before me, and it re-emerged so piercingly shrill that even these amorphous night prowlers flinched.

I jerked my foot back under the sheet and pulled the thin cover over my head, the unsophisticated reaction of a child who was afraid of the boogeyman hiding in his bedroom closet, imagining that this insubstantial layer would be protection against the haunting. But cowering there, body quaking, I felt their weight through the material, felt their proddings and their jabs, tormenting nudges that sought to draw me out so that I would face their full horror. I resisted though, denied them their claim, and I prayed for reality to return, for part of me knew that this could not really be happening, that my mind must still be captive of my dreams, that somehow consciousness had not wholly escaped nightmare fantasy.

And so eventually, and in their own time, they went away, whispering and mumbling their discontent as they faded. Yet I still remained hidden and only the gradual dawn light filtering through my flimsy but shielding cloak finally drew me from cover. Only that and the sane, welcoming sound of the telephone ringing in the next room.

21

It had been Louise Broomfield who had called me in the early hours, rousing me from the chilling after-effects of the haunting, bringing me back to the natural world of cold hallway floor, stubbed toes, and insistent telephones, a conventional place uninhabited by ambiguous, shape-changing chimaeras. It had turned out that Louise had also been having a bad time of it, but her dream – her sleep-sensing, as she would have it – was about me and the nightmare *I* was going through. She had observed me cowering beneath a white shroud while shadowy, spectral demons had roamed the darkness around me, flailing me with ill-formed fists, screeching and berating me as they did so. Although the imagery was confused, she was acutely aware that I was in grave danger, for this was in her own dreamscape, one from which she herself could not escape. Louise had called my name, but I had not responded; she had chastised my tormentors, but they had not listened. All she could do, the clairvoyant told me, was to watch over me until the abuse ended. As had happened with me, the nightmare eventually had faded and early light had awakened her.

Her immediate thought had been to make contact with me, the idea that the dream was hers alone not even entering her head; the psychic link between us had been so strong, she said, and she was desperately afraid for my state of mind. I was both pleased and relieved to hear her voice when I answered the phone for, together with the pain in my stubbed toe, it helped vanquish the lingering remnants of the nightmare (yes, mentally I was already rationalizing the whole experience as a terrible and vivid dream, refusing to accept that for much of it I had been conscious. It's an example of how a frightened but pragmatic mind will alter perception to minimize the anguish). Louise had warned me that danger was hovering close by, that the dream was either a threat or a desperate message; ultimately, though, it was I who was trying to calm her. Although I was frightened and shaken, my natural cynicism offered a hubristic shield behind which I could take refuge, bravado my only weapon of defence.

Later, when I left the flat for the office, I saw that the skies were overcast, the sunlight grey, another dismal beginning to the day. So early in the morning the streets were quiet, with only a few shop assistants and office staff making their way to work. Seagulls swooped and circled overhead, searching for snacks, impatient for the first appearance of food-gobbling tourists with sandwiches to be snatched, crumbs to be beaked from the kerbsides. The alleyways and narrow passages I took as short cuts seemed particularly bleak and intimidatingly empty, and I hurried through them, the unfamiliar quietness increasing my unease. The broader thoroughfares were more comforting, but still not busy enough for me to feel totally safe. As much as I resisted the notion, the night had left me wasted and vulnerable.

When I finally slid the key into the agency's ground floor door, I almost stumbled inside. There in the gloom of the stairwell I wedged my hump into a corner and drew in exhausted breaths, my journey being more like a flight through suspect territories. I gave myself time to steady my breathing and for my trembling to settle, then began the climb up the creaky stairs to my office. I paused when a noise from the rooms above came to me.

After the night I'd just been through, I suppose I had the right to feel a little jumpy, even though I stubbornly (and perhaps necessarily) continued to dismiss the whole thing as a wild dream prompted by the worrisome events of the past few days. I peered up at the landing at the top of the stairs and debated with myself whether or not to carry on or turn around and head back outside into the living world again. Part of me was aware that I was being old-maidishly ridiculous, while the other part remembered another ascent to upstairs rooms, those in the repossessed house at the beginning of the week where a shattering mirror filled with agitated monstrosities (self-reflections, I'd later rationalized) had awaited me. I was reluctant to advance further, fearing yet another shock might be in store, and with that nervousness there came the acceptance of what had truly happened during the night. Those terrors that had invaded my bedroom, although perhaps instigated by a dream, had been real: they had materialized into something perhaps less solid than you or I, but nevertheless palpable, entities that could touch and use their weight, wraiths that could be heard and so feared as actual though unnatural beings. The pounding of giant wings, heard not just by myself, but by the clairvoyant and Shelly Ripstone too, had been no illusion, and neither were these night creatures. If I believed in one, then I had to believe in the other. And as I stood there on the stairway it came to me as a dawning recognition that the 'phantasms' had not been there to torment but were there to warn me. Louise had been partly right: their message was desperate. But somehow I knew – and God knows I was no psychic, but I *knew* – that their desperation was for me! And of course, this answer led to another question: Why? What *was* the message?

Another noise from above. The scraping of furniture. Then it hit me: Was the answer to the other question waiting for me up there?

The urge to turn and flee back downstairs was immense and, in fact, almost overpowering when I heard a door open on the landing above. I had turned, one foot already on the step below, when the voice came to me.

'Dis? That you?'

Henry. Bless his lovely Yiddisher heart, it was Henry! 'Uh . . .' was all I could reply.

He appeared at the top of the stairs, red braces brightening the gloom, his sky-blue shirt a little wrinkled, his gimlet eyes boring through thick, gold-framed spectacles.

'You gave me a fright,' he complained, shaking his head in irritation. 'I heard someone come half-way up, and then nothing. What happened – you run out of breath?'

'Jesus, Henry,' I managed to say.

'You all right, Dis?' He bent down, hands on knees, to get a better look. 'Bloody hell, you look awful.'

'What?'

'You look as if you've seen a ghost. What was it – a bad night?'

I hadn't realized the dread inside showed so plainly. 'I didn't expect anyone to be here at this hour, that's all. You took me by surprise.'

He cocked his head, still scrutinizing me. 'No, it's more than that. You really don't look at all well. Come on up, let me get you some coffee.'

I resumed the climb and he disappeared back through the door. When I entered the office, he was already by the filing cabinets, pouring boiling water into two mugs. 'I was making myself a cup when I heard you,' he said. Looking at my face, he shook his head again. 'You're as white as a sheet, Dis.'

'As it happens, I did have a pretty bad night.'

'Want to tell me about it?' He gave me a steaming mug, then took his own over to his desk. He sat and swivelled round to face me again. 'So. Talk to me.'

'Hmn?' I blew into the coffee before sipping. I scorched my lips, but it felt good; it felt real.

'Why are you looking so . . .' He searched for an adequate description. 'Well, so bloody grim and haggard. You look as if you've reached your first century and aren't looking forward to the second. Has someone upset you, Dis?'

Over the years, Henry and I had shared quite a few
confidences over a few pints and gins and he had proved a
good and comforting friend when my own burdens, those
mostly to do with my stature and other people's attitude
towards it – an odd remark in a bar that might have caught
me off guard, chortled derision in the street that had been
unexpected, the kind of slings and arrows that came with
outrageous fortune, and stuff that as a rule I'd learned to
cope with. Sometimes though, the word 'freak' got through
to me and, as independent as I kidded myself to be, I needed
some amicable words of compassion, someone to let me
know that ignorance was a minority commodity and a sure
sign of sickness of soul. He'd always matched me drink for
drink, listening to my whining, always agreeing with me, but
never trying to kid me that things were not as they seemed.
He knew and *almost* understood the problems I faced, never
ever suggesting they were in my own imagination, never
once pretending I was anything other than I was: he was too
shrewd and respected me too much for that. Henry was
invariably sympathetic without ever becoming maudlin and
because of that, and because of his honesty with me, I
listened and accepted the point when he advised me I had to
be what I was and never to imagine I could be anything else
– that could only lead to further fantasy and further disappointment. His reasoning was that what I was was incredible
enough: I had brains, I had determination, and I ran my own
business, I had good friends, excellent associates, and I
owned my own home; I was in relatively good health, despite
my handicaps, and I was physically strong; I took shit from
no one and anybody who knew me properly would never
give it. In short, I had a whole lot more going for me than
many people who had perfect physiques and good looks.
That kind of sugared his words, although his initial advice
was a little hard to take; but when I took time to think on it,
to *really* think on it, I realized he made a lot of sense. My life
was as it was and even among the harsh realities there was

a fair amount of good. I had much to enjoy and good people to enjoy it with. Because of Henry's pearls of wisdom, my expectations over the last few years had never risen too high; but then, neither had they been too limited. (What Henry wasn't aware of as yet was that a new light had entered my life in the person of Constance Bell, someone whose love would counterbalance every bad thing that had come my way. *If*, that is, she was free, and *if*, as my instincts told me, she was interested in me.)

The only regret I had as far as Henry was concerned was that although he'd confided in me about some things – the love-hate relationship he had with his mother and the frustrations of still living with her, the grief his hard-nosed father had given him when Henry was a young boy, this followed by further grief from a subsequent stepfather who had taken the place of his natural father when the latter had kneeled over and died from a heart attack at the age of forty-eight, the time he'd fled from the school playground because of bullying and had wandered the streets in the pouring rain so that he'd caught pneumonia and nearly died – he never once touched on his own homosexuality and the problems denial had caused him (I mean denial regarding his friends here, not self-denial: as far as we were concerned the closet was firmly padlocked and not even Ida, who freely admitted her lesbianism, had managed to find Henry's key). I found his reticence odd, especially in these enlightened times when homosexuality was accepted more and more as a life-choice (or, more accurately, a life-directive), and also because his preference was so obvious to those who knew him. Pocketbook Freud maybe, but I'd always surmised that the relationship with his mother and her old-school, die-hard, attitude towards what she considered deviant behaviour was the root of the problem: he hated to appear less than perfect in her bigoted old eyes. I also got the feeling that in keeping the true nature of his sexuality from his mother, he was in some way keeping it from himself; in refuting the reality, there was no reason to act upon it. Of course, this meant ignoring emotions and passions as well, so it was little wonder that beneath the exterior of prissy and acerbic coolness, Henry was pretty screwed up.

'Dis? I said has someone upset you?'

'Uh, no, Henry. Just a bad night.'

Who was holding back now? Should I let him in on the whole thing, perhaps allow a voice of sanity into the debate, or would my bookkeeper merely think I'd finally flipped? Wasn't I playing the same game as Henry, denial leading to self-denial? Whatever, I decided my friend and associate wasn't quite ready for this yet, and neither was I: I was too vulnerable at that time to risk his derision.

Henry's expression told me he wasn't convinced by my explanation, but he shrugged his shoulders. He swung back to face his desk and opened up an accounts book.

'No movie question this morning?' I asked to get the daily challenge over with and out of the way.

'I was too busy last night to give it any thought,' he replied distractedly, his brain already engaged in figures and balances.

'All work and no play, Henry,' I warned.

'You're a fine one to talk.' His voice was distant, because by now he was already in his other world where truth was in facts and nothing else. A clear world for clear thinkers. How lucky he was.

I left him to it, going into my office and closing the door behind me. I needed to think and now, before the daily grind began, was a good time. Later, when the working day for others had commenced, I would ring Dr Leonard K. Wisbeech, MD, FRCS, FRCOG, FRCP, DCH at PERFECT REST, for I was determined to visit Hildegarde Vogel again, no matter what her condition. My mind was going off on another track now, you see, wondering if the 'desperate message' contained in the nightmare (real or otherwise) was, in fact, a warning about the frail old ex-midwife. Was she the one that was really in danger?

The ringing of the phone startled me in the quietness of my office and I stared at the receiver for a few minutes before picking it up. I suspected Louise Broomfield was the caller, checking up on me again, and possibly with some outrageous new idea as to the relevance of last night's little episode. I was wrong though, it wasn't her.

'Mr Dismas?'

I drew in a breath. 'Constance?'

'Yes, it's Constance Bell . . . from PERFECT REST.'

You don't need to tell me that, Constance. I said: 'I was hoping to come over today.' Butterflies in my stomach? Well, something was fluttering around in there.

'I know. That's why I'm calling you.'

She sounded fraught and I suddenly had a cold, ominous feeling. 'What is it, Constance? Is it something to do with Hildegarde?'

'How . . . how did you know?'

I closed my good eye and allowed a slow breath to escape me. 'What's happened to her?'

'I'm afraid . . .' She seemed lost for words.

'Is she dead?'

There was a short silence before Constance replied. 'She died during the night.'

Why wasn't I surprised?

'Mr Dismas?'

'Please call me Dis. Or Nick. Call me Nick.'

'Nick.' Despite the gravity of her message, I felt a touch of warmth when I heard her say my name. 'Hildegarde passed away during the night,' Constance went on. 'We found her early this morning in one of the corridors.'

'She'd left her bed?'

'She often did. We often used to find her roaming the home until her illness worsened and incapacitated her almost entirely.'

'But not recently?'

'Not in the last couple of years.'

'Had she fallen, is that what killed her?'

'We're not sure at this stage. Dr Wisbeech thinks her heart just stopped beating.'

'A heart attack?'

'It seems likely. Inability to breathe correctly or confusion in unfamiliar surroundings may have induced a panic attack. In recent years her heart has been very weak.'

'I'm sorry, Constance. I know you liked the old lady.'

'I'm not sure that I did.'

Another surprise for me, but I let it go. 'How could she have left her room? Surely you have night staff to check on your patients from time to time?'

'Of course we do, but generally it's just one person, with others on standby. Unfortunately, the nurse can't be expected to be everywhere at once.'

It wasn't a rebuke, nor even a defence; it was more a deep regret over the situation. But a brittleness in her voice conveyed something even more to me: I sensed a slight anger and, inexplicably, a kind of dread also. It worried me.

'Look, I'd still like to come over there,' I said. 'Maybe I could see you, we could talk.'

'You mustn't!'

I was startled yet again, almost flinching from the telephone. It was the insistence rather than the shout that alarmed me. 'I need some questions answered,' I said, recovering quickly. 'If Hildegarde can no longer answer them, then perhaps you can. Or I could talk to Dr Wisbeech.'

'Nick, please don't.' The dread was more evident in her voice now. I felt her desperation when she said: 'Let me come and see you. Tonight, I could meet you tonight.'

'But I can easily get over there. It might be easier for you . . .'

I hadn't meant to patronize, but she cut me short. 'I have my own specially adapted car and I'm an adequate driver.'

'I didn't mean – '

'I know you didn't. Please, let's do it my way, Nick.'

'What's wrong, Constance? What the hell is going on at PERFECT REST?'

'Nothing. Honestly, nothing.'

'Then why are you so afraid?'

'I don't understand. What makes you think I am?'

Intuition? Years of experience dealing with all kinds of folk, discerning all kinds of nuances? An unspoken *connection* between the two of us? 'It's just a feeling,' I said.

There was no reply.

'Constance?'

A further pause, and then: 'Yes?'

'Okay, look. Do you want to come here, to the office?'

'If you don't mind, I'd rather come to your home.'

Mind? Oh Lord, that sounded good to me even though I was mystified. 'I'd still like to talk to Dr Wisbeech again, though. There are questions that maybe only he can answer.'

'You can put them to me, Nick.'

'I'm really not sure you'll have the answers. Tell me something, how long have you known the Doctor?'

'Why do you ask?'

What was so difficult about the question? 'Just curious, Constance.'

'I've been employed at the home for many years.'

'But did you know him before that?'

She seemed uncomfortable. 'Leonard was a family friend. He knew my parents when they were alive.'

'They're both dead? God, I'm sorry, Constance, I didn't know.'

'Why should you have known? It happened a long time ago, so the worst of the grieving is over for me. They died in a motoring accident eleven years ago – the other driver was drunk. He paid the price though – a five hundred pounds fine and an eighteen months' driving ban. It seems he was not entirely to blame for the crash.' Her bitterness was apparent, but she didn't dwell on it now. 'Dr Wisbeech took me in. He was wonderful to me, Nick. He paid for my education as well as my upkeep, financed the operations I've had over the years and then for my training as a nurse and care-supervisor.'

'He sounds like a good man.'

She took my comment at face value. 'I have to go. Arrangements have to be made about poor Hildegarde, our other residents have to be reassured . . .'

'Wait, can't you talk to me a little longer?'

'I think I can hear Nurse Fletcher calling me.'

I couldn't understand her urgency to end the call. Was she worried she'd be overheard?

'You'll see me tonight?'

'I'll be there, but I only have your office address.'

I quickly gave her the location of my flat and rough directions on how to get there once she reached Brighton. I heard another muffled voice from the earpiece, one that I vaguely recognized as belonging to the senior nurse-cum-administrator I'd met during my first visit to PERFECT REST.

Without another word, Constance rang off, but it was another minute before I replaced my own receiver.

The next call actually was from Louise Broomfield. She was checking on me, anxious to know if I was all right, that I'd recovered from my nasty experience. I assured her I was fine, the shock had worn off, the memory already blunted, and she wondered what my intentions were now. I told her I wasn't sure.

'Dis,' she said, her voice taking on an even more serious tone if that were possible, so that I guessed I was in for another warning. 'You must be careful. I sense terrible danger and somehow it's all connected to Shelly's missing son.'

'You were wrong about last night.' I felt no satisfaction in correcting her. 'It wasn't me at risk, it was Hildegarde Vogel, our little sparrow. She died at the nursing home last night.'

I caught the small gasp.

'Look,' I added, 'she was old and infirm. I don't think you can read anything into her death.'

'Are you sure, Dis, are you really sure? You don't see these visions you've been having as premonitions?'

'They're too crazy for that. Surely I would have seen some sense to them if they were.'

'They led you to Hildegarde Vogel.'

I couldn't argue with that.

'Are you going to drop the case again?' the clairvoyant persisted.

'I told you, I don't know. Something tells me that this Dr Wisbeech and Shelly's missing baby are linked, so maybe I'll do some more digging.' For some reason, I felt disinclined to mention Constance Bell's forthcoming visit that evening.

'But you don't know why or how.'

'It's partly instinct. The other part – and I'll admit it's kind of flimsy – is that Wisbeech has a stack of qualifications behind him. One, an FRCOG, means that he's a qualified obstetrician and gynaecologist.'

'What does that tell you?'

'It tells me he used to have something to do with pregnancy and births. Yesterday I got information from the BMA regarding his other medical specialities. FRCS – Fellow Royal College of Surgeons; FRCP – Fellow Royal College of Physicians, which apparently encompasses treatment of geriatrics; DCH – Diploma in Child Health. Wisbeech is somewhat over-qualified to run an upmarket old folks' nursing home, wouldn't you say?'

'I don't understand what you're getting at,' was Louise's response.

'I'm not sure myself. But those capabilities are far-ranging and I'm wondering how they led his career in the direction of caring for the elderly. Maybe that's where the money is these days, with the majority of the population living longer that ever before. I'd like to find out where he got the money to finance such a Grade A establishment in the beginning even if the house itself belonged to his family.' Or maybe I just didn't like the man and it would give me great satisfaction to rake up some dirt on him. It was a mean and petty motive and I don't think I really believed in it myself; certainly it wasn't worth mentioning to the clairvoyant.

'Oh dear,' I heard Louise say, 'this seems to be becoming more than I expected.'

'Don't worry, it's routine stuff to me.' Routine? Broken mirrors, illusionary wings – well, you know the list, so no point in reiterating. There was nothing routine about this business.

'You will take care, won't you, Dis? I've told you this before, but from the moment we first met I sensed that there is something depleted about your aura . . .'

'Don't do this to me, Louise. I don't want to get into that kind of stuff.'

'Whether you do or don't, it doesn't change things. I've never met anyone like you before, I've never had such a feeling of . . . of . . .' She let out what I took to be an exasperated breath. 'I can't put a finger on it, it's something I've never before encountered.'

'I don't know if that's supposed to make me feel special or not.'

'Don't joke with me, Dis.'

'Who said I'm joking? I'm giving off bad vibes, is that it?'

'Not exactly. I told you, I can't explain.'

'All right, so I'll just have to live with it. Thanks a heap, Louise, you've really helped my mood.'

'I'm sorry, I didn't mean – '

'Yeah, yeah. I'll let you know if anything develops with this Wisbeech thing.'

'Dis – '

'Goodbye, Louise.'

I brooded for the next ten minutes after I rang off.

*

Next, I made a call. It was to the Prince Albert Hospital in Hackney.

I already knew that their employment records would not go further back than ten years, but I hoped to speak to someone who had worked there for much longer. And for once, I was in luck: the woman I spoke to was from the hospital's personnel office and she had been around the place for quite some time.

'Oh yes, nearly thirty years since I joined Prince Albert,' she told me, evidently with some satisfaction.

'Then you might remember Hildegarde Vogel. She was a midwife there, probably in the late Seventies.'

'Vogel?' There was a pause. 'Hildegarde ... ? No, I'm afraid I don't recall. The name sounds familiar though. So many staff have come and gone in my time, as you might imagine. Vogel ... Well, the name definitely rings a bell. Foreign, was she?'

'German.'

'Unfortunately, we don't keep records for more – '

'Yes, I know. It was just a chance you might remember.'

'Can you tell me what this is in regard to?'

I explained that I was a PI trying to trace a missing person whom Ms Vogel might know. I didn't say it was okay that she didn't remember Hildegarde, that I was more interested in someone else right then. 'You don't remember,' I ventured, 'a doctor by the name of Wisbeech being there around the same time, do you?'

'Wisbeech. Wisbeech, Wisbeech, Wisbeech. Oh yes, of course I do. What woman would forget such a distinguished and charming man. But no, he wasn't a resident doctor.'

'I don't understand.'

'Dr Wisbeech was a consultant. Oh, how the nurses used to fancy him. Had film-star looks, that man. I took a shine to him myself, as I remember. Of course, that was over twenty years ago. Is he still handsome? I hope you're not going to tell me he's died since.'

'No, he's still alive and well. Tell me, did he have a practice nearby?'

She gave a short laugh. 'In Hackney? Oh no. I think his rooms were in Harley Street or Wimpole Street, one or the other. No, Dr Wisbeech was more like a roving consultant – he used to visit hospitals all over the country as I understood it. Always brought in when a difficult birth was expected. I've never been on that side of things, so I don't know why precisely. He was a very well-respected man, I do remember that. But if you do need to contact him, I should contact the BMA, dear. They're bound to know where he is nowadays. Retired, I'd imagine. Has that been of any help to you? I do like to be helpful.'

'You've been terrific,' I assured her. And I meant it.

Most of the rest of the day was filled with the normal business of running an enquiry agency and we all shared the workload, although the heavy-duty paperwork and client contact was left to myself and Henry. It was around 4.30pm that I received the call from Dr Leonard K. Wisbeech.

'I'm afraid I have some rather sad news to tell you, Mr Dismas,' he said after announcing himself.

For a heart-stopping moment I thought something dreadful had happened to Constance, but it soon became apparent that the doctor wasn't aware that his care-supervisor had already been in touch with me earlier.

'I'm afraid our guest, Ms Vogel, passed away in her sleep last night.' He continued before I could put in a word. 'I'm so sorry that we cannot be of any help in your enquiries, but I doubt very much if Hildegarde would have remembered anything useful to you anyway. Of course, I'm not putting any blame on you, but I do believe the unfortunate circumstances on your first visit to her might somehow have precipitated her sudden demise. I'm afraid you did rather upset her.'

Whoa, wait a minute, I thought. 'I'm sure nothing I said or did would have caused her to leave her bed in the middle of the night to wander the corridors,' I said bluntly. I could almost sense his stiffening.

'How did you know she was found outside her room?'

There was a sharpness in his tone and I could have kicked myself for my stupidity. I recovered quickly. 'I didn't know. I just assumed she'd taken a fall and it must have happened when she was unsupervised.' It was pretty lame – she might just as easily fallen out of bed – and I don't think he was fooled. Wisbeech appeared to let it go, although I was certain he wasn't satisfied.

'Very well then, Mr Dismas. Again, I'm sorry that you were unable to find the information you were seeking. Your client, no doubt, will be disappointed.'

'The investigation isn't over yet.' I guess I wanted to rile him.

'But surely there's nothing more you can do?'

'Oh, there's plenty more. I can contact all the hospitals Hildegarde worked for as a midwife, for a start. You never know, I might strike lucky and dig up some long-termer who even worked with Hildegarde at Dartford. They might have some answers.' I wondered if he would fall for the bluff.

'Then I wish you luck.'

That was disappointing. 'It'll be interesting to discover if any other babies died under her supervision,' I said, almost in spite.

'I'm not sure I understand what you are implying by that.'

'I've just got an idea that quite a few babies failed to survive their birth when Hildegarde Vogel was in charge.' It was a hasty remark, but a deliberate insinuation. To my own surprise, wild though it was, the speculation was suddenly a suspicion in my mind.

'I would be extremely careful about making such preposterous accusations, if I were you,' Wisbeech said, rather severely, I thought. I couldn't help but smile.

'She's not going to sue me, is she?'

'Let me caution you again, Mr Dismas – be very careful with what you say and do.'

That was more like it. Civility had taken on a harder edge.

'I have to earn my fee,' I said amiably. 'And I've always believed in client satisfaction, you know what I mean? That's why I run a successful little business. We're not super-sleuths, but we're dogged; we don't give up easily. Incidentally, Dr Wisbeech, I'm very impressed by all those letters after your name. They must cover almost everything in the medical field, but I'm particularly interested in your work as an obstetrician.'

'I can't see that my career in medicine has anything to do with you. In fact, I believe that your own ... shall we say, shortcomings? ... are rather clouding your vision. Might I suggest that you stick to your own profession, Mr Dismas, and leave mine alone? Is that, at least, clear to you?'

I was too aroused by my own train of thought to take umbrage. 'Oh yes, that's very clear, Doctor. But you see – '

He didn't give me the chance to say anything more. The line went dead and to be honest, I was relieved, because I'd had no idea what I was going to say next anyway.

22

I was like a jittery kid on his very first hot date. I kept glancing at the clock to check the time and more than once I lingered over my stash, tempted to calm my nerves the illegal way. I resisted though and stuck to regular smokes, not because of noble resolve, but because I didn't want the distinctive odour of cannabis stinking up the place. I'd been on edge all day, not just because I was going to see Constance that evening, but because I was frustrated with the stop-go progress (or lack of it) of the Ripstone case; also I was still frazzled by the previous night's drama – in fact, just about *all* of my experiences over the past week! Life itself had never been particularly normal for me, but now it had turned positively *weird*. Everyone at the office was aware that something was up with me, but when their probing was constantly met with short, sharp responses, they soon gave up. There had been other times when I was just plain unapproachable, times I developed headaches so bad I wanted to scream, and I guess Henry, Ida and Philo assumed this was one of them. I was grateful when they left me alone.

I checked the clock again, then my wristwatch for corroboration. 8.15pm. She had said she would try to get here by 8pm after I'd given her directions. Had she got lost? Or had she changed her mind? Surely she would have phoned? Perhaps I should ring PERFECT REST, maybe she'd been told she had to work late at the last moment. Or maybe she'd forgotten our meeting – our date. No, I didn't think so for one moment: Constance wasn't the cavalier type.

243

I paced the sitting-room, the air blue with cigarette smoke. Had Wisbeech somehow found out about her plans and forbidden her to see me? Yeah, that wouldn't surprise me. He had that kind of arrogance. But wait, I was getting in a tizz for no reason at all. Maybe she couldn't find a parking space – Lord knows, the crescent was always filled with double-parked vehicles, so maybe she was touring the area, searching for somewhere to leave her car. Even parking spaces for the disabled were at a premium in Brighton. And if she had managed to find somewhere far away, it would take her a while to make it back to the crescent on crutches. Or it could be that she was circling the crescent right now, driving round and round until a parked vehicle gave up its space and she could nip into it. As I headed for the front door, the bell rang.

She was on the doorstep, petite and vulnerable, and I wanted to gather her up in my arms and tell her I was crazy about her.

'You found somewhere to park then?' I said.

'Yes, close by. It wasn't a problem.'

'I was anxious . . .'

'I'm sorry I'm late. I didn't allow enough time for the journey.'

'It's okay. I'm just glad you made it.'

Was that a flush on her cheeks? Light from the hallway wasn't too good.

'I've had a busy day,' she said by way, I thought, of saying something. 'There's always so much to do when one of our guests passes away.'

'I'm sure. Please, come in. Are you hungry? Have you eaten? I could rustle up something . . .'

'No, I'm fine. I managed to have something quick before I left.'

I stepped aside so that she could enter and I caught her perfume as she brushed by: Anais Anais, I guessed. The fragrance battled with cigarette smoke drifting along the hallway.

'Straight ahead, to the right,' I told her. 'Can I get you a drink?'

'Just coffee, please.'

Constance was wearing a pastel-green dress, its hem reaching her ankles, the skirt flowing gracefully despite the awkwardness of her steps. Over it she wore a simple beige jacket, a thin gold crucifix chain adorning her neck. Her make-up was minimal, practically non-existent, and she wore no other jewellery: no earrings, no rings on fingers. Her hair was tied back in its usual tail and I had to resist the urge to reach out and stroke it as I followed her into the sitting-room.

She stopped in the middle of the room and jokingly waved a hand in front of her face. 'You must enjoy bar-room atmospheres,' she said.

'Sorry,' I apologized sheepishly. 'I didn't realize it'd got so bad. Let me open a window.'

I rushed to the barred window, pulled it open, and began to flap at the smoky air with both hands. She gave a little laugh at my antics.

'It'll clear on its own, Nick. Please don't worry.'

I smiled, delighted again at the sound of my own name from her lips. 'Make yourself comfortable while I get that coffee. How d'you like it – milk and sugar? Cream? Only instant, I'm afraid.'

Constance returned my smile, but I could still detect a tenseness in her eyes, an apprehension that was scarcely veiled.

'White, one sugar, milk rather than cream,' she replied.

'Right. You're sure you wouldn't like something stronger?'

'No, but please don't let me stop you.'

Did I look as though I needed one? I had to admit, a good malt would have been welcome right then.

I left her settling into the lumpy sofa, going through to the kitchen and switching on the Morphy Richards, which I'd filled with water before she had arrived just for something to do.

'You sure I can't get you something to eat?' I called back through the doorway.

'No. I'm fine,' came the reply. 'Thanks anyway.'

While the water boiled I poured myself a large Dalmore, loading the tumbler with ice first so that the whisky didn't look excessive. It was a poor ploy – the dark brown liquid reached the brim of the glass and I had to gulp down some of it just so my guest wouldn't think I was an alcoholic. Then I realized I had swallowed too much and decided to top the drink up again to a decent level. By the time this rigmarole was over the plastic kettle had boiled, so I poured the water into the best mug I owned, only to remember I hadn't put in coffee grains beforehand. This remedied (and making sure I opened the *correct* coffee jar), I placed the mug on a tray with the sugar bowl and small jug of milk, added my whisky tumbler, and returned to the sitting-room.

Constance seemed to be taking an interest in the framed prints on the walls, but when I looked directly into her eyes, I realized she was distracted, that interest only superficial, her mind apparently on other matters.

'Coffee,' I announced needlessly, taking the mug from the tray and placing it on the low table by the sofa.

'Yes,' she replied, equally needlessly.

I couldn't make up my mind as to whether I should sit beside her or in the armchair opposite. The former might appear presumptuous, I reasoned, it might even make her more tense – nervous? – so I plumped for the armchair. It was growing dark outside by now and I switched on a standing lamp before I sat down. Its glow was soft, the shadows around us deep.

Constance lifted the mug and sipped. 'Hot,' she said.

'Sorry,' I replied.

'It's good,' she said. Then she began to weep.

I held her close to me, fingers lightly brushing the dampness from her cheeks. We had talked for a long time, Constance and I, and by now she was visibly growing weary, her emotions drained. She had spoken of her life, how disability had closed so many doors to her, but how she eventually had managed to overcome the worse aspects of other people's unthinking intolerance and carve out a decent and worthwhile career for herself. She had been sixteen years old, a time of psychological and hormonal changes that confused and frustrated even the most normal of adolescents, when her parents had been taken from her in the horrendous road accident, leaving her alone in the world, no siblings, no relatives there to offer support or comfort. Fortunately, Dr Leonard K. Wisbeech had been a close friend of her father's, who himself had also been a surgeon, and had for years taken an interest in Constance's progress, encouraging her in her resolve not to allow the spina bifida to ruin her life totally. Unmarried himself, with only one dependant, the doctor had brought her to PERFECT REST, where she had been trained to look after the sick and the elderly. It was obvious to me that Constance was deeply grateful to her guardian and mentor, but I sensed something more in her attitude towards him, something she did her best to hide. Again, the tell-tale signs were in her eyes, the shadowy veil that descended over them at each mention of his name. She was afraid of this man.

This did not account for her tears that evening, though, and I pressed her as gently as I could to discover what had upset her so. But she countered my probing with questions about myself, one leading to another, and her unselfish concern encouraged me to talk, her soft, searching gaze ripping through barriers maintained for longer than I could remember. I talked – perhaps I rambled – without rancour, following her example of truth without bitterness, recounting the hardships as facts, the difficulties as part of my history. And the good thing was, we were able to share the feelings of those moments, Constance knew, really *knew*, how certain things, certain slights, certain incapabilities, affected me. I was talking to someone who was *inside* my emotions, who had experienced *my* experiences, perhaps in different ways, but nevertheless with an understanding of the instances and the consequences. She knew how the tiniest indignities imposed by the oblivious few could make you want to hide away into the darkest recesses of your own space; she understood how the most trivial remark from the unwitting dimwit could resurrect barricades you thought you'd long since dismantled. Yet we spoke of funny incidents as well, those times our shortcomings had led to hilarity – not many, I grant you, but enough to share with humour and enough for us both to recognize mutual methods of coping. We both laughed, Constance through her tears, me through my top-ups of whisky, and we gradually broke down whatever safeguards there were between each other. We reached out and touched – or so I thought – each other's inner self.

I told her of how I had been found, a deformed swaddling discarded by an uncaring or frightened mother, how I had been reared in a home whose guardians were not unkind, but whose regime was not based on love. I explained how I had lost my eye, asking not for sympathy but for compassion. I related my early years as kitchen help, street market runaround, furniture shifter for the local council offices, all jobs I had while studying for a career as a private investigator, saving money week by week, month by month, year by year, until I'd learned enough and gathered enough to set up my own business. And why a private investigator? she had asked, and my reply had been that I really didn't know, but I enjoyed snooping, that my own curiosity had always been a driving force, that I always seemed to be searching for answers even when the questions were not themselves clear.

One important thing we discovered about each other was that neither one of us had experienced romance before. Constance had known what she had thought to be mutual love, but which had turned out to be pity on the other person's part, and once, when she had thought she had found someone she thought truly cared, it had turned out to be curiosity on his part, and both those relationships had been the cause of her own reservation, her resistance to anyone who might try to penetrate the emotional and, admittedly flimsy, shield she now hid behind. PERFECT REST had become her physical fortress and she rarely ventured far from its confines. The walk along the lane each evening was her own way of telling herself – *deceiving* herself – that she was free of such self-imposed constraint. I had begun to understand how difficult her decision to come to me had been. While not exactly a recluse – her job meant journeys in her car, various non-live-in staff to take backwards and forwards on occasions, errands to run, things to buy – Constance's whole life was based around PERFECT REST, and it was not just a place of work: it had become her home. She hated driving, she was timid (shy, I think) of people she didn't know. The journey to Brighton had been a challenge.

As we got to know each other and spoke of things never told to any other person before, it didn't seem quite right to sit so far away, and when Constance wept once more, I moved nearer, taking a seat at the opposite end of the sofa. Soon, both of us had edged even closer and gradually I held her in my arms. She hadn't resisted.

We fell silent for a while, both pondering each other's confidences and perhaps, she, like me, wondered at our own trust in a person hardly known before, at the mutual honesties disclosed, the private thoughts shared. Now she lifted her head from my shoulder and looked deep into my one good eye.

'You must never visit PERFECT REST again,' she said.

I was taken by surprise by the foreboding that was so apparent in her gaze. 'You have to tell me why, Constance. What are you so afraid of?'

She pulled away, turning her head aside. 'I can't tell you, Nick. It's better that you don't know.'

I spoke quietly and my anger was not directed at her. 'How bad can it be? It's a nursing home for wealthy old folk, for Christ's sake.'

'You don't understand.'

'So explain. Whatever is going on, I'm on your side, Constance. I'll do anything to help you. So tell me – is Dr Wisbeech running some kind of scam, is he getting his hands on their money before they die? Or working his way into their wills?'

'Of course not! Please, *please*, don't ask me any more questions.'

'Then why did you come all this way tonight? If you had no intention of saying anything about PERFECT REST and your precious doctor, why make the journey? I know it wasn't easy for you.'

'*Please*, Nick.'

'You came to warn me.'

'Yes.'

'But you won't tell me about what.'

'No. I can't.'

Another suspicion, a wild one, was beginning to form. I took a chance.

'Dr Wisbeech used to steal babies, didn't he? That's why he was so indebted to Hildegarde Vogel. As a midwife, she used to help him.'

Constance swung round to face me again, but I could not understand the look in her eyes: surprise, shock, anger. It could have been any or all of these.

I went on, not giving her the chance to speak. 'I contacted a London hospital earlier today, one where years ago Hildegarde was employed as a midwife. It seems that Dr Leonard Wisbeech was a consultant in the same place, around the same time. I know from the letters behind his name that just two of his specialities are obstetrics and gynaecology and that he was consultant to many hospitals around the country. I'll bet that included the Dartford General Hospital until it was razed to the ground by fire. I think both he and Hildegarde were present at certain allegedly difficult births, both in Hackney and Dartford, and for all I know, plenty of others too. I also think that if I asked my client, whose newly-born baby went missing eighteen years ago, she'd probably remember the distinguished looking doctor who had attended the birth. She'd probably remember his name too, if I prompted her.'

Constance was shaking her head. 'What are you saying, Nick?' She was also trembling. 'What are you implying?'

'New-born babies have always been in demand by infertile couples. Even all those years ago they fetched a high price. I'm just wondering, Constance, if that's how Wisbeech grew rich. Setting up PERFECT REST must have cost a small fortune.'

'The house belonged to his family,' she protested.

'But converting it to a nursing home must have been costly.'

'Leonard has a wealthy brother who financed everything.'

That stopped me in my tracks. I recalled that Constance had spoken of Wisbeech as having a dependant relative, but I'd thought no more of it, assuming she meant someone older, a parent or uncle or aunt. A brother hadn't come into my thinking at all.

'So where is this brother?' I asked a little too belligerently. I guess by then I had got carried away, not realizing how much I was upsetting Constance. 'And who's to say they weren't both in it together?'

'You've got it wrong, Nick. Leonard's brother is an invalid. He hides himself away.'

'Where? At the home?'

She nodded. 'I haven't even seen him myself for three years. Only Nurse Fletcher is allowed to take care of him these days. Oh God, Nick, how could you suggest such a thing?'

She broke then. She threw herself away from me and buried her face in her hands against the arm of the sofa.

Already regretting my persistence, I reached out to her and she flinched when my fingers touched her misshapen back. I didn't pull away though: it would have made matters worse.

'Okay, Constance,' I said as gently as I could, my hand softly stroking, letting her get used to my touch. 'I just got carried away. It happens sometimes when I'm desperate for a result in a case. I won't do anything that could hurt you.'

She stirred from the sofa's arm. 'Do you mean that, Nick?'

She was weeping again and I felt like an all-time rat. 'I'll back off, if that's what you want. You're more important to me than any case I'm working on.' And I meant it. I didn't want to lose this woman, not after such a long search. Missing babies couldn't compete.

Constance came into my arms once more, her forehead snuggling into the space between my neck and shoulder. Her arm reached around me and for the first time in my life I was in someone else's embrace. Someone who might . . . eventually . . . learn to love me. My vision was blurred by welling tears and for a while I could not speak, too afraid my voice might break with a sob. I stroked her hair, her lovely neck, her arm, my hand finally falling to her waist so that I could pull her towards me. The pressure was soft and slow, because I feared she would resist, feared she might reject me. But she didn't, she came with my urging, she committed herself to me. She pressed against me, lifting her face, offering her lips. And then, sweet God, we kissed.

The bliss was perfect. My head felt alive with light and my senses reeled and soared so that I felt giddy with the happiness of it. For a moment I felt I might pass out, so exquisite was the sensation, so *rare* was the occasion; but no, this was a pleasure from which I had no wish to abscond. I maintained the pressure and went with the sensations.

We were equals: there could be no pity, and no condescension; our imperfections were a bond rather than a barrier.

Eventually, our lips parted, but not for long, only to give us time to draw in new breath; then our mouths brushed against each other's again, softly, searching, tasting the sweetness before developing into a second kiss. I relished the moistness there and almost gasped when her lips opened, inviting me to taste more, to explore with my tongue, the intimacy almost overwhelming to a novice like myself, the gentle probing that followed intoxicating to such a fledgling lover. When my tongue met with hers, every nerve seemed to tingle, every part of my body came alive, and when her hands moved over me, caressing, touching me in a way I'd never known before, I felt another part of me stirring. Although her touch was innocent and our kisses pure, the arousal was inevitable.

'Constance . . . ?' I said, pulling away a millimetre or so.

She murmured something as she kissed my cheek, my nose, my chin.

'Can we . . . ?'

'It's difficult for me, Nick.'

'I know, but . . .' It was just a 'but', nothing I could follow it with.

She took my hand and slid it over her body so that it lay upon her small breast. I breathed something, probably her name, this new intimacy sending me into rapture. My fingers – surprisingly not trembling – found buttons, undid them, lay material aside. I touched the wonderfully soft skin beneath the thin cotton of her underwear, felt the tiny mound that swiftly grew into a nipple, and heard Constance catch her breath. She gave a little moan.

'No, Nick, not yet.' She seemed close to tears once more.

'It's all right, Constance. There's nothing to be afraid of. I'm a learner too.'

But she had tensed and the glow had gone from her eyes to be replaced by that shadowy veil I had observed before. I understood her fear, but wanted her to know it was mutual, that I was just as afraid of exposing my twisted body to another, that a lifetime's shame could not be overcome in a moment. I wanted to tell her it was an experience we could go through together, our nervousness shared, and that would make it even more special; but instead I slipped my hand from her breast and drew her into my embrace once more, because I was just as scared that my body might offend. I dare not risk repulsing this woman I loved so dearly.

'I'm sorry,' she said, her voice muffled against my chest. 'I'm so sorry.'

'It's okay,' I soothed. 'Nothing's going to happen, nothing that you don't want to happen.'

'But I do.'

'Then . . .'

She huddled even closer.

'It's all right, Constance, it's all right.'

'Let's wait, Nick. Let's get to know each other first.'

Get to know each other . . . ? I soared, I wept, I smiled, I moaned (all inwardly, apart from the smile). The implication was that there was a future for us, we, together. Friends, lovers. I can't remember a time, a moment, when I was happier.

We stayed that way for a long time, holding each other, our pleasure coming from compassion rather than passion, our joy from whispered intimacies rather than sensual caresses. How long we would have remained that way, locked in sometimes tight, sometimes loose, embrace I've no idea, but it was that stark, interfering sound of the bloody telephone that shattered our peace.

23

The Ford's tyres squealed, burning rubber as I pulled to the right and jammed on the brakes, the car coming to a juddering halt by the kerbside. Strolling pedestrians turned in alarm to see what the emergency was, then continued on their way, shaking their heads and muttering something about idiot drivers who should never have been given a licence. A figure detached itself from the shadow of a doorway and hurried over to me.

Louise Broomfield peered into the open side window. 'I've only just arrived myself,' she said, taking in short breaths between words. 'Thank God you're all –' She noticed my companion.

'Louise, this is Constance Bell,' I said quickly, already beginning to open the car door and forcing the clairvoyant back on the pavement. 'Constance, this is Louise Broomfield. She's a friend of my client.'

Still crouched, Louise's gaze lingered on Constance a moment longer than necessary. She straightened as I emerged from the car.

'What the hell is up?' I almost barked at her, annoyed that my precious moments with Constance had been interrupted, but concerned with the urgency in her voice when she had phoned.

Louise grabbed my arm. 'I thought it was you! The voices weren't clear, but I was sure they meant you! It was only when I spoke to you on the phone that I realized the trouble was here.'

'You've never been to my office before.'

'I didn't need to. Once I heard you speak and you told me you were all right, I understood the message.'

I was rapidly losing patience. 'Come on, Louise, what's this all about? You didn't explain anything, you just said there was a problem at my agency.'

'You didn't hear them yourself? The voices, the whispering?'

'Maybe I was too preoccupied with other things.'

It was meant as a jibe, but I immediately wondered if it were true, that my thoughts had been directed solely on Constance to the exclusion of all else that night. Could everything else from outside sources, other thoughts, other *sensings*, be blocked by the sheer power of a person's emotions? In the light from a nearby café's windows I could see Louise's eyes were wide and staring, her trepidation genuine; even the fierce grip on my arm was an indication of her inner turmoil. Further along the street, people were spilling from the old Regency theatre's open doors and for a moment I thought I might be going crazy. Among the departing audience were odd figures, people so bizarrely garbed they might have escaped from one of my own weird dreams. They played and giggled amidst their ordinary companions, masked and painted faces grotesque in the streetlights. Fishnet stockings and sequined cloaks, humped backs and demented eyes – the exotic adornments of fools and funsters. With relief I remembered that the all-new, revised and improved *Rocky Horror Show* was back in town. Even so, even though I knew this was the audience's ritual pantomime of affinity with the show, I shuddered at the sight of all those grotesques mingling with the usual theatre-goers.

'The warning was linked to you,' Louise was saying insistently. 'I saw shadows and shapes moving among them and I sensed that they hid because they were ashamed to be seen. I couldn't understand, Dis, it was all so confusing. But there were no wings this time.'

My right leg felt weak, anxiety rather than fatigue taking its toll, and I leaned back against the car, one hand resting on its roof.

'I tried to see them more clearly,' the clairvoyant went on. 'I tried to see into those shadows, using all the power I possessed, but each time I focused on one it seemed to dissolve before me. It was as if they didn't want to be seen. I sensed fear and shame, but most of all I sensed that you were being threatened again.'

'But I wasn't. I was with Constance.'

'That's why I asked you to meet me here. It had to be connected to you somehow. This is the only other place . . .'

I was already looking up at the windows of my offices, two floors above the street. A dim light shone from one of them. Louise was still talking as I broke away and limped across the pavement towards the front door.

'Be careful, Dis. Please, I urge you to be careful. Let's call the police.'

I whirled on her. 'And tell them what? That you *think* there might be something wrong, that I'm being threatened by shadows in your own mind? Come on, Louise, get real here.'

I turned back to the street door, fumbling for the right key on my keyring. The buzz of conversations and music came from the cafés and the Colonnade Bar next to the theatre, and people strolled the pavement; vehicles were parked diagonally to the kerbside on the other side of the broad roadway, behind them the dark area that was the small park, gardens that led to the Royal Pavilion and museum. All appeared so normal on this warm summer's night, yet my hands shook as I found the right key. I could not be sure if I had been contaminated by the clairvoyant's panic, or whether my own inbuilt alarm system had been triggered by something else, a feeling that something was horribly amiss.

'Nick?'

Constance had followed from the car and was standing

behind me, a tiny figure relying on metal crutches for support.

'Stay here with Louise,' I told her and heard the shakiness in my own voice.

'Please tell me what's wrong.' Under the glow from street-lights and windows she looked delicate and appealing. I wanted to take her in my arms again.

'I don't know myself,' I said to her. 'Not yet, anyway.' She had insisted on accompanying me after the clairvoyant's phone call and for some reason I was glad she was there with me even though I didn't want her involved in anything unpleasant or dangerous. I guess she made me feel braver than I really was. 'Will you stay here with Louise while I go up and check out my offices?'

'No, I'd rather come with you.'

I had to resist embracing her and smothering her face with kisses. I'd never had someone to show that kind of concern for me before, not in this way.

'Constance, my agency is on the top floor and it's a long haul. I can do it more quickly on my own.'

I could tell she didn't like the condescension, but at least she saw the sense in it. She remained quiet as I turned back to the front door.

Even as I inserted the key into the lock, I realized it wasn't necessary: the door was already open, the latch off, the heavy wood only resting in the frame.

'Be careful.' It was Louise who gave me the warning as I pushed the door.

I entered and waited for a moment in the darkness of the short area before the stairs, a feeling of *déjà vu* coming over me. Hadn't I been through this that very morning, or had that merely been some kind of presage of what was to come? Was this now the real thing? Outside, I had noticed the dull light shining from the window of my office and I realized that the reason it was dull was because it came from next door, the outer office whose windows did not overlook the street. But I always closed my door each evening before leaving, so who had opened it again?

Reaching for the light-switch beside the door, I flicked it on. The bulb over my head had never been efficient, throwing more shadows than spreading light. The turn in the stairs above me was just a pitchy void which did not look welcoming. Unfortunately, the second light-switch was on the next landing.

Telling my two companions to remain outside until I called, I moved to the first step and began to climb. This was almost becoming tedious, I said silently to myself. These days I was climbing too many flights of stairs with dread in my heart and lead in my shoes. The unnatural events of the past few days had put the fear of God – well, the fear of *something* – into me, and tonight Louise Broomfield's over-reaction had reinforced it. Exacerbated it, in fact, because now as I climbed, I was twitching, my legs soft at the knees, a tic under my good eye, and my breathing kind of shivery. This is ridiculous, I informed myself, and so it was: I was a fully-grown – okay, *almost* fully-grown adult sneaking tremulously up a creaky staircase to my own office, expecting to find – *what*? That Henry had forgotten to turn off the light when he'd decided to work late just so he could get the books straight and please his boss? The VAT returns were due soon and Henry always got into a tizz about that. Some women suffered from pre-menstrual tension, Henry suffered from pre-VAT tension. VAT, the accountant's PMT.

My hand scrabbled over the wall in the darkness of the first-floor landing for the light-switch I knew was there. I found it, clicked it. Nothing happened, no light came on, and I remembered that the light-bulb had needed replacing for at least two months, the light summer evenings the reason for our tardiness. At least there was enough street-light coming through the window for me to see my way. The atmosphere wasn't improved though.

'Henry? Are you up there, Henry?'

I waited in silence. Deafening silence.

'Henry!'

I was forcing myself to get angry. Still nothing.

'Okay, I'm coming up!' It was meant to sound threatening, but my voice cracked on the last word so that 'up' had two syllables. Nevertheless, I hoped that if there was an intruder in the offices above, he realized he'd received fair warning. I rushed the next flight of stairs, boldness my friend, exclusion of further trepidation my ally. My limp slowed me a little, but I quickly reached the half-way mark, V1 to air pilots, the point of no return, full take-off an imperative. I couldn't go back, but when I saw the half-open office door, light from it brightening the way, I came to a breathless halt.

I supposed I was sick and tired of being a victim, fed up with being intimidated by things beyond my control, because I paused for only a second or two before rage boiled again, sending me clambering onwards, stomping stairboards to show I meant business. I barged through, slapping the door with the flat of my hand so that it banged against a filing cabinet behind, then bounced back. I blinked against the light's full blast.

I blinked against the horror that was laid out before me.

24

I'd smelled the blood even before I'd entered the office and it should have forewarned me, but my fear had made me reckless, had given impetus to my charge, knowing that to falter was to stop and that to stop was to turn around and scurry back down those stairs like a coward from confrontation, a rat from a wreck.

My feeble leg nearly gave way completely and I think I swooned as I grabbed the doorhandle for support. The sour, coppery stink of liberated gore was almost overwhelming and the sight before me was almost heart-stopping. I caught my breath and held it there somewhere between my lungs and my throat.

The half-naked body was lying across Henry's desk, one grey tartan-patterned sock hanging loose from the toes, the other covering a foot, but ruffled around the ankle. The legs were long and skinny. They were hairy around the calves and thighs. They hung over the desk, the toe of the loose sock touching the floor.

The body's head was out of sight over the other edge of the desk. The pink shirt was sopping with still-shiny blood and it was pulled back over a smoothly stretched belly, a belly so rounded it would have been a paunch in a standing position. The flamboyant shirt and socks should have been my clues, but I was still in the first stages of utter shock, where the mind is numbed and the senses insensible. Another clue was the charcoal-grey trousers neatly folded over the back of the visitor's chair, flashy red braces a tangle on the chair's seat, but, although I'd taken them in along with everything else in this newly-appointed charnel chamber, my attention now was concentrated on the blood-bubbles softly erupting from the well of pumping liquid trapped between the body's closed thighs. The groin's pubic hair appeared thickly gelled with red dye and more blood trickled over the fleshy walls to join with other flows, the main ones from below, from under the upper legs, forming a surging lake that expanded towards the desk's cliff edge, flowing around objects, making an island of a glass paper-weight, a jetty of the yellow pencil that jutted from the open crimson-soaked accounts book, one side of this squashed by the mutilated corpse's buttocks.

'Oh . . . dear . . . God . . .' I whispered, the words releasing the small breath I had left.

I held even more tightly to the doorhandle, at last forced to gulp in that bespoiled air.

Despite the evidence, I suppose that I did not want to acknowledge that it was Henry's poor body lying there like some unfortunate victim on the stone of a sacrificial altar, and the shock, disbelief, encouraged my beleaguered mind to play along with the game. No, this wasn't Henry, not my acerbic, bigoted, *caring*, mother-dominated, movie-interlocutor, *amusing*, identity-denying, *good friend* Henry. No, this was a stranger, someone who had wandered in from the street below. For what reason – who knows? Whodunnit – who cares? Just so long as it *wasn't* dear Henry. One way to make sure though, one way to eliminate Henry from the scene-of-crime. Take a look at the face. Walk around the desk, tilt your own head just to be sure, and observe the corpse's features. Then you'll see it isn't – couldn't be! – Henry. All you need is the courage.

So said the voice in my head, the voice that was my saner, wiser, softly-commanding, self. And I would do as it bid me. Because I had no other choice. I had to know.

Blood overflowed on to the floor, a slick stream that was

soon forming another swelling pool on the office's cheap lino floor, one border sliding towards another little crimson lake that I hadn't noticed before, this one seeping around the desk itself. Spilling, it seemed, from the body's head or throat. I forced myself – I *had* to force myself – towards the corner of the desk.

And it was Henry, all right. The hooked nose was the giveaway. It was Henry, except his glasses were missing and his eyes were gone.

Blood still flowed from those empty sockets, streaking his forehead and sparse hair red before falling to the floor to form the second radiating pool. Henry's mouth was still gaping as if in death-screams and I fancied I could still hear them, as if their echoes continued to bounce off the walls, suffusing the air itself. Hadn't anyone heard his cries? Had no one in the street below caught the sounds of his distress? I remembered the revelry outside, the bizarrely camp audience leaving the theatre, the almost carnival-like jollity, the voices from the next-door bar, music from restaurants and café, the footsteps and passing traffic – had they all conspired to smother the exclamation of mortal terror? Could life be so oblivious to the nearness of death?

I thought I could see the tip of his bloodied tongue resting against his upper lip, but I didn't want to look too closely. Dear God, dear Henry . . .

A noise from the room next door. From my office.

The door was ajar, enough light spilling in to throw a dim flush against the window – the glow I had observed from the street below.

A scuffling. Something dragging across the floor in my sanctum.

My first impulse was to flee and rejoin the rest of the world. But a whimper caused me to stay. At least, I thought it was a whimper.

I knew I should be hurtling down the stairs from whatever lurked in the gloom of my office, and perhaps I would have had not the clump of ungainly footsteps come to me from the stairway. I heard my name called. Not Dis but Nick, so I knew it was Constance's voice.

I stayed where I was, unable to move. I wanted to warn the two women to keep away, or at least to let them know of the terrible shock that awaited them; and I wanted to throw open my office door and face whatever whimpered in there, murderer or no. But I remained perfectly still, too traumatized to make the decision.

Louise came through first, Constance a few paces behind. Now I tried to shout the warning, but no sound came, I was voiceless. The two women stared first at me, and then at the bloody carcass on the desk.

I thought they would scream at the sight and they didn't. I thought at least one of them would faint away (as I nearly had) and neither one did that either. They just stared, their faces at first numbed with shock before creasing into rigid lines of revulsion. Before they, before I, could say a word, we all heard the muted sound from my darkened office.

Perhaps it was because I was no longer alone, perhaps I thought I had to be brave in front of Constance, but I jolted to my senses and quickly looked around for a weapon of some kind, anything I could use to protect us all. All I could find was a hard, wooden, straight-backed chair, the uncomfortable one reserved only for Philo and the VAT man on his yearly visit. I raised it high over my shoulder and turned back to face my office door.

'Nick, please, no!' Constance reached out for me but, like myself a few moments ago, seemed unable to move any more than that.

'Stay there,' I commanded with all the false authority I could muster.

I strode forward and kicked the door back with a foot, my bad leg almost collapsing under its burden – the chair plus me. Light flew in ahead of me and I stalled in the doorway, the chair quivering in my grip, my eye swiftly searching the shadows.

Something moved behind my desk, something low but with no discernible form, shuffling towards a far corner where the shadows were thickest.

For a moment, the whimpers stopped and I saw the white – greys – of two wide eyes watching me. My own one quickly adapted to the semi-darkness and I saw a skinny kid cowering there, a *naked* skinny kid, his shoulders and stick-arms trembling uncontrollably. He seemed to observe something in me that was terrifying, because now his whimpers graduated to screams.

Jesus Lord, I wanted to get out of there. The boy's screams were cutting through my head like aural daggers, reactivating my panic so that I wanted to back away – no, I wanted to turn and *rush* away, self-preservation my justification, cowardice my mentor – and only the figures of Constance and Louise Broomfield gathered behind me prevented me from so doing. Constance looked up at me questioningly, then back at the person huddled in the corner, his knees drawn up, naked arms over his head.

Even in the gloom he didn't look much, but I didn't know what kind of weapon he might have concealed behind him or somewhere close by. It would have had to be something horrifically vicious to have inflicted that kind of damage to Henry ... poor Henry. As was the way with me, anger helped me overcome the worst of the fear, and I snapped down the light-switch by the side of the door. I heard Louise gasp and felt Constance's hand on my arm.

He wasn't entirely naked, only from the waist up, torn baggy combat fatigues covering his legs, scuffed trainers on his sockless feet, the skinny ankles that were revealed almost the colour of bleached bone. And he wasn't really a kid, he was a youth, a teenager, his wavering arms occasionally exposing spiky blond hair, a young man's pallid face, a cheap metal earring studded through his ear. His frightened eyes protruded so much I thought they might easily pop from their sockets. Like Henry's. Although his had been ripped from their sockets . . .

I was still more than nervous, despite my growing rage but I took a step forward.

Wrong move. The intruder began gibbering and sobbing, sliding himself up the wall and towards the window. As he moved behind my desk he kicked out, sending it scudding a couple of feet across the floor, distracting my attention for a second or two. Before I could move around the desk to reach him, the youth had climbed on to the broad windowsill, clutching his trousers to his stomach with one hand (it seemed they were undone and threatening to drop) and pushing at the top of the lower window frame with the other. Fresh night air and noise from the street below rushed past his kneeling figure, invading like a hit squad sent in to break up a private party.

'*No, no, no, no!*' I yelled, staccato fashion, blindly rushing forward and half-sprawling over the desktop, knocking pens, pads and filing trays aside.

'*No!*' One last time as the boy scrambled through the black opening on to the window ledge outside.

I think all three of us must have stared in disbelief, listening to the sound of muted voices and a heavy bass beat now mingled with the intruder's – *out*truder's? – sobs and pitiful wails. Still half over the desk, I moved around it, heading for the window, praying I would not be too late to drag the boy back. And even as I did so, I heard shouts and calls from the pavements below as the figure on the window ledge was spotted.

My nerves were stretched to breaking point as I stood on tip-toe and stuck my head out the window, both my anger and my fear considerably diminished now that I knew the

intruder, murderer, mutilator, was more afraid of me than I
of him and that he was merely a skinny man-boy, with no
weapon that I could detect. In fact, my emotions were
somewhat mixed at that point: this creature had slaughtered
my friend and yet what was he? A pathetic, scared-witless
juvenile, is what he was, a miserable, shivering, punk
perched on the end of my windowsill. One part of me wanted
to push him off; the other part, which was just as sincere,
wanted to calm him down and coax him back into the safety
of my office. If he had shown aggression, then perhaps I
might have acted differently; but I had spent a good deal of
my life trying to convince others, especially but not exclusively children, that there was nothing to fear from me. I
think that yet another part of me, the rational, logical side of
my nature, told me this kid was too frail and sorry-looking to
have inflicted the damage I'd just witnessed. I spoke soothingly as I reached a hand towards him.

'Take it,' I said to him, aware of the shouts and pointing
fingers from below. 'Come on, just take my hand and let me
help you back inside. Nobody's going to hurt you.'

'*Keep away!*' he shrieked. '*Keep away!*'

Putting a knee on the outside sill, I pushed my shoulder
through the open window. I kept my voice low and soft,
surprised by my own coolness. 'It's all right. I promise, no
one's going to hurt you. Come back inside before you slip.'

But he edged further away and there really was nowhere
to go. He stood erect, face to the wall, fingers digging into
the cracks of the old brickwork for purchase. His combats
began to slide over his bare buttocks and down his scrawny
legs, and as he reached for them with one hand, he looked
my way once more, his eyes still bulging and wide, but
opening even wider when they took in my shape, the hunch
of my back, the fall of my jutting forehead, the black,
shrivelled hole where my own eye used to be. Even though
it was night, I saw every dark-stained tooth in his head as he
opened his mouth to scream, this scream louder than any

that had gone before, its horror more intense than I thought could ever be possible. His fingers scrabbled at the wall as he lost his balance.

Then he was gone and I was looking at empty space.

His scream was cut off as if stolen by the rushing air even before his body reached the pavement. Instead, the unified cry of the watching crowd in the street came back up to me and I closed my eye, unwilling to look over the edge, disinclined to witness the inevitable, the *unavoidable*, consequences of a fall from that height.

But I couldn't close my ears against the short wet crunch of shattered bones and crushed flesh as the kid hit the ground.

25

No more Henry. It's the finality that gets to you. One day someone you know – even worse, someone you love – is there, the next they've vanished. That's the hardship. Not sorrow or pity, just the sudden and irrevocable emptiness. It's shocking and it's wretched. Nevertheless, it's something we all have to go/grow through at some stage in our lives, usually more than once. Unless you die young yourself, of course, which is the best way to avoid mourning others.

Curiously, you still worry about them, your departed ones. Where have they gone to? Who's looking after them? (If you've lost a child, that's the concern that can easily destroy you.) If there are destinations called Heaven and Hell, which train did your friend/relation/loved-one (not always in combination, these) catch? And if you do fear the worst, can your prayers help them change track mid-journey?

So how much better to believe that there is no life after death, that there can be no soul because there's no place for it to go once the body has withered to dust. Sure, you'd still grieve for the one you've lost, but you wouldn't have to *worry* about them any more, because that wouldn't make sense. All you'd have to do is remember them and miss them. Wouldn't that be easier?

Why then, do most of us cling to the idea that there is more to follow, that death truly isn't the end of the road? Because we can't stand the idea of nothingness? Because we won't tolerate the notion that all our life amounts to at the end of the day is a heap of dirt? Or does society itself realize that to live tolerably well together we must have higher resolutions that will be rewarded when the end comes? A kind of inbuilt subliminal stick and carrot. Can it be a misconception whose purpose is to encourage us to be civilized? Maybe. But maybe, also, everything around us speaks of regeneration, that things may appear to die, but they never quite cease to exist. Flesh corrupts to dust, which becomes particles, which becomes atoms, which become energy and energy is the magic that binds everything together, and energy is invisible ... just like the soul. Unconvincing, of course, unless you *want* to be convinced, and for that, you have to believe. Which leads us back to why we *should* want to believe. After all, oblivion means peace – of a kind – so why not yearn for oblivion? Because ultimately it isn't enough. We think we're yearning for peace – peace of mind, tranquillity of heart – but really we're yearning for something better (after all, if there is no mind and no heart, their peace is irrelevant). And by better we really mean something better than we have now, in this life. Despite times of great joy and even contentment, we know it's not finite, that it cannot last. It's a brief intermission between the bad parts. So we seek – perhaps even pray for – something better, which ultimately means something more than any of us really has, and oblivion isn't more, it's goddamn *less*. And who the hell wants something *less*, something that is actually nothing at all?

Catch my drift?

Anyway, here's the point: all my life I'd known – okay, I'd *believed* – there was a better existence waiting for me somewhere, although I'd never been particularly religious, never attended church much (I'd always been saddened, sometimes angered, at the way great causes and religions had been tempered, often distorted, by mankind itself, how even the noblest of intentions invariably had been tainted by mind-pygmies and politicians with their vain hierarchies, petty doctrines, and absolutist dogma); yet in my thoughts, and